A Conversation with the Client's Wife . . .

When I turned to face Sonja, I could see tears welling below her blue eyes. She was staring at me as if I were about to say something devastating. But it was she who spoke.

"Nobody knows better than I how unstable she is. I shouldn't have taken a chance, leaving them alone. But she's been hurt so much. I thought, if she could have a relationship with her son, perhaps it would give her a reason to care about herself."

"Sounds reasonable."

"I didn't want her to think I don't trust her."

"Even though you don't."

"No."

"Tell me about your grandson."

"He was my second chance. 'Was,' Christ, listen to me! I think Ben and I both wanted to make up for Melanie through little Ben. Melanie's lost to us. . . ."

"Do you think your grandson's in any physical danger from Melanie?"

"My daughter is irrational, self-d̲_____ full of hate—totally out of control as far _____ ̲hink he's in danger. Don't you?"

BODY OF EVIDENCE

DAVID A. VAN METER

JOVE BOOKS, NEW YORK

BODY OF EVIDENCE

A Jove Book / published by arrangement with
the author

PRINTING HISTORY
Jove edition / January 1990

ISBN: 0-515-10207-5

Jove Books are published by The Berkley Publishing Group,
200 Madison Avenue, New York, New York 10016.
The name "JOVE" and the "J" logo
are trademarks belonging to Jove Publications, Inc.

PRINTED IN THE UNITED STATES OF AMERICA

10 9 8 7 6 5 4 3 2 1

•• For Robin ••

· · Chapter One · ·

Maggie is an artist in all things, as vigorously creative in sex as in her painting. Our lovemaking, even after five years, was never routine. But this time was different from the rest. I felt it first; then I saw that tears had darkened the loose red curls in front of her ears. I asked her what was wrong. She turned her head in the blue-gray light and looked at me with eyes that made me wish I'd kept my mouth shut. "I'm leaving," she said. "This was supposed to be good-bye." It was dawn. She cried harder. It was the middle of the afternoon in Europe. I was still there. My head hurt. Maggie was making a sentimental gesture. It wasn't like her to use sex to say good-bye. It wasn't like her to cry. Before, she'd just lobbed a few expletives in my direction and walked out. There had been no fight this time.

"You mean it," I said.

"Yes."

I put my arms around her and, without effort or self-consciousness, our bodies found a close and comforting posture. I felt her soft, moist exhalations against my chest as I gently stroked her back with the palm of my hand. Loving her had never felt so lonely.

I was just back from Vienna. Arthur Wormsey, respected engineer and family man, had stolen plans for an advanced, three-axis industrial robot from his employer, and I'd been hired to retrieve them. The plans represented not only millions in research and development but the company's future. I barged in on Arthur's big sale and, after a brief spree through midnight streets, recovered the plans from the bloody pocket of his customer. When I got back to the fire escape where I'd shackled Arthur, all that remained of him was the lower half of his right arm, hanging like wolf bait from my Swiss-made handcuffs. If they let him live, he'd spend his days in interrogation and menial labor. At night, he could practice tying his shoes with one hand.

Maggie and I showered separately and dressed without saying much. Breakfast was perfunctory. Despite all our love and understanding, I resented being left. As I looked around my little house for the first time with clear eyes since I got back, I could see that Miss Bly hadn't waited for her big announcement to start packing. There were boxes stacked in front of the fireplace. Her loom and the big canvases were already gone. She put on the old Neil Diamond record she always played when she was hurt or sad, and went about her business, filling more boxes and making piles of her belongings. I felt out of place in my own home.

Home in my case is a quirky old house overlooking Half Moon Bay, thirty minutes south of San Francisco. The place had been built by an eccentric Stanford professor during the twenties, a kind of poor man's Jay Gatsby. Before the crash, Sea Crest had been infamous as a hotbed of debauchery and scandal. It was ready for the bulldozer when I found it. I bought it for the value of the land.

Fixing up the old place was probably more expensive than rebuilding, but I didn't have the heart to tear it down. I had the old front porch glassed in and opened up the front of the house to take advantage of the sweeping view of coast and sea beyond the trees. Within a week of the day she assumed resident status, Maggie had turned my sun porch into her own little Garden of Eden. The fruit trees and flowering plants were gone now, and the place where they had been looked worse than empty. The lady herself would be gone in a few hours, to a little rented condo over the Cahill ridge near Palo Alto. The smell of her art would be the last thing to go. Sometimes the air had become so thick with the fumes of paints and thinners that I'd threatened to throw her out. Now as I watched her preparing to remove all traces of herself from my life, I was comforted to think that the biting scent of her work would remain for weeks like some small part of her.

It was September, the one month of summer we had in our odd chunk of the U.S. I went outside for a quick tour of my two acres. The good people of California own the wooded hillside around me, which they intend to maintain as green space now and forever. My access is a half mile of dirt road. The heirs of the wacky professor were the only property owners in the area who refused to sell out. In the shade of a favorite live oak tree, I stopped to admire the spectacular view of curving coast that forms Half Moon Bay. Maggie's melancholy music caught up with me there.

Maggie and I met during what may have been the worst period of my adult life. She had some paintings in a sidewalk show in Monterey. I'd gone down there hoping to outrun a black mood and there she was. We talked for an hour about her work. I was impressed. Here amid the saucer-eyed puppies and trite seascapes was actual talent.

Her work was defiant, yet it touched a small, hurt thing deep in my soul. I bought a painting, my first. And I fell wildly, unexpectedly, in love.

Had it not been for the perfidy of my ex-business partner, Charlie Neihardt, Maggie and I might never have met. Maybe I should be grateful to him for that, but I'm not, any more than I'm grateful to the folks who brought us the Vietnam War. Yet without their contribution to history, I never would have met old Charlie and the life of Gardner Wells might be a very different package these days.

My army unit field-tested experimental weapons, trying them out on the Viet Cong as often as possible. They told me I had lucked into the job because I was brilliant, courageous, and educated in electronics. I figured my number came up. Neihardt's company had sent him over with a laser-guided rocket. Depending on how it performed for the brass, he could look forward to a hero's welcome or a pink slip when he got home. I supervised the setup, field work, and the official demonstration; and I made it go. Neihardt's gratitude embarrassed me. As soon as he'd notified his bosses, we did Saigon, four days' worth. His company treated us repeatedly to the city's pleasures. Between innings, we learned we had things in common other than our baser instincts: training in intelligence work, fondness for baseball, and a tendency to laugh at the same things. A friendship of sorts developed. During the next year, he wrote me occasionally about his plans.

When I got out, we started Wells-Neihardt Security in Santa Clara. It had the makings of a perfect marriage: I'd learned computer science at MIT; Neihardt knew the big guns in the business, their strengths, their weaknesses, even their misdeeds. We were convinced high-tech companies would pay people with our backgrounds to protect them from each other and dishonest employees. And they did. Silicon Valley was exploding. Not only did I love the work, I was right for it. Nam had taught me I'd never make it in corporate lockstep.

The honeymoon lasted two years, until the day two men in polyester suits showed up and took Neihardt away. It turned out he'd started his own export business with one client, the KGB. I felt like an ass. We hadn't worked a case together since the second month. We rarely conferred, except to divide the spoils. Still, I blamed myself. I'd had a feeling about him, but I was so busy solving everyone else's problems, I never checked it out.

The news that our company was a pipeline to Moscow got around with predictable speed and consequences. Wells-Neihardt folded. It took eleven bleak months for the feds to clear me. Maggie helped me survive. She was beautiful, kind, and somehow able to tolerate my spells of bitterness.

In some ways, we're opposites. I run the beach and work out when I can. Maggie's favorite exercise is poker. I'm a little over six-three and broad-shouldered. She's only five-six, but it's all energy. Her hair is the color of ginger. Mine's bourbon-colored. Her eyes are Irish Sea green; she says mine are the color of moose piss. Maggie's the extrovert, no secrets. Almost. Beware what Maggie keeps inside.

In those early days, the romantic in me came charging from the adolescent place where I'd abandoned him and took over. Whatever the calendar may have said, it was springtime. The world bloomed. She eclipsed Wells-Neihardt and my loneliness and became everything to me. It seemed not only right, but inevitable, that we set up housekeeping.

And now, it seemed not only right, but inevitable, that we say good-bye. Caught up in our romance and embittered by the collapse of Wells-Neihardt, I thought I was ready for another kind of life, a life with her and kids, in which our family and the things we believed in would always come first. I talked a great game until the office phone started ringing again. At first, Maggie was jubilant. Our

dark days were over. Now we'd have the money and
stability to get on with our plans. But no. Not until this job
is over and the next one and the one after that and don't
you realize it's impossible for me to do my job without
leaving for weeks at a time? I don't know why we ever
thought it would work. . . . Yes I do.

In time, another sort of relationship developed between
us. Less idealistic. Less romantic. The love was still there,
and the laughter, but the expectations had changed. I guess
we liked each other too much to give up quickly. There
were fights. She'd leave and come back. I'd chase her out
and then go after her a day or two later. As I rebuilt the
business in my name, she developed a more pragmatic
attitude toward her own work. In time she had quite a list
of clients among the local ad agencies and publishing
outfits. I suspected that loneliness and disillusionment motivated the change. She'd given up her calling for a career
path. I blamed myself.

By late morning, we'd finished the mine-yours sorting
of possessions and had wedged a laughable amount of stuff
into her convertible. She declined my offer to follow and
help her unpack. We kissed and had a long hug standing in
the driveway. I told her she was brave and that I loved her.
She had to work at holding off the tears.

As she drove down my narrow lane toward the main
road, the overstuffed car kicked up a cloud of dust that
filled the tunnel space beneath the dense overgrowth of
trees. It settled slowly in the absence of wind and several
minutes passed before I could see clearly to the first turn.
She was gone.

There's a path from my place to the beach. Without
making a conscious decision to do so, I started walking it.
I turned south on the empty beach and walked mindlessly,
allowing the sounds and smells of the sea to work their
magic on me. Soon I was unaware even of the sensation of
wet sand beneath my bare feet. I don't know how many

hours or miles it took, but when I got back to the house, I felt better. And very tired. I found some of the salmon I'd had smoked and canned at the end of a fishing trip to Alaska a couple of months earlier, washed it down with a cold bottle of St. Pauli Girl and went to bed.

When the phone woke me a little after ten, I rolled over to check on Maggie. The place where she belonged was flat and cold. The damn thing kept ringing. Maggie, a light sleeper, had always handled the wrong numbers and old pals looking for a party, while I slept on like the dead. No more. I was becoming annoyed at the caller's persistence until I realized who it was. Who else would give me two dozen rings to wake up?

"Maggie?" I could feel myself smiling as I said her name.

"No such luck, Wells. It's Maitland."

I yawned.

"I didn't mean to wake you. I figured you and Mag had that damn stereo blasting away like you do."

"Not tonight. What can I do for you?"

"Have lunch with me tomorrow at the Mission Club."

"One o'clock?"

"Make it noon."

Maitland, ordinarily the gregarious type, was obviously in no mood for conversation and neither was I, so we said good night without discussing whatever weighty matter was on his mind.

Going back to sleep was not among my immediate options. I had made the mistake of switching on the Tensor on my side of the king-size bed and in its light, I was newly confronted by her absence. Everywhere I looked, something was missing. Her clothes, her pictures, her bureau things, her. After a few minutes of trying to visualize an image of her on the ceiling, I got up and fed the Nakamichi a cassette of an old Caruso recording of "De Tempio al Limitar" from *The Pearl Fishers*. It's a duet about love and loss and friendship, things very much on my mind. Maggie did not share my taste for opera and it usually took only a few notes to send her lunging for the volume control or the door. Tonight I was blessed with complete musical freedom. I turned the sound up loud enough to shake the dust from nearby objects and poured myself a beaker of Glenfiddich.

· · Chapter Two · ·

If Maggie was part of my salvation in the aftermath of Wells-Neihardt, so was Ben Maitland. One afternoon during the time when it seemed like everyone in the Valley thought I was a Russian spy, he waved me over on the Stinson Beach road and introduced himself. It was gratifying to think that such a famous character wanted to meet me, but Maitland wasn't the least bit interested in Gardner Wells. He wanted to buy the old Morgan 4/4 I was driving. I've been restoring the old beast inch by inch for several years now, but back then I'd had Myrtle only a few weeks and to most people, I suppose, she looked like a well-qualified candidate for the scrap yard.

I recognized Maitland before he introduced himself; he was a legend in our business. One Monday night, as the story goes, Ben was watching football with the sound off (we called it "Cosell mode" in those days). For no particular reason he started doodling and, before the two-minute warning, had invented a disk drive that changed the industry; put him among the Forbes Four Hundred; and led to the formation of Data Matrix Industries, currently doing $300 million a year in sales and growing, while other hot dog companies of the early Eighties have joined the ranks of Pac Man and Frogger.

Maitland and I walked circles around the homely roadster for twenty minutes while he tried to buy her from me. When I turned down three times what she was worth, he gave up. We spent the rest of the afternoon on the beach, trading tales and surf-fishing. That evening, over a pitcher of brew in Sausalito, I told him the story of Wells-Neihardt. He had me checked out, and a week later I was hired to give Data Matrix a going over.

We both got lucky. There were the usual weaknesses in plant and procedure. I expected that. But there were also two cousins named Lusano cannibalizing defective units and building their own drives for the black market. And who should turn up in finance but one "Leon Gilbert" better known to law enforcement agencies as Louis Gilman. "Louie the Leech" had a new name, but the games he was setting up were the same ones he'd used to bleed other young companies to death. When I finished my exorcism, Data Matrix had the clean bill of health it needed to keep growing. Ben was grateful, and so was I—for the opportunity to reward his trust. As word spread of my triumph, the phone started ringing again and within weeks, Wells, Inc., was turning away business.

The Mission Club is as staid as anything you'll find in the land of fern bars and mellow. The nucleus of the club complex is, in fact, an old Spanish mission, and that architectural motif has been maintained throughout the club's newer structures and in the gracious gardens and patios that surround them. But inside, there are no mariachis, and *taco* is a dirty word. The atmosphere is emphatically Boston Brahmin. Grim portraits of grandfatherly gentlemen hang everywhere. There are also grandfather clocks and waiters who remind me of my grandfather. It's quiet enough to hear a name dropped in the next room.

I arrived a few minutes early for my appointment with Maitland, but found him waiting for me in the main bar, looking every bit as dispirited as the glass of flat beer in front of him. Our handshake seemed to revive him. We went to the dining area and there followed the headwaiter on a brisk march through a series of cozy rooms in which the titans of California's electronics industry were pondering the day's menu. Several greeted Ben and a few invited us to sit down. With the finesse of a master politician, Ben declined each invitation without missing a step. He was a diamond in the rough when we first met, more socially inept computer genius than polished CEO, but a decade at the top had transformed him.

Only one of the four tables in the last dining room we entered was set for lunch. The headwaiter seated us graciously while murmuring menu information in a Slavic accent so thick I couldn't make out anything he said except, "Enjoy your lunch." On the way out, he closed the seven-foot, oak double doors through which we'd entered. And there we were, a dining room to ourselves in the Mission Club on a day when the place was packed and $750K board chairmen were being wait-listed. Our table overlooked the club's pool and beyond it, the polo field where a young girl was exercising a white stallion.

"I know you'd prefer Wendy's, Wells," Ben said, "but I like showing you nonconformist guys what you're missing. All is not compromise on the inside."

"Actually, I'm a Burger King man, Ben, but this will do." Sometimes Ben dealt with the twenty-year difference in our ages by treating me like a rebellious son. I didn't mind. We made small talk and kidded each other while they filled our water glasses and took our drink order. The usual flush of good health was missing from my friend's

broad, freckled face. His mind was on whatever he wanted
to see me about. The dining room number wasn't meant to
impress me or to insure our privacy. He was scared—of
something his wealth and power couldn't fix. I guess
booking the room made him feel better. When they'd
brought our beers and taken our lunch order, he handed me
a wallet-sized photo of a cute blond kid with freckles and a
turned-up nose.

"It's my grandson, little Ben."

"We met when I ran into you guys at that 49ers' game
last winter. You'd bought him so many souvenirs, he
looked like a mascot. He's grown, not so much the baby
anymore."

"Sorry, I'd forgotten about the game. He turned four in
June. I guess I spoil him; baseball, football, the circus,
fishing. At that football game, I don't think he knew what
the hell was going on. But it's better now. He's a real
Giants fan." It was hard for Ben to tell me what was
wrong. I studied the picture. The boy looked a lot like his
grandfather. The older Ben's hair was still mostly blond,
but turning silver. They had the same deep blue eyes. A
handsome kid.

"You've met Melanie."

"About a year before you and Sonja split up and again
afterward. Sonja was having a party. Melanie was fourteen
then."

"Well, she's twenty now, and I'm afraid she's pretty
screwed up. I don't know what the hell happened. People
get divorced every day. Melanie couldn't handle it. She
hates me, hates her mother, hates herself. It's hard for me
to talk about it, but things have gotten out of hand."

Ben took a couple of long swallows from his beer and
continued. "Sonja blames Melanie's problems on me, on
the divorce. I suppose if I hadn't gotten . . . involved, we
might still be together. I didn't feel like I had any control
over it at the time. I was like a kid. I don't even know
where the hell she is now, you believe that?"

"Bess?"

"Yeah. I think of her as my mid-life crisis. Sonja's better off now than I am. It was pretty rough on her for a while. I still haven't gotten over the suicide thing. I left her well-fixed; she was attractive. Sometimes I wonder if she really meant to kill herself at all. You know what I mean? Maybe it was a gesture to get back at me. It's what really set Melanie off. There's no doubt of that. She ran away for keeps after her mother came home from the hospital."

"She was gone about a year as I remember."

"Yeah. She had Ben while she was away. I guess that's what brought her home. We tried to find her. But kids disappear. New York. L.A. They're in another world. They can stay lost as long as they want to. Melanie wouldn't say who Ben's father was. She wouldn't even tell us where she'd been. After a while, I didn't want to know."

"Had she named her son when she came back?"

He nodded and turned to stare out the window. "She gave her son my name, but she didn't want me anywhere near him." He paused momentarily; then he went on. "One day early last month, Melanie showed up at her mother's house. Sonja had been keeping Ben. Thank God for that. Melanie didn't have any interest in him. I sent her a check every week. She usually wrote some little insult below the endorsement. It was the only contact we had. She went from one psychiatrist to another. Got picked up for drugs at least twice that I know about. Of course, Sonja was suspicious about Melanie's sudden interest in little Ben but I guess she hoped Mel might start acting like a mother. The three of them had a nice visit. Milk, cookies, the whole bit. Ben showed Melanie some of the stuff he'd been doing at preschool. After about half an hour, Melanie asked Ben if he'd like to play in the yard with her. They never came back. I'm frightened, Wells. I can't stop thinking she might hurt him . . . and herself. Ever since Sonja tried to take her own life, I've worried that Melanie might get it in her head to try the same thing.''

''Any idea where she's gone?''

''We think Mexico City. Sonja's husband called me that evening. I guess she was in pretty bad shape. We talked about what to do. Sonja didn't have legal custody. There was nothing illegal about Melanie taking her own son. Jack, Jack Ridgely, and I decided to give it twenty-four hours. As soon as I got off the phone, I drove over to Oakland. Melanie had been living there for a year. Once I crossed the bridge, it took me fifteen minutes to find her address. I couldn't believe the neighborhood. God only knows why she wanted to live like that. She didn't have to, Wells, believe me. Anyway, she wasn't there. A black family had rented the apartment. The next day, I hired a detective, Mel Berry.''

''He's a good man.''

''That's what I heard. Berry found out that Melanie had given up the apartment about three weeks before she showed up at Sonja's and took Ben. There had been a guy living with her in Oakland. From what Berry said, I guess there had been a lot of guys. She had quite a reputation in the neighborhood. Berry didn't pull punches. Her latest live-in was a Mexican kid named Ramon, Aguirre, I think. Called himself a 'filmmaker.' According to the grapevine, he supported himself selling stolen TVs and stereos, things like that. He had quite a reputation, too. 'Reckless, antisocial, given to fits of rage,' that's the description Berry gave me. You ready for another beer?''

''Just keep going.''

''Okay. Mexico City. This creep Ramon had been telling all his cronies that he was going down there to direct a documentary about Bobby Barron. You know, the singer.''

''The Chairman of the Boardwalk. The Lord of Las Vegas. I've got all his records.''

"You should have all his money."

"I should have all your money."

"Nobody Berry talked to believed Ramon was going to direct anything, anywhere, but Berry didn't have a hell of a lot else to go on. When he found out that Barron was actually down there appearing at the El Dorado, he thought he ought to check it out. He asked me if I'd go a plane ticket and couple of nights in a hotel, said there was too much chance of spooking Melanie if he tried to track her down over the phone. I wondered how he would have handled it if I was Joe Blow from Redwood, but I said okay."

"You should have. Berry is no hustler."

"He was supposed to locate Melanie; find out if she had Ben with her; and only then was he supposed to approach her. I told him to offer her anything within reason if she'd send the boy back to her mother. I said visitation was no problem. I didn't want to cut her off from her son. But she's unfit to look after him, Wells."

"So what happened?"

"Berry disappeared. He went down there a week ago. Yesterday, his secretary called me, practically in tears. He's five days late calling in. The people at the hotel where he was staying haven't seen him in at least that long."

"Luggage?"

"Still in his room. I don't know what the hell to think. His secretary's called the police and sent them a picture."

"You have no idea whether he got anywhere trying to find Melanie?"

"None." He shook his head and swallowed hard. "I love her, Wells. I need to say that because maybe it doesn't sound like I do. I just can't deal with how she is now. When she was little, there was no sweeter kid in the world. She was always bringing home these bugs and birds. Sometimes she said they were sick or hurt; sometimes she claimed they were lonely. Her room smelled like a pet store. She was the same way about people. We were out in the car one time when she was four, and for no reason she said, 'Daddy, does God know there are people starving in the world?' I said yes, and she said, 'Well, why doesn't he do something about it?' Four years old, Wells. She had this incredible sense of right and wrong, yet she was so tenderhearted along with it. Her mother used to say the world would break her heart. . . .'' He fussed with his flatware for a few seconds; then turned to look at me with sad eyes.

"Do you remember Gretchen?" he said.

"Sure. Some people at work gave her to you and you griped about taking care of a dog. Now you've got her picture on your desk."

He sighed heavily and lowered his voice, though we were alone. "I haven't told anyone this," he said. "A few months ago, I came home from work one night, late. I went out in the back to let Gretchen out of her run. I knew right away something was wrong; she always barked to say hello. It was so quiet. . . . She was dead, Wells. Someone had poisoned her. God help me, I can't get the idea out of my head that it was Melanie. I don't know why. There's no proof. I just think it was. . . ." Ben took a couple of deep breaths and went on. "We found out she got involved with some pretty rough people that year she was traveling around. I don't think life is very important to her. Hers or anyone else's.

"She's had every opportunity in the world for help the last few years, and as far as I can tell, she's rejected it, along with her mother and me. I know I failed her as a father and I'm going to have to live with that the rest of my life, but you get burned out, Wells. You cut your losses. It hurts, but what else can you do?"

"I'm sorry, Ben," I said. "I'm sorry about the whole thing."

The Fates had found Ben's Achilles' heel and moved in for the kill. He wasn't used to feeling vulnerable, let alone helpless or afraid. I don't accept personal cases. I assumed that was why he hadn't asked directly for my help.

"Ben," I said, "if you don't mind taking a chance on someone without much experience in these matters, I'd like to fly down to Mexico City and look around. I won't promise anything." The look of gloom on Ben's face broke suddenly into a smile and he shoved his big mitt across the table.

"Thanks, Wells," he said.

I hadn't expected Ben to be very hungry but he shoveled in the veal and fettuccine like a starving steamfitter. Between mouthfuls, he added some detail to the picture. The trout and salad in front of me were passable. I glanced at my watch. It had been an hour since I'd thought about Maggie.

Coming from the cool and shadowy depths of the Mission Club, the afternoon seemed brighter and hotter than it was. I'd neglected to park the Morgan in the shade, so I grabbed a map from the glove box and covered as much of the seat leather as I could, trying to spare myself a severely scorched butt. Myrtle's eager growl when I started her became a resonant purr as we made our way over to the freeway. She was hungry for the road and was letting me know it as any well-bred machine will do from time to time. Unfortunately, she had picked the wrong moment. My mind was hunting for the tape of my last meeting with Melanie Maitland.

Not long after the Maitland's divorce, Sonja threw a big "coming out" party for herself at the suggestion of some well-meaning friends. It was a disaster. She'd invited a hundred or more of "the best people." Fewer than twenty showed up; and of those, about half stayed less than an hour. I didn't blame Sonja for getting smashed.

When I dropped in, there was enough food going begging to feed a family of Ethiopians for a year. A trio was playing feebly in a corner; and in the middle of the vast, open space that was her living room, the hostess was dancing with a friend's husband. I waved to Sonja, then spent the better part of fifteen minutes talking baseball and Scotch with her bartender. We'd just replayed the '86 series when I saw a man I remembered as an Olympic class bore heading straight toward me. Sonja had left the room. The bore had an empty glass and the eager look people like that get when they spot an audience. I abandoned my drink and ducked out the nearest exit, which led to the swimming pool. From there, I intended to circle the house to my car and take off.

As I cut through Sonja's rose garden, I heard a whimpering sound coming from a nearby cluster of flowering shrubs. I decided to check it out. The shrubs surrounded a small grouping of wrought-iron lawn furniture. The loveseat was in use. He was all over her, pawing and groping. Her whimpers said no, but her body looked undecided. My voice startled them. He sprang away from her as if he'd just read "AIDS positive" tattooed on her breast. I recognized them both. He was Al Garner, perennial free-lance marketing man and professional party animal, married to an heiress of some sort. She was Melanie Maitland, all fourteen years' worth. In short shorts and a half-T, she looked like the midsummer night's wet dream of any teenaged boy with his fair share of hormones.

When he recognized me, Al quickly became a sputtering blob of embarrassment. He appeared not to notice as Melanie rose self-consciously from the seat beside him. She thanked me through a sheepish, tearful smile, then slipped into the shadowy darkness of her backyard. I hesitated, then went after her. I wanted to say something, a few kind words. But she was gone.

Less than a week later, a UPS guy with a package to

deliver heard Sonja's Jaguar idling inside her closed garage. If he'd stopped for coffee or cigarettes on the way, the lady of the house would have been completely dead instead of close when he arrived.

The time since has been much kinder to Sonja than to her daughter. A couple of years after the suicide attempt, Sonja married a wealthy diet doctor who built her a three-million-dollar love nest in Los Altos Hills. I called her there from the Mission Club after Ben and I signed off. She had welcomed the prospect of a visit. For a moment, it felt like old times.

There are still some places where, for three million dollars, you can have your own palace and a square mile or so of land to keep the riffraff at bay. Not so on our little peninsula, where cardboard split-levels with a ten-minute mow can bring a quarter million. Still, even in the pricier sections like Los Altos Hills, three mill makes an impression. Sonja's house juts like a giant sugar cube above the lush greenery on her choice morsel of hillside. After the obligatory electric gate, the drive swings behind a stand of catalpas and you are face to face with the result of six months of meetings between Sonja and a Japanese architect. On opposing corners of the house, there are two-story, wraparound windows of smoked glass. Other than that, the structure is pure white, unbroken even by a peephole or a dryer vent. Not huge, but impressive. Clearly not something Joe Handyman built on weekends from a set of Sunday supplement plans, and I guess that, more than anything else, is the point.

You enter through a door set in the bottom of the northeast glass section. Sonja answered the bell herself. I hadn't seen her in nearly two years, but she'd aged more than could be accounted for by the passage of time. Still, she looked great, not a pound over or under her ideal weight; raven black hair swept back fashionably behind her head. After a quick hug, she led me from the marble

entryway to the sunny side of the house and a living room
with a twenty-foot ceiling and an arrangement of upholstered furniture that looked like it had come straight from
the Museum of Modern Art. While I tried to arrange
myself comfortably in something that looked like half a
tulip, Sonja went to ask the housekeeper to bring lemonade.

She was opening a pack of cigarettes when she came
back; I'd switched to a footstool. She laughed at the sight
of me. "That grouping won three international awards,
Wells. Would you like to get a straight-back from the
other room?" She sat ladylike on one end of a persimmon-
colored loveseat and dropped the cellophane from her
cigarettes into an alabaster ashtray the size of a fruit bowl;
maybe it *was* a fruit bowl.

"I'm suspicious," I said, "of furniture that makes me
feel like I missed half the joke."

"And isn't very comfortable," she admitted. "Jack's
quite an art fancier. Quite a change from good, old you-
know-who." Neither of us laughed. She lit a cigarette and
pulled the first drag deep into her lungs. I'd never seen her
smoke. "I'm surprised Maggie hasn't taken you off to live
in Tahiti by now. How's she doing?"

"Better, I suppose. She moved out yesterday."

"Permanently?"

"It looks that way. She wasn't made for the widow's
walk."

"Who is? I always hoped you two would work it out. Is
playing cops and robbers really that satisfying, Wells?"
She took another long drag while I ignored her question.
"Sorry, I shouldn't have said that."

"You're right. Maggie and I had something exceptional
for a few years. The time had come for her to move on."

"And you?"

"I'm where I belong."

"Are you really so fatalistic that you can just let her
go?"

"I don't mean to make it sound easy or painless. It isn't. I'm just not in the mood to disembowel myself this afternoon."

"It's none of my business."

The housekeeper served lemonade and some little sesame things. Despite the smoked glass and air conditioning, it was hot in Sonja's living room. I stood and took my glass to a shady corner. When I turned to face Sonja, I could see tears welling below her blue eyes. She was staring at me as if I were about to say something devastating. But it was she who spoke.

"He blames me, doesn't he?"

"I don't think so."

"Nobody knows better than I how unstable she is. I shouldn't have taken a chance, leaving them alone. But she's been hurt so much. I thought, if she could have a relationship with her son, perhaps it would give her a reason to care about herself."

"Sounds reasonable."

"I didn't want her to think I don't trust her."

"Even though you don't."

"No. I used to leave her alone deliberately when she came. She'd take things. I never mentioned them. She has her father and me to thank for the way she is. We can never make up to her for that. I suppose he told you about the psychiatrists."

"There were a lot of them."

"One of them told me to put her away. I should have listened to him. I couldn't bear the guilt so I changed psychiatrists instead."

"A lot of kids have made it through an ugly divorce. . . ."

"And a parental suicide attempt?"

"That, too. Tell me about your grandson."

"He was my second chance. 'Was.' Christ, listen to me! I think Ben and I both wanted to try to make up for Melanie through little Ben. I'm not sure which of us tried harder. In the last twelve months, while he was here, I think Ben spent more time with his grandson than he did with his daughter in fourteen years. Too often with kids, you realize your mistakes when it's too late to correct them. Melanie's lost to us. I hope she's not lost to herself."

"How did little Ben feel about being separated from his mother?"

"He loved it here, I think. When Melanie first reappeared, with Ben in her arms, there were times when she doted on him like a kid with a new pet, but for the most part, I think she resented him. He slowed her down. She seemed delighted to let me take him. Ben was only three then, but I honestly believe he was relieved to get away from her. He was so eager to start preschool and settle in. Of course there were some adjustments. He had quite a vocabulary and I don't think Melanie had taught him any manners. . . . Damn it, Gardner, I miss him so much I can't stand it. Sometimes I wonder if she let him stay here just so she could hurt her father and me by taking him away."

"It was your idea, wasn't it?"

"Yes. I was prepared to insist, but she agreed before I had to. She'd been living in some counterculture hideaway near Big Sur, doing God knows what. One day, she came to the door with her hand out; I told her I thought Ben should stay with me."

"Do you think he's in any physical danger from Melanie?"

"My daughter is irrational, self-destructive, full of hate— totally out of control as far as I can tell. Yes, I think he's in danger. Don't you?"

· · Chapter Three · ·

The 747 slipped through the sulfurous layer of crud that
hangs over Mexico City and landed on schedule at Benito
Juarez International about ten minutes of seven local time
the following evening.

I have mixed feelings about Mexico City; almost all of
them negative. On my last visit, I had to identify one of
our Treasury agents in the city's morgue. When I got
there, they were doing an autopsy on a little girl with coat
hanger arms and a stomach that was still packed with the
newspaper she'd eaten for dinner. There are severe short-
ages of food, water, and air in Mexico City. But there are
plenty of people—eighteen million of them, whose hometown
is about to become the most populous city on earth.

El Pescador is not my favorite hotel in Mexico City but
it's modern, centrally located, and the phones there are
more likely to work than in the places I've stayed that push
charm and great service. I wanted this trip to be strictly
business. The mint-on-the-pillow routine would only re-

mind me of Maggie and all the pleasures great and small
that had been part of life with her.

The room was high in the back of the building as I'd
requested. King-size bed, comfortable sitting area, full
bath. It might have been the Dubuque Hilton except for the
flashy weaving that hung over the headboard. I decided
not to take a chance on the in-house water treatment
system and ordered two six-packs of Perrier sent to the
room. Montezuma had had his revenge on me once and I
wasn't about to give him another shot.

I tried calling Pete Velasquez, a guy I knew in the M.C.
Police, but he'd gone home to his family in Cuauhtémoc.
A long shower rid me of the grime of my travels and I
climbed into some linens I'd had made on a trip to Hong
Kong. Navy jacket, ivory slacks, and a very white shirt
that showed off my tan. I looked mah-velous, dahling.

I decided to take a chance on La Tertulia, a restaurant
near the hotel that the desk clerk had told me was popular
with local fatcats. My immediate impression was highly
favorable. There was a good crowd, mostly domestic business types. It looked cozy, lots of carved wood and a guy
in the corner making love to a twelve-string guitar. I fed
the maître d' a small bribe to assure that I would not be
seated next to a sextet of drunken Texans who were the
one blight in an otherwise inviting landscape. He rewarded
me with a comfortable booth at an agreeable distance from
the guitar player.

Much as I like it, I didn't want to inflict tequila on an
empty stomach so I ordered a favorite Spanish red. The
menu was limited, but interesting. I settled on steak au
poivre, rare. It came surrounded by fresh, steamed vegeta-
bles and was magnificent. I could have settled in very
happily with a snifter of Carlos I, and let the guitar man
work his magic, but, alas, it was time to punch in.

I paid the restaurant a quarter of what the meal had been
worth to me and set off at a brisk pace for the El Dorado.

It's a fifteen-minute walk, from one side of the hotel district to the other. The thin air at 7,350 feet aggravates Mexico City's pollution problems, but it makes for pleasant night temperatures during even the hottest months. The sidewalks were bustling. There were beggars and beautiful people, old men stretching their legs, and hookers stretching theirs. I found a hole in the flow of people going my direction and jumped in. It's like Manhattan, but you don't get the same feeling that the sidewalk crowd consists of predators and prey.

El Dorado is one of the newest and most successful hotels in Mexico City. It was conceived and constructed in the grand tradition of the world's legendary pleasure domes. Bigger than big. Gaudier than a drag queen imitating Dolly Parton. No service or comfort it can't provide. Three palatial penthouse suites; each with its own swimming pool. They opened it at the peak of Mexico's oil boom, a fitting symbol of the country's new power and prestige. They've said the last rites for Mexico's flirtation with prosperity, but El Dorado has a life all its own. Among those with a taste for showy self-indulgence, who can afford it, El Dorado is a "must" on the tour. It's not my taste, but it struck me as a perfect showcase for Bobby Barron.

Barron was a frequent guest on programs like "The Ed Sullivan Show" when I was in first grade. He had a man's body, but the face of a twelve-year-old, and a voice like a girl. I could not understand why people would want to hear a freak like Bobby sing. I still can't. His voice had changed between the time I first remember him and his transformation to middle-aged sleazeball, but the reason for his popularity continued to elude me. I can understand why my fellow baby boomers develop a taste for vintage Sinatra, Glenn Miller, and the likes of Thelonius Monk when they hit thirty. They're all good, and somehow "Jumpin' Jack Flash" doesn't make it with that first martini after a rough sales meeting. But Bobby Barron? Give me a break.

Barron was somewhere near the middle of his final show of the evening when I arrived in the El Dorado's lobby, a temple to bad taste ringed by towering, anatomically-correct marble statues, set against acres of crushed red velvet. Between seventy-five and a hundred of the faithful were gathered around the three entrances to the Club Casanova, hoping, I guess, that someone inside would drop dead and liberate a seat. Looking grim and purposeful, I worked my way through what appeared to be the smallest knot of women. On the far side of the silver-colored doors in front of me, Bobby was getting an ovation. A muscular young man in a gladiator costume was on guard duty. I flashed him my best smile, whispered that I was Bobby's cousin, the movie director from L.A., and showed him one of my special green business cards with the picture of Andrew Jackson on it. He immediately returned my smile, took the card, and opened the door for me. As it closed, young Spartacus told the grumbling women I was Bobby's brother. It made their night.

Onstage, a section of the tinsel curtain was swaying where, I guessed, the star had just made his exit. In the pit below, a thirty-member band began storming through a medley from *Man of La Mancha*. It was break time. Waiters in black tie scurried through the thirsty crowd taking drink orders. A thousand people had jammed into a space meant for half that number. Groups of five or six were crowded around tables with tops no bigger than manhole covers.

I dodged the stampede for the bathrooms and made it to one of the banana-shaped bars at the back of the hall, where husbands and boyfriends were standing three-deep. I now had two impossible dreams: spotting Melanie Maitland in the unlikely event she was in that crowd, and getting myself a slug of tequila. After a few minutes, I spotted a guy at the bar shifting his butt and glancing anxiously toward the men's room. When he made his move, I was ready.

After a fanfare fit for God himself, two unctuous male voices—one English, the other Spanish—came on the P.A. system to proclaim in tandem the pride of the "world's greatest luxury hotel" in presenting "the world's greatest entertainer, the sensational, sensual 'Mr. Enchantment' himself—THE MAGNIFICENT BOBBEEEE BARRRRON!" Grandmotherly types jumped out of their seats, squealing like fourteen-year-olds. The band dug into "Get Ready" and Bobby Barron burst through the tinsel like some bimbo jumping out of a cake. To say the place erupted is like saying the ground shook a bit down there in 'eighty-five. For what seemed like several minutes, Barron, in top hat, cape, and pants that looked sprayed on, strutted like a gloating gamecock on the stage. He looked good: tan, trim, radiating a kind of lecherous glow. He was taller than I would have guessed, about six feet or a little more. His thin mustache tilted wickedly above an unchanging grin. Housewives, secretaries, and a lot of women who looked like they would know better tossed flowers, notes, and assorted undergarments on the stage. The grin never varied, the hysteria never ebbed . . . until Mr. Enchantment passed his wireless mike from his left hand to his right. Then, as if it had all been planned, the music and lighting changed, the crowd got quiet, and Bobby Barron switched on the quivering tenor voice for a medley of love songs. I counted five languages including English and Spanish. The selection was eclectic—"Yesterday," "Crazy for You," "What Now My Love?" The only Spanish song I recognized was "La Paloma." The hat and cape went fairly early on, during "Rescue Me," I think. I must have been ordering another drink when he ripped open his shirt. One minute his chest was covered by white silk and a very proper little bow tie; then, before you could say

"male stripper," he'd exposed a glistening expanse of
flesh and hair. I could tell no amount of tequila would help
me take the screaming. It got worse when he dropped to
one knee—as luck would have it, in exactly the right spot
to give the maximum number of people a prime view of
his crotch. He was a regular Niagara of sweat by now.
There were women near the stage trying to catch some of
it. Halfway through "Go Away Little Girl," the undulat-
ing sex serpent had even the most self-conscious of them
on their feet again. Me, too. I had to get out of there.

To get some air in Mexico City, you really have to leave
town, but I settled for what I could find outside the hotel.
It was pushing 1:00 A.M. The show would be over soon.
Mr. Enchantment wasn't the type to do encores. I wondered what he did for a finale. Drop his pants while
singing the national anthem of his host country? Hump
some bloated senior citizen at her table to the strains of
"All the Way"? Whatever it was, taste and subtlety would
not interfere.

In the next block, there was an empty lot where one of
the old hotels had been, the Diplomatico, I think. Several
of the old hotels, including the Principado and the Regis,
were victims of *El Grande,* the monster quake. I remember the remark of a Mexican cab driver about the collapse
of ten major government office buildings in the disaster.
"Maybe there is a god," he said. That guy should be
running the country.

I had little hope of finding Melanie Maitland in the
crush of Barron's worshipers, but if there was a connection
between the king of sleaze appeal and the missing girl, I
wasn't going to discover it or anything else by counting
cobwebs in my hotel room.

Predictably, Barron's backstage security was geared to
hysterical women. I had no trouble getting through. I don't
think my aviator shades and a throaty whisper convinced
the guy at the door I was Clint Eastwood, but I know he
liked my smile and the feel of my money in his palm.

The door behind the security guy opened onto a short hall at the end of which about twenty people were milling around in a kind of lounge area. The mostly pink decor probably reflected some Mexican designer's image of a fashionable Beverly Hills sitting room, yet I had the feeling every table lamp and ashtray was bolted down. There were a couple of richly paneled doors in the far wall. On one of them was a removable plaque with Barron's name painted on it in gold script inside a border of stars. From the expectant murmurings of those around me, I gathered he was closeted on the other side, recovering from his performance. There were big bucks visitors, hotel gophers, people I guessed were on Barron's staff, and a few press types. One of these attracted my attention immediately.

She was tall, beautiful, and angry. The beauty caught my eye but the anger held it. I dropped the shades into a jacket pocket and sidled over to see if I could find out what had her steamed. A smiley type, three inches shorter than the lady, with gray hair and a blue velour turtleneck, was doing his oily best to calm her down but she was having none of it. There was a formation of beaming businessmen stage right of the drama. I fell in at one end of it and tried to listen behind me. It seemed that the reporter was having access problems. There had been an interview with Barron in which her questions were "invasive" according to the man in the blue turtleneck. Now she felt they were denying her access. She was Mexican; he American, Upper East Side speech pattern, undoubtedly fake. Her English was better than his. So were her eyes, like eight-balls in cream. The rest of her looked pretty good, too.

She worked for *Excelsior,* the biggest paper in the country, which must have been why Mr. Smiles was trying so hard to be diplomatic. By now I had him pegged for an ex-arm breaker from Newark who'd worked his way up to the executive suite. I had a feeling the poor guy was sweating bullets trying to stifle the urge to tell her to fuck off.

They went at it inconclusively for a few more minutes, until Barron's guy finally got red in the face and lapsed into the old vernacular. "Look, I don't got time to mess with this!" he snarled. "This man is like a god to women all over the world and you ask him questions like he was applying for welfare or some goddamn thing. What the hell do you expect? Orchids?" The lady from *Excelsior* stood her ground as the angry little man went off like a string of cheap fireworks. "If it was me, I'd have you thrown out," he sputtered, "but Bobby's not like that. If you'd just cool it for a couple of days, I'm sure he'll see you again, but come on like you did before, honey, you'll be the one applying for welfare! Barron's got more clout in this country than the oil wells. Comprendez?"

"Si, Señor D'Ortona," she said sweetly. I thought I saw her curtsy out of the corner of my eye. "You know, I'll bet our readers would be fascinated by your personal history, Vincent. 'I Work with a Star,' that kind of thing. It's amazing what you can find out with just a few phone calls to the right people." I turned toward them just in time to see Vincent's complexion turn from red to scarlet as he stormed away from her. She was fighting the desire to laugh.

I said, "I guess he couldn't wait to call his mom and tell her about the article."

"I guess not." She smiled cautiously.

"I'm Gardner Wells," I said as I offered my hand, "president of the Peoria chapter of the Bobby Barron Fan Club and chair of the National Committee for Canonization." She laughed and shook my hand as I fessed up. "Actually," I said, "I'm looking for someone and being here is one of the indignities of the task."

"I know what you mean," she said. "My name's Dolores Aguilar."

"How do you do?"

"Fine, thank you."

"I apologize for listening to your conversation, Dolores. It looked to me like you're as happy to be here as I am. I'm always attracted to kindred spirits."

"My editor wants me to do a series on Barron, but all I get out of them is press-kit hype. I can't work that way."

"A dedicated reporter?"

"I'm not getting rich. Who are you looking for?"

"I'm looking for someone who might make herself disappear if she finds out I'm here before I get to her."

"No names, right?"

"Some close friends have been hurt. The woman I'm looking for is unstable. There's a child involved."

"So no names."

"No names. Sorry."

"I had to ask. You're a detective?"

"I help high-tech companies hang onto their secrets. This job is something of a favor." I could see she thought I was evading again. "Yeah, I'm a detective." I said it, but I didn't mean it.

"Look, if you come across anything . . ." She handed me one of her cards.

"You'll be the first to know. Now it's your turn. I'm told there's a film being made about our friend, Mr. Enchantment. Do you know anything about it?"

"Are you kidding? They've tried to make it seem like the biggest thing to hit Mexico City since the earthquake. Sometimes I wonder if there's actually film in the cameras or if the whole thing's just a publicity gimmick for his nightclub appearance."

"I don't get the feeling he'd need something like that to fill a house."

"No, you're right. I just resent the way they manipulate the media and we bend over to cooperate."

"Not you."

"I've been wondering if I'm foolish to make an issue of it. The people in this city practically worship him."

"All the more reason for you to make an issue of it."

"Thanks."

"You're welcome."

"Barron's tied into a lot of charities. Clinics, orphanages, a couple of schools. He's been doing benefit concerts for a new hospital. Some people want to get it named after him. Supposedly the film will be used to encourage contributions to the charities, but it strikes me as a giant ego trip. Sorry, there I go again."

"Who's making the film? Where did he get the crew?"

"Oh, that's one of their publicity things. Everyone's Mexican. No Hollywood talent."

"How about some names?"

"José Romero's directing, I know that. Let's see . . . the cameraman is Luis. I don't know his last name. They're the only ones I can think of. There's a woman assistant."

"Mexican?"

"Yes. They all are. At least they didn't lie about that." I ran half a dozen Mexican-sounding names by her including Ramon Aguirre, Melanie's boyfriend. She gave no indication of recognizing any of them. "Sorry I can't help. I went to one of their locations with Barron two days ago—before he cut me off."

"What was your crime?"

"I think he's used to having everyone fawn over him, reporters included."

"Surely you weren't disrespectful."

"No." Ms. Aguilar's ebony mane danced behind her slender shoulders as she laughed. "I was just trying to get behind the image. The questions were pretty routine—childhood, sex, marriage . . ."

"Is he?"

"No."

"Bad for the image, I guess."

"Who knows? I thought he might welcome a chance to do an honest interview. Obviously not."

"Seems to me he should have been flattered by the suggestion that integrity could coexist with sequins and spandex tights."

"I should point that out to his P.R. man." Applause suddenly crackled through the crowd as Bobby Barron and another man came charging out of his dressing room. Barron led the way. His red face and grim expression were an odd contrast to the white turtleneck, blazer, and pleated slacks he was wearing. The guy following him—undoubtedly a high-ranking staffer—was straight out of central casting: the graying CEO whose boyish charm miraculously survived his rise to the top. He was trying not to look frazzled. Barron was gunning for someone. The applause and cheering continued despite Barron's indifference. He finally acknowledged it with a half smirk and the kind of hand movement that might have chased a fly from his cheek. The room got quiet. Barron's mood spread through it like a poison. His expression darkened further when he noticed Dolores. She took a step back as he passed by us. A few feet away, Barron stopped in front of a short fat man with a red short-sleeved shirt and the face of a dissipated cherub. People drew back to give them space.

"I need Paul Santori, Joe. Have you seen him?" Barron spoke in a low voice, but the rest of the room was dead silent. He was easy to hear.

"Sorry, Bobby." The pudgy face shook woefully.

"That kid blew three cues in the second show. I want him out."

"I'll tell Paul, Bobby."

"I'm not going to have a million-dollar production screwed up by some zit-faced piece of teenage crap."

"Paul will get rid of him. There's lots of guys can run lights without messing up."

"You tell Paul I want to see him."

"I will, Bobby."

"That kid's history." The cherub nodded solemnly and the CEO-type began cheerily introducing Barron to an expectant knot of VIP's standing nearby. The chance to mouth off had done Bobby good; his mood brightened. The rest of the room followed his lead. A couple of guys appeared from nowhere with trays jammed with glasses of champagne. I grabbed a pair, for myself and the lady. She thanked me.

"I'm glad to see Barron hires guys who aren't afraid to speak their own mind," I said.

"When I'm around this scene for more than an hour, I feel like I need a bath. Salud!"

"Cheers."

"At least they don't buy cheap champagne."

"Would you let a gringo detective buy you dinner tomorrow?"

She said, "I don't know," but she smiled. "I've been working a lot of nights. Barron usually doesn't show his face to the world before two in the afternoon." I gave her my look of wry puzzlement. It worked. "Well, maybe," she said. After the official exchange of personal phone numbers, she shaped the lightly glossed lips into a terrific smile. "Good luck with your detecting," she said. She had movie star teeth.

"Thanks, Dolores."

"Doe."

"I like that. Every spare minute, I plan to direct my deductive powers to figuring out how you learned to speak American-style English like a native. You aren't, are you?"

"I'll never tell."

"We'll see." I could see that she was fighting off a yawn as we prepared to work our way through the growing crowd to the door. The free-flowing champagne was having its way with the multitude. I turned in to Barron as we maneuvered across the room. Some sweaty staff guy in a cheap suit was trying to introduce his girlfriend, and Barron was doing his best to make hamburger out of them.

". . . But Mark," Barron lisped as the man tried to hide in his shirt, "when did you switch to girls? And what about you, honey? When did you and Kermit break up?" The crowd loved it. Mark didn't. I think he would have loved to take a poke at Barron, but the prospect of unemployment can be very sobering. Then there was the baboon with the sledgehammer fists slouched in the corner.

"What makes Barron so insecure?" I asked Doe as we stepped into the hall.

"I've thought a lot about that," she said. "He came from nothing; maybe he can't believe his own success."

"He's had it a long time."

"True."

"Maybe he thinks he doesn't deserve it, so it makes him feel guilty, you know, and he acts like that to show the world what a rotten guy he is."

"Highly speculative, Dr. Freud."

"I suppose. A nightcap, Ms. Aguilar?"

"Bed, Mr. Wells. You in yours; me in mine."

"Good night, Ms. Aguilar."

"Buenos noches, Señor Wells."

·· Chapter Four ··

I met Pete Velasquez back in the days of Wells-Neihardt. Neihardt and I had a group of clients who were losing shipments of Japanese components to a guy with an international chop shop in Mexico City. Our Treasury agents and the Mexicans were working on it, but too slowly. The chopper sold everything: cars, guns, computers, anything he could move, whole or in pieces. He was big. I knew I couldn't shut him down by myself, but I thought there might be a way to get him off our clients' backs so I went to Mexico.

One night, I spotted Pete following me tailing the bad guy. I had no idea who he was. We tangled briefly but wound up having several beers and talking shop till the wee hours. He is a true rarity among the cops in the Big Tortilla: bright, competent, and honest.

I'd called Pete before I left California to ask him to find out what he could about the disappearance of Mel Berry. I also gave him the names of Melanie Maitland and her boyfriend to see if they'd attracted the attention of his colleagues. After breakfast, I called Pete from the hotel to see what he'd been able to find out.

"I've pulled together as much information as I could," he said when we'd exchanged amenities. "There isn't much to tell about your detective, Melvin Berry. He checked into the Excelaris on the 17th at 6:00 P.M. He slept in his room that night and the two following. He paid nothing in advance and gave no indication he'd be staying elsewhere. His things were untouched as far as we could tell. They've packed them up and will hold them for a month if he doesn't turn up."

"What do your guys think?" There was a pregnant pause. I could guess why. "This is a very solid chunk of humanity we're talking about," I said. "Ex-marine, twenty years on the police force. Detroit, I think. He has a top reputation as an investigator, hard-working, reliable. Definitely not the guy to whisk some bimbo off to Acapulco to help him spend his client's money."

"No one said that, Wells."

"So what do your guys think?"

"It would help if you had some perspective on how things are in this country. . . ."

"If you're saying you can't assign a special investigative team to check out the mere disappearance of one, measly gringo detective, neither can we."

"I don't want to bullshit you."

"I appreciate that, Pete. What about Melanie Maitland and Ramon Aguirre?"

"They were questioned in the investigation of Berry's disappearance. Berry had business with them, but you know about that. We know where they were the day he disappeared. Aguirre works as a technician in the film crew making the movie about Bobby Barron, but it's no big job or anything, like you said he was telling people back there. He and the girl say Berry talked to them a few

times about her son. They said Berry was working for the
girl's father and he tried to persuade her to take her son
back to the States. She refused. Berry's assistant confirms
that that was his assignment.''

"That's it?''

"Yes. Your man was reported missing just a week ago.
We've checked the hospitals and talked to the people we
know he contacted here. There is no evidence a crime has
been committed. If something has happened to him, he'll
turn up. Be patient. It's a very big city.''

"Where do I find Ramon and Melanie?''

"The Camino Real.''

"At a hundred and fifty dollars a day?''

"More like two or two-fifty. It's a suite.''

"They lived in a roach motel in Oakland.''

"I understand her father is very rich.''

"Yeah, but you can bet neither of her parents is paying
for this joyride. How much could Ramon be making with
Barron?''

"In a month, not enough to pay for one night at the
Camino.''

"How long have they been there?''

"Don't know.''

"Thanks for your help, Pete. I'll keep in touch.''

"I'm sorry I didn't have more for you.''

"More? You've given me everything but the room
number.''

"Two-eighteen.''

"You really know how to make a guy feel useless,
Velasquez.''

"Don't disappear like Berry, my friend, okay?''

"Unless he is in Acapulco with a girl—I promise.''

There was no answer in Room 218 at the Camino Real,
but the switchboard operator confirmed that it was regis-
tered to a Mr. Aguirre. They'd been there a week. The
luxury hotel didn't fit what I knew about Ramon and

Melanie's financial circumstances, but I decided not to let my natural curiosity get the better of me. I wanted to locate little Ben as quickly as I could; report on his condition to his grandfather; and go home.

Dolores Aguilar was glad to hear from me. I welcomed the excuse to call her and realized that it might not be all bad if things took longer in Mexico City than I'd planned. She had a press-kit production schedule for Barron's epic and dug it out of her file while I tried to negotiate a commitment for dinner later. She pleaded work overload.

"I'll cater it," I said. "Just tell me where your desk is. I know a soprano who works newsrooms, or would you prefer a violin?"

"I'd prefer Thursday, Mr. Wells. Here's the schedule. Let's see, Sacred Heart Pediatric Clinic, all day today and tomorrow. Barron did a benefit for them last year. I think he donated some lab equipment, too. Would you like to know when he's going to be at the clinic *in person* today? I noticed you forgot to get his autograph last night."

"Go ahead, tell me."

"Two-fifteen."

"May I call you later?"

"About dinner?"

"Mind reader."

"Maybe around six."

"You can set your watch by it."

"No promises."

"Gotcha."

The clinic was in Netzahualcoyotl, "Netza" for short, one of Mexico City's cozy satellite communities. Population: a mere two and a half million or so, many of them immigrants from the countryside, come to the big city looking for the good life. If a person's definition of the good life includes open sewers and families living in vermin-infested spaces smaller than any self-respecting yuppie's walk-in closet, then Netza's the place. The Good Life, Calcutta style.

The cab ride was long and uneventful. The use of the term "gridlock" as it applies to traffic may have been used first in connection with Mexico City. People read, knit, write Christmas cards, learn another language, and occasionally shoot each other in traffic jams. For those who can't amuse themselves, there are usually jugglers and fire eaters at the intersections. No mimes. All the mimes have been shot.

I got out of the cab a couple of blocks from the clinic and told the driver to wait. A huge crowd waited in the sulfurous midday glare for Mr. Enchantment. *"Medico,"* I said, *"con permiso, por favor."* They parted politely for the doctor. *"Medico, perdona, gracias."* I guess the gray suit helped. *"Medico, perdona me."* A squat old woman eyed my empty hands suspiciously and demanded to know what kind of a doctor carries no little black bag.

Double rows of police barricades blocked the street above and below the clinic. There were maybe a dozen cops on the forbidden ground, four police cars, and a couple of shabby vans I assumed went with the film crew. The clinic was to my left, a one-story cement structure about three storefronts wide. The dark-blue paint job appeared to be brand new. The three large plate-glass windows in front had been painted white on the inside except for a ten-inch clear space across the top, through which big movie lights were visible inside. One side wall of the clinic was exposed; the other adjoined an empty commercial building of similar size. On the exposed side was a fresh thirty-foot mural that showed Bobby Barron leering godlike above a series of scenes of men and women in white coats helping sick children.

Near the front of the crowd, I found a good vantage point in the shade of what looked like a four-story housing project. A sudden breeze swirled hot dust and smells of rot along the street. To the west some promising thunderheads were building among the foothills. The place ached for rain.

Half an hour before Barron was supposed to arrive, they began carting movie gear outside. A wave of excitement surged through the crowd. There were about ten people in the film crew. On the basis of appearance alone, two of them might have been Ramon Aguirre—five feet ten, swarthy, medium build, about twenty-eight years old. One was a sound technician, who did his job with skill and confidence. The other guy hung at the back of the pack, waiting for orders. He was making an effort to look bored. He wanted the world to know that behind the oversized aviator shades with the mirror lenses was someone destined for much more important stuff than stringing lighting cables and holding the cameraman's coffee. His loose-fitting tan slacks and jacket belonged in Bloomingdale's, not on some hard-luck street corner in Netza, Mexico. The slippery smile to the crew's cute production assistant was made to sell CD players that happened to fall off a truck. If this wasn't Ramon, it should have been.

At two-twenty, the people in the back of the crowd section opposite me began cheering. I could just make out the top of a white limo nudging past frenzied onlookers toward the clinic. "BOBBEEE . . . BOBBEEE . . . BOBBEEE . . ." The chant swept the crowd. Two policemen on motorcycles were parting the jam of people for the big Lincoln. The cops who'd been standing by at the clinic moved a section of barricades aside. As the limo nosed past them into full view, a couple of dozen women charged it in small groups from the crowd. With a degree of finesse I wouldn't have expected, the motorcycle cops herded them out of the way. The chanting got louder. The six-door star barge swung toward the clinic and stopped in the middle of the street. The cops set the barricades back in place. The chanting got louder still, and more demanding.

But nothing happened. Nobody got out of the custom stretch. It just stood there smugly chugging the soot of unburned gasoline into the atmosphere. The passenger windows were so deeply tinted, I'm not sure a guy washing them could have seen inside.

After a few minutes, just as the chanting began to fade, one of the middle doors of the car opened, a huge cheer erupted, and a fat guy with gray hair stepped from the cool darkness into the glare. There were a few boos as he slammed the door behind him and walked over to confer with the film crew. That was the first of several comings and goings from the car over the next half hour as the crowd's excitement gave way to frustration. The crew was ready; even the guy I figured for Ramon was doing his best to look sharp. I could only guess what was keeping Bobby inside. Catching the end of an old movie? Waiting for his makeup to kick in? Who knows? All I can say for sure is that when Mr. B did emerge from the car, any resentment among the faithful was gone instantly. He was wearing a studded blue jumpsuit, open across the chest, tight in the ass. His shades were as impenetrable as the car windows. He waved soft, manicured hands and flashed perfect, keyboard teeth at the jubilant throng. This is what they had been waiting for. The fat guy started barking ground rules at the crowd through an electric bull horn, but I don't think anyone was listening. All eyes were on Bobby, who was leading a parade of himself and two goons along the perimeter of the barricaded area. Just before they made the far turn down my side of the crowd, I slipped around the end of the row of barricades closest to the clinic and headed straight toward the guy I'd picked to talk to. He was manning a stack of playback equipment, a dour sort in his mid-thirties with thick glasses and a yellow short-sleeved shirt so dirty I think the buttons had ring-around-the-collar. I interrupted him as he was previewing a cassette through one side of a pair of studio-type earphones.

"Howdy," I said, "I'm Skip Evans, Evans Advertising, Houston, Texas? Do you speak English?"

"Yes," he said and slapped the stop key of his tape deck.

"That's good news!" I said in my best drawl. "We're gonna shoot some location footage down here in a few weeks and I'm looking for a crew. I knew old Bobby would have the best, am I right?"

He looked at me like I was crazy. "He's very happy with our work."

"Must be great working for a big star, huh?" He nodded. "I thought it was just gonna be Big Bob here today but I was lookin' at that fella in the tan outfit over there. That's Tony Orlando, ain't it? Tell the truth, now!" For the first time since I started watching him, the guy smiled, then he laughed. "Hey, what's so all-fired funny?" I said. "You-all surprised I recognized him without Dawn?"

"That's just Ramon," he said. "He's on the crew."

"Come on," I said. "I won't say nothin'. Him and Bobby gonna do 'Tie a Yellow Ribbon 'Round the Old Oak Tree,' or what?"

"That's Ramon Aguirre," the guy assured me. "He's nobody. That's his brother, Chaco, over there, the lighting man."

"Well you sure could have fooled me," I said. "Y'all have a nice day, now." I went back to my spot in the crowd. People around me were yelling out song titles. Barron was huddled with the director and cameraman in front of the clinic. Behind them, a group of freshly scrubbed kids in wheelchairs and braces were being displayed for the camera. One of them, a wheelchair-bound boy about six was unhappy as hell about something. He was shaking his head furiously as the production assistant Ramon had smiled at tried to appease him.

The fact that Ramon had a brother in a responsible position on Barron's crew helped to explain why he was there. The brother didn't look or act anything like Ramon. He was much older, ten years or more, I guessed; balding, with a once-angular face that now drooped slightly with the weight of time. He handled his lighting gear like a seasoned pro. His body looked hard, unlike Ramon's. Big Brother, I guessed, had been doing physically demanding work for a lot of years.

My pal on the P.A. system cranked it up for a run through of Bobby's Spanish/English rendition of "A Spoonful of Sugar." Mr. B was going to lip sync it to the handicapped kids. There was a burst of delighted applause as he grabbed a mike for effect, I guess, and took his position with the children while the P.A. guy recued the tape. I wanted to leave but I felt the tug of morbid curiosity. They slated it; Barron fell to one knee and switched on the polyester smile. They rolled the playback, and just as Bobby started to mouth the first lyrics, the kid in the wheelchair who'd been so unhappy jumped up and ran off camera crying like a baby for his mom. The crowd went crazy. Barron mouthed a popular expletive that is not among the lyrics to "A Spoonful of Sugar" and made like a torpedo for the clinic door. When I got back to the cab, the driver asked me why everyone had been laughing.

Our first stop was a public phone from which I called the Camino Real again. There was still no answer in 218. Where was Melanie? At the circus with little Ben? Researching her Ph.D. thesis at the library? Or maybe smoking a joint in the back of Bobby Barron's limo down the street. I decided to try to catch the little family that evening at their hotel.

I got there a little after six and tried calling Doe from the lobby. Her extension was busy. Two-eighteen was at the end of the hall and, as I remembered the layout of the Camino Real, probably had a view of the pool and tennis courts. My first knock was unproductive. I made it insistent. Melanie answered. The identification was purely cir-

cumstantial. I remembered Melanie Maitland as a pretty
fourteen-year-old; I did not want to believe that she'd
become the stone-eyed woman standing in front of me.

"Melanie?" I said. She held the door open about a foot.
There was a glimmer of recognition that faded quickly into
a frown.

"Who are you?" she said. Her raspy voice went with
the eyes. She stood across the opening with one hand
ready to close the door.

"Gardner Wells. Do you remember?" She started to
smile, then caught herself. I could hear a shower running.

She sighed. "What do you want? Did my father send
you?"

"I offered to come. Your parents are worried about
you." She laughed.

"That's bull."

"You're right. Actually, you've won the Publisher's
Clearinghouse Sweepstakes and I'm here to give you your
prize. Congratulations!" She laughed a little as I took the
hand she had on the door and started shaking it. "Yes,
little lady, you've won a hundred-thousand dollars," I
said, slipping past her like an encyclopedia salesman, "a
luxury car, your dream home on Marco Island, and an
extra ten grand for beating the earlybird deadline. May I
come in?" I was in the middle of the room.

"Get out of here, please." Her voice was firm. She
glanced over her shoulder toward the shower noise.

"Don't judge me by what you think of your parents,
Melanie," I said. "Give me ten minutes and I'll leave, I
promise." She put her hands on her hips and shot me an
appraising stare. Her blonde hair was swept up in a beauty
salon punk. She was wearing a kelly green designer
sweatshirt with dolman sleeves and blue graffiti markings
all over it. The sweatshirt drooped down to her butt; below
it were tight black stirrup pants and bare feet. When she'd
had enough of looking at me, she pulled a cigarette from a

pack on the coffee table, lit it, and dropped into an easy chair. It was a very nice suite. I could see into a big bedroom with a chaise, a king-size bed, and a couple of ornate chests. The furnishings throughout were whites and grays; the walls were rose-colored.

"How much are they paying you?" she said, exhaling a deep drag. The room where we sat had a desk, a small bar, and a big TV, in addition to the mandatory sitting equipment. In fact, the place appeared to have everything but a four-year-old boy.

"I don't know yet," I said, settling into the end of the couch beside her chair.

"Bull."

"It's true. Your father and I didn't discuss money. My rates vary, depending on the size of the job, where I have to go, what I have to do, and the exposures . . . the risks. This kind of thing really isn't my specialty. I'll probably just charge him expenses." She laughed again.

"You must think I'm a real head job," she said, "but I do remember you. Daddy's friend."

"I'm sorry your family life has been so unhappy, Melanie. For your sake, much more than for your parents'. I'm not here to try to change your feelings about them or to take your son away from you. When I go back, I'd like to be able to tell his grandparents that I've seen him and that he's okay. Anything after that is between the three of you." A plume of cigarette smoke curled in front of her face. The shower noise stopped.

"He'll just keep sending people down here, won't he?" she asked.

"Until he knows something about little Ben." She rose slowly from the chair and went over to the desk. From the center drawer, she took a fat clasp envelope and tossed it to me.

"Tell him he doesn't have a grandson anymore," she said, standing beside me as I opened the envelope. "His precious little pride and joy has been adopted. I gave him up. He was mine and I gave him away. Tell Daddy 'Merry Christmas.' " Her voice was ragged.

The envelope contained a wad of legal documents. While I went through them, she sat next to me on the couch, as if we were perusing an album of family photos. Although Mexican lawyers, like the American variety, are inclined to make things unintelligible, it did appear that Melanie had legally relinquished her little boy. The dates were fresh, only a few days after she made off with him from her mother's backyard. There were names: an agency, an officer of the agency, and various bureaucrats. It looked very official, and permanent. She could have set it all up before she brought him down.

"I met his father in Lauderdale," she said somberly. "He was like really rich and great looking. We had a terrific time. Then he disappeared, no good-byes or anything, just gone. I looked all over for him. He said he went to Boston University. I called there; they never heard of him. . . . I don't know; I thought it would be really neat to have a baby." Her expression hardened. "But now, Ramon and I have a great thing going. There's no room in it for somebody else's kid. I'm not exactly the mother type as you probably heard from the old man. My parents fucked up my life. I won't let them do it to my kid. You think it's wrong for me to protect him?" Her wet eyes discredited the sneer and jutting chin.

"Who has little Ben now, Melanie?" I asked. She looked up, at something behind me.

"None of your fucking business." Ramon reached over me as he spoke and snatched the papers out of my hands. Still dripping wet, he was wearing a powder-blue velour robe, open across his bare chest. He stepped back from me as I stood, rising half a foot above him. I don't think he liked being outsized.

"You're dripping on the papers, Ramon," I said.

"Who is this guy?" he demanded of Melanie, as he wiped the papers on his sleeve. She went to the bar.

"This is Mr. Wells. He's another one of my father's flunkies. I thought I ought to give him the bad news." Melanie lit herself a fresh cigarette and was opening a wine cooler. "Want one?" she asked me.

I shook my head. "Your father won't accept this," I said.

"That's tough shit," Ramon said, as he helped himself at the bar. "It's all legal. Good lawyers, believe it. It's her kid, not his. She can do what she wants and she wants to get rid of him. That's it. Tough titty for your parents, right, chickie?"

I ignored Ramon. "Just tell me where he is, Melanie."

"No. I don't know. . . ."

"Your dad will find him eventually. You know he will."

She took a long pull from her wine cooler, and said, "I only told you what I did because I used to like you." She laughed coyly and vamped her way across the room to me. Behind her, Ramon shook his head grimly as she put her hands on my shoulders and cocked her hips. Underneath the Giorgio and cigarette smoke was a sour, musty smell. She needed a bath. "Wanna fuck?" she said. She threw Ramon a sly look and waited for me to answer. I laughed and stepped away from her. "I'm serious," she said. "Ramon and I have a very free relationship." She turned back again and caught him smirking.

"Hey, that's right," he said. "Go ahead and fuck her, man. I'll lend you a rubber." He was laughing at both of us. The joke disappeared suddenly from Melanie's eyes, leaving only a vacant sadness and the question.

"I'm sorry, Melanie," I said. I was very sorry.

Fifteen minutes in a hot shower flushed away the external crud of an afternoon on Mexico City's streets, and at least some of the emotional sludge I'd accumulated in

Suite 218 at the Camino Real. It was a little after seven-thirty. I put on fresh slacks and a clean shirt and tried both numbers I had for Doe Aguilar. There was no answer at her home number, and the guy I talked to at the paper didn't think she'd be in again before morning.

It took twenty minutes for my call to go through to Ben Maitland. I split the time: thirty seconds of Mexican TV, and the rest reading a new book about emotional illness among research and development people in the computer industry. A truly poor choice for the old suitcase. After seeing Melanie, what I really needed was *Tom Sawyer*.

Ben had very little to say as I described the encounter with his daughter, and when I finished, there was a long silence. After half a minute of listening to the line buzz, I said, "Ben, are you there?"

"It's hard, Wells," he said. His voice was dead flat. "It's hard being hated that much by your own kid. I guess I'm not surprised she's pulled something like this. Maybe I should be relieved she hasn't killed him."

"I don't think she's capable of that."

"Get him back for me, Wells. I don't care what it takes."

"My business card doesn't say 'kidnapping,' Ben."

"The people who have my grandson are the kidnappers."

"Call the best lawyer you know. Tell him to hire you the best lawyer in Mexico City. That's what it's going to take . . . and a bucket of bribe money."

"Bullshit. It can't be legal. It happened too fast."

"Don't be so sure. She had the right, legally. The wheels of bureaucracy in Mexico can turn very quickly with enough grease, properly applied. The paperwork looked very professional. There's every reason to think a hefty chunk of money was involved. Melanie and Ramon checked into the Camino just a couple of days after the adoption. They didn't win the suite on "Wheel of Fortune," and he sure as hell isn't paying for it out of earned income."

"So she sold him. That's not legal anywhere, Wells."

"Ben, I'm not suggesting there's a bill of sale. Healthy WASP kids, even four years old, can bring twenty-five or thirty thousand dollars, especially if they look like your grandson. It's a business down here, but the money's all under the table."

"Everything you're telling me makes me think you should find him and bring him home. I'll make sure she doesn't get within a mile of him after that."

"I'll be happy to cooperate with your lawyer, Ben. If you want the boy kidnapped, I can't help you. If it turns out there is no legal adoption, we can look at other ways of solving the problem, but for now, I think we must assume that the letter of the law has been followed. I have no reason at all to think it hasn't. Now I'm going to tell you something else you don't want to hear: I think you and Sonja should cease hostilities for seventy-two hours and fly down here to talk to your daughter. She needs you, Ben. I don't think she knows who or what she is. She's suffering. The boyfriend is just along for the ride. Tell her you love her to her face. Tell her it's not her fault you guys split up. Hug her and ask her to let you help." Ben sighed when I finished talking. Then he hung up.

I knew Ben would forgive me in time for delivering the bad news, and for not wanting to risk a prison term for snatching little Ben from his new home. Still, as an inveterate dragon slayer, I was sorry I hadn't set things right for my friend.

Or Mel Berry. Velasquez said Berry would rise from the Sea of Time. Maybe. Were Ramon and Melanie behind the disappearance? My gut said yes. If Mel Berry had lived his life in a way that inspired other people to be fond of him, someone would make an issue of his disappearance. If not . . . well . . . lousy things happen every day. I already had a backlog of evil deeds to avenge.

There was a poisonous silence in my hotel room. I

endured it for thirty minutes, during which I made several futile attempts to connect with the lady reporter. At twenty of nine, I put in a call to Miss Maggie. Her line was busy. I decided to go for a walk.

It was a good decision. There had been a cloudburst while I was inside. The streets were wet, but there were stars overhead and the thunder was moving away. Frisky breezes following the storm cells smelled of rain and the clean places where they'd been. For a night at least, breathing wasn't hazardous in Mexico City.

I walked the Zona Rosa like a beat cop, past the discos, fancy restaurants, and nightclubs; sidestepping knots of affluent young Mexicans out doing the town. On broad, near-empty sidewalks, I circled the National Palace, a mammoth architectural and historic treasure doing double duty as a flophouse for a million pigeons. I kept walking for nearly three hours. It was chilly when I got back to the hotel. And I was tired enough to face my empty room.

I woke at seven and shopped the airlines. The best I could do was a 1:00 P.M. on Continental. The day beyond my window looked bright and packed with potential. Below, the streets and sidewalks bustled with people in business clothes. Worlds waited to be conquered, and I had six virgin hours ahead of me. It seemed like a golden opportunity: I went back to bed.

The phone rang at nine-fifteen. I considered not answering, but you never know when you've won something. "Mr. Wells, did I *wake* you?" She sounded as if the possibility amazed her.

"No, it's a drug overdose," I said. "When I couldn't reach you last night, I decided there was just no reason to go on living."

"Well, as long as I didn't wake you," she laughed. "It's so embarrassing."

"How are you?" I asked, trying to sound alert.

"Fine, thanks. I am sorry about last night, but I told you not to count on it."

"It's okay."

"The wife of one of our big industrialists is running for the senate. I'd asked for an interview. Last night turned out to be the only time she could do it before next week."

"Demands of the job. I understand." I sat up in bed and tried to will a cup of hot, black coffee to materialize on my night table.

"How did you do yesterday? Have you found what you're looking for?"

"The 'what' is a four-year-old boy. No reason not to tell you now. He's my client's grandson. The boy's mother is mentally ill, potentially dangerous. She grabbed him from his grandmother's house a few weeks ago and brought him down here. He's a beautiful kid; it looks like she sold him."

"Black market adoption."

"The papers looked very legit," I said. "Mom and the boyfriend are at the Camino. They'll probably blow the whole payoff in a few weeks."

"And start over again?"

"Not with this boyfriend."

"He's Mexican?"

"No offense."

"None taken. You're right. She'll have to go back home and find herself a nice, blue-eyed blond boy if she wants to sell her babies. I guess this means you'll be going home." She sounded disappointed.

"I'm on a one o'clock flight. Send me your series on Barron, okay? The address is on the card I gave you."

"If I ever write it, sure."

"Philadelphia! That's it. You've got a Philadelphia accent."

"You're incredible, Gardner."

"I'll take that as a compliment. Am I right? Did you learn English in Philadelphia, or from a Philadelphian?"

"Both. My father was Consul General there for six years. I went to the U of P and then did graduate work in journalism at Columbia. After that, I went back to Philadelphia and got a job reporting at the *Bulletin*."

"And when the paper folded, you came home. Right?"

"Nobody's ever told me I have a Philadelphia accent."

"Don't be defensive. Lots of otherwise nice people have Philadelphia accents. It's from the cockney, you know."

"How do you know so much about it?"

"Kind of a hobby."

"I'm really sorry I have to miss out on dinner."

"Next time, Doe."

"It doesn't sound to me like you're planning to rush back."

"I'll see you again."

"I hope so, Gardner. Good luck."

"I'm glad you called, Doe."

I was sorry to say goodbye to her. I took a shower, packed, and called Pete Velasquez to thank him for his help. He said he'd let me know if Mel Berry turned up.

Knowing it would probably be the last edible food I'd see before I set foot in my kitchen, I ordered a medium-sized breakfast of fruit, cheese, peasant bread, and black coffee in the hotel dining room. Adequately fortified, I paid my bill and got a cab. The day had gone from bright blue to yellow gray. The rain-fresh air of the night before had given way to Mexico City's standard haze, rippled by gas fumes and heat. I wanted to call Doe and tell her to move out of there, but I was certain the lady had long since weighed the health risks of living in Mexico City against whatever she regarded as the personal benefits.

When we reached the airport, I felt like I needed a shower though it had been all of two hours since I'd had

one. . . . After I checked in, I found a cool, dark place
and a Tecate to keep me company until it was time to
board. I carried the beer to a corner table and stretched my
legs out in front of me. My mind was flitting in and out of
a Buddhist meditation exercise I used to do when the
newspaper went by under an elbow. For a second, it didn't
register. It was one of the afternoon tabloids. The picture
was about three inches square, lower left-hand corner,
front page. Ramon Aguirre. Either a very unflattering
likeness or Ramon was dead. I caught up with the guy and
borrowed his paper. The story was on page eleven. Latin
America's answer to Steven Spielberg had been shot six
times in the face, chest, and groin. . . . Police are investigating. No mention of Melanie Maitland. The article was
smaller than the picture. . . . I returned the guy's paper
and paid for his drink.

I knew what I'd want Ben to do for me if the situation
were reversed. Even so, I couldn't help thinking that the
hand of fate had just raised its middle finger at me.

· · Chapter Five · ·

I had fifty minutes and a fistful of change from the bartender. From a pay phone, I called the Camino Real. Somehow I didn't think Melanie Maitland would be hanging around her hotel room grieving for Ramon, but sometimes miracles happen. Sometimes. The woman in 218 mistook me for the manager and told me I was crazy if I thought she'd "come all the way from Orlando to stay in such a Plain Jane suite."

Pete Velasquez answered on the third ring. I told him I had little time and a large need to know the condition and whereabouts of Melanie Maitland. He said he'd call me back in fifteen minutes. It was twenty and Pete wasn't happy. He started saying he was sorry before I got the phone to my ear.

"It's okay, Pete," I assured him, "I can still catch the plane."

"It's not that, Wells."

"She's dead?"

"No. I mean we don't know. We're not sure where she is."

"So what is it?" I knew the answer before he could speak. I felt their body heat behind me and smelled the sweat they'd worked up finding me. I hung up the phone, raised my hands above my head and turned toward the waiting barrel of a thirty-eight. We live in a time when it's wise to play the lamb with airport cops. There were two of them —young and nervous; three more were running toward us. I held out my hands for the cuffs. Nobody was smiling.

A virtually wordless journey ended in the interrogation room of a police station near the Zona Rosa. Pete Velasquez and a Lieutenant Portillo were waiting for us. Ramon had been murdered on Portillo's turf; when Pete called him to ask about Melanie, Portillo decided that I was the one who should be answering questions and ordered me brought in. I could see that Pete felt rotten about it. He was taking a chance by leaving his responsibilities to chaperone me.

It had been a few years since I'd seen Pete. He looked good, a little taller and thinner than I remembered. Same thick, curly dark hair, and broad, ingratiating smile. His handshake, strong and self-assured, reminded me that he was trouble on the tennis court. He was wearing a light blue Izod shirt and tan slacks. The informality surprised me. Portillo had on the more traditional shiny gray suit textured with little tufts of black thread and ubiquitous wrinkles. I suspected he was close to Pete's age, mid-thirties, but he looked much older. The suit, pale complexion, and receding hairline were part of it; the rest was attitude.

Pete started things off by ordering my escorts to remove the cuffs. Portillo resented the friendly gesture. Portillo did the questioning, in Spanish—though he spoke English as well as Pete did. Pete chimed in occasionally as a character witness. I told them everything.

The room was hot, the air rancid from decades of

cigarette smoke. We sat around an orphaned metal desk on cast-off chairs. By three-thirty, Portillo seemed convinced of my innocence, and anxious to be rid of me. During the interrogation, I learned that they'd found traces of cocaine all over Suite 218, but no Melanie. The place had been totally trashed. Portillo's theory was that Ramon had been killed in a drug deal gone sour and that Melanie had been abducted, either in the hope that she could be made to reveal something, or so that she could be raped under more secure circumstances, or both. In any case, Portillo figured, she was dead.

Pete Velasquez and I were headed in opposite directions when the party broke up, but he commandeered a patrol car to take me to the destination of my choice. The cop driving was not happy to learn that I wanted to go to Netza, but when I reminded him that I might have said Los Angeles, he flipped on his siren and did an impressive job of making what might have been a long, tedious ride short and suspenseful. When we reached the Sacred Heart Pediatric Clinic, the crew was loading their gear into a van.

Chaco Aguirre found it hard to believe that the police would play taxi for someone interested only in buying him a drink. I explained who I was, in Spanish, and why I was there. That Melanie Maitland's father had become worried about her and little Ben, even prior to Ramon's murder, seemed entirely reasonable to Chaco. He accepted my offer and invited me to ride along while he dropped off people on the crew.

We wound up in the Aristos, a tourist hotel on the Paseo de la Reforma. The thirsty crowd seemed about evenly divided between local office workers and hotel guests. There was an empty bandstand and dance floor at one end of the room. I led the way to a table beside the bandstand where I thought we could hear each other above the canned mariachis. The waitress was about twenty-two, with sparkling eyes and D-cup boobs cruelly confined by her black uniform. Chaco ordered pulque, a bitter, milky liquid produced by fermenting cactus juice. I ordered Mezcal and told her to make them both doubles.

Chaco looked more like Ramon in the subdued light of the bar. They had the same sharp eyes and high cheekbones. In Ramon, the eyes were marks of crafty insincerity. In Chaco, they were honest eyes, curious and intelligent, not for hiding, but for taking in.

"It's too bad you have to work today," I said, trying to sound comfortable with Chaco's language.

"I speak English," he said, looking up at me. He was running his thumbnail under the opposing nails of his right hand.

"Glad to hear it." I said in English. "A couple of drinks will play hell with my Spanish." A corner of Chaco's upper right incisor was missing and several of his front teeth were capped with silver, a characteristic common among people raised on the local water.

"I learned my craft at a TV station in L.A. KNXT. Started in film processing and worked my way up. There was a big push on to hire minorities. They didn't know I was a wetback." He smiled. The bad teeth coarsened his appearance, yet he was good-looking in a rugged way. "I came home when they switched to video. I wanted to stay in film, and make movies." He laughed at himself.

"Sorry about your brother."

"We weren't close." His eyes dropped to the empty ashtray in front of him. He started turning it with his left hand.

"But you didn't like it that way," I said.

He looked up at me again. "What do you want with me, Mr. . . ."

"Wells. Call me Gardner. As I mentioned, your brother was involved with the daughter of a friend of mine, Ben Maitland. Ben and Melanie had been estranged for some time, but he was very close to her son. I came down here to find the boy after Melanie took him from his grand-mother's house. Little Ben had been living there. Melanie wasn't much of a parent.''

"I'd go along with that. Are you a cop?"

"No. I do investigative work for a living, but this isn't my line. I'm just trying to help a friend." Chaco dug an unopened pack of cigarettes from the pocket of his blue plaid shirt. He was looking for the waitress. "Have you seen Melanie or heard anything about her since the murder?"

"No." He answered quickly. "I didn't see much of her before. Sometimes she and the boy would hang around while we were shooting. Sometimes not. I didn't know anything about her. He just showed up with her."

"When he came down to work for you?"

"Yes." The waitress was headed our way. Chaco settled back in his chair.

"Have you made funeral arrangements?"

"Saturday. Ten o'clock. St. Theresa."

"Where is that?"

"Cuauhtémoc. Are you coming?" He sounded incredulous.

"Would you mind?"

"No." The idea seemed to please him. We took a break from conversation to admire the waitress as she set the drinks in front of us. I paid for the first round and another.

"To Ramon," I said, raising my glass. We drank. "What got the two of you interested in filmmaking?"

"Our father was an assistant director and a cameraman. He was getting ready to direct his first feature when he died. Our mother was an actress. She gave it up when they were married."

"She's still living?"

"Yes. She was so excited when she heard Ramon was coming back. Then he didn't go to see her for three weeks. I know it hurt her, but she didn't say anything about it. He bragged that he was going with this rich American girl, but he didn't bring her with him to meet Mama. Mama asked me if I thought Ramon was ashamed of her. A fine son!''

"Her favorite?'' Chaco nodded and emptied his glass.

"He couldn't do anything wrong in her eyes. Two days after the first visit, he came back for a few minutes and barely spoke to her. I think he must have taken something, jewelry, maybe. Mama had some old silver, too. Ramon liked cocaine.''

"How much?''

"I don't think it was too bad.'' Chaco put the pack of smokes between his thumb and index finger and turned it.

"He lived well.''

"The Camino? Hah! She paid for it.''

"How?''

"She's rich.''

"No,'' I said. "Her parents are, but it wasn't their money. She sold her kid.''

"Shit. That sounds like one of Ramon's schemes. He loved the fast life.''

As the waitress deployed fresh drinks, I put a tip on her tray. She cocked her head to one side, said she'd be back, and flashed me a pretty smile. When she was gone, I popped the question. "Who killed him?''

"I don't know. Ramon lived a dirty life. I took a chance getting him the job with me, but the way things were going, I thought we would lose him completely.''

"The family.''

"Yes. But it didn't help. He liked working with a big star. That's why he came back. Not to be with his family. I only saw him while we were working. I think he wanted Bobby Barron to *discover* him or something. He dressed like the pimps in L.A.''

"The police think Ramon went down in a drug deal.''

"It could be. If Ramon was dealing drugs he wouldn't have told me. To tell the truth, I hope they just let it go.

Our mother's heart is broken. What good would it do to
have more bad things come out about Ramon?''

"What about his killers? Don't you want them punished?''

"I don't care about that. They weren't killing Chaco
Aguirre's brother. They were just killing another punk like
themselves. It's their way. Ramon wanted to live like that.
I see you think it's strange that I don't want revenge.''

"I do, a little. You Mexicans are very fatalistic.''

"We are, but don't think every Mexican would feel the
way I do.'' He dropped the pack of cigarettes back into his
shirt pocket. I took a large bite of Mezcal; I could feel my
face flush as it hit home.

"Are you married?''

"Divorced. She fell for a Pemex executive during the
oil boom. He was rich.'' Chaco laughed and took a knock
from his pulque. "Now he's in jail.''

"Kids?''

He shook his head. "She was carrying our first when
she met him. A few weeks later she told me she'd miscar-
ried. I think it was an abortion.''

"Sorry.''

"I celebrated when they put the bastard in jail. He's got
six years to go and she's getting fat. So you see, sometimes there is justice.''

The six o'clock glare put my eyes in a hard squint as we
emerged from the cool darkness of the hotel bar onto the
sidewalk. I gladly accepted Chaco's offer of a ride. He
took me first to El Pescador and waited patiently at the
curb while I checked in. I welcomed the chance to off-load
my luggage and wash my face. Our next destination was
Excelsior, Doe Aguilar's newspaper. The Mezcal had inspired thoughts of a romantic dinner with a beautiful woman,
and Ms. Aguilar had said she would be free this very
night. It seemed only fitting that I present myself and my
invitation in person. Turn-downs are too easy over the
phone.

When we got to the paper, I thanked Chaco and got a phone number. Doe was in the library, going through a microfiche of back issues. She was delighted to see me. Visions of a lovely evening shone brightly in my crystal ball. I spoke eloquently of Taittinger, rack of lamb, and dancing under the smog.

"Tomorrow night, Gardner, I promise." The tone was consoling; the big eyes were full of regret; the sweet lips were tilted in a sympathetic smile.

"I won't get violent," I assured her, "but I am disappointed as hell." I was suddenly aware of the dull, utilitarian space that surrounded us. It reminded me of the Army. Rows and rows of floor-to-ceiling metal racks were jammed with files, books, papers, and periodicals. At one end, were the librarian's desk and a half dozen large gray tables each surrounded by four or five chairs. I'd grabbed one of them and rolled it to the reader where Doe was working.

"I know a wonderful place where we can go," she said excitedly, and touched my hand as if to prove it. "It's an old Carmelite monastery, Desierto de los Leones. It's up in the hills west of the city. There are beautiful gardens and a great restaurant. We could take a tour of the monastery, if you like, before dinner." She had on a becoming beige dress, high-collared, long-sleeved, with layers of ruffles cascading from the neckline.

"Sounds nice," I admitted. "Do the monks take American Express?"

"Oh, it's a public park now. The monastery hasn't been active for years."

"Well, I think we should drive up there tonight, before it loses any more of its charm."

"I've got to research this Barron series. My editor is losing patience with me."

"I thought you were going to rewrite their handouts."

"I just can't. What I'm doing will be almost as bad, but at least it will be true."

"Do I have to buy a paper to find out what you came up with?"

"I'm profiling each of his major charitable interests in the city. Lots of case histories, photos of cute kids."

"A string section playing in the background?"

"I'm afraid so."

"So write the good news now and the bad later on when you can back it up."

"I intend to. Actually, I haven't turned up anything really sensational. Just a lot of inconsistencies. He calls Mexico his 'second home'; he says his mother was Mexican. But I found out he was raised in an orphanage near Los Angeles. He never knew either of his parents and there are no records about them. I have a friend on the *L.A. Times* who checked it out."

"Genetic memory?"

"Good thought. I'll get some DNA from him and see how it responds to green chile."

"What do you think?"

"I have nothing but guesses and rumors to go on. The fact is that his interest in our country has been a positive thing. He helps support charities all over the city; he's down here two or three times a year doing benefit concerts. He raised a fortune after the earthquake. The people love him, especially young people—a lot more so than in the States. He's a role model—the flashy free spender, the hero with a heart."

"What's his real name? Not Bobby Barron."

"Yes, believe it or not. My friend in L.A. said he was what they used to call a Doe baby, a foundling—abandoned during the Depression. I guess someone at the orphanage picked the name, and his first name isn't even Robert. It's actually Bobby. Oh, and based on his official estimated date of birth, he'll be fifty in a couple of months. His bio says he's forty-two."

"Stop the presses."

"I told you . . . ," Doe scolded.

"Sorry. Go on."

"Well, the main thing is the connection to organized crime. I should say 'alleged connection.' "

"You're among friends."

"I hope so. The rumors have been there for years. Some of Barron's friends are not exactly altar boy material. Carlo Rossano, Meyer Sakin, Sylva Mendez down here. There are many others. These people are into drugs, pornography, all kinds of political corruption."

"Where does Barron fit in? According to the rumors." She bit her lower lip and looked strangely at me. "I don't work for him," I said. "And if I did, you've already hanged yourself."

"How did you know what I was thinking?"

"Where did we meet? Barron's dressing room. What do we really know about each other? Not very much. And here I am pumping you about Bobby Barron. But then I've told you what brought me back into your life and you know that Ramon was killed. Your suspicion is reasonable but incorrect. So talk. Where does Barron fit in?" She smiled and shrugged. I'd won her confidence. I just couldn't get her to go out for dinner.

"I don't think he does fit in. Not as a real part of the organization. If anything, I think he's a tool, and a toy—a plaything for the big boys. They've probably helped him more than he's helped them—money for his shows, bookings at their hotels in Las Vegas and Atlantic City. . . ."

"Reno, Tahoe, New York, Miami. Movie work. Probably minority ownership of a casino."

"Exactly."

"He adds a little glamour to their dreary lives; they like showing him off to their women and political friends." She nodded. "And every so often, he moves some coke for them—under the false bottom of a wardrobe trunk or stuffed in the gas tank of his Rolls." She nodded again.

"And I'll just bet he's got a production company that comes in handy now and again for laundering money."

"And I can't prove any of it. Here, just look at this, Gardner." She motioned me over to the viewer. "There, see, lower right-hand corner. The picture. This was five years ago, the ground-breaking for the orphanage I'm visiting tomorrow. That's the Mayor holding the shovel with Barron. Behind them in the front row of the crowd, that's Sylva Mendez, our local cocaine king. The one with the funny mustache is Carlos Romero; he buys and sells politicians. . . ." Her shoulder pressed against mine as we stared into the viewer. Her perfume was making me crazy.

"Aren't you hungry, damnit?" I asked, showing more frustration than I intended. She laughed and took my hand as she turned to face me.

"Gardner, tomorrow night. You will come to my apartment at seven, we will have a drink or two, and then dinner. I will even make the reservations."

"Okay," I said. We shook hands. In a less liberated time, I might have said it concerned me that doing an exposé on a character like Barron could have an adverse effect on her health and career, but I was sure she knew that. I returned my chair to the table where I'd gotten it and said, "At least recommend a restaurant."

"Magritte," she said. "Two blocks west, one south. Excellent French food." She sounded like someone working the front desk at a hotel. My cue to leave.

"Thanks."

"And not too many single women." She smiled and waved as I swung the door open to go. I took a last look and realized again that I could grow very fond of this lady.

Magritte was not a place one would ever confuse with Friday's, but whatever it lacked in conviviality, it paid back handsomely to the palate. My red snapper was fresh and boneless. It had been buttered, lemoned, and herbed by someone with a knowing hand, and then baked in a golden crust fit for the gods. I was truly sorry to see it, and the last of a cheerful Riesling, disappear.

There was a message waiting for me at the hotel from Pete Velasquez. He'd left his home number. The hotel had given me a room two floors higher and one door south of the one in which I'd spent the previous two nights. The decor was identical except for the art behind the bed. A still life of a turquoise-colored pottery with bright flowers hung in the space that in my previous room had been occupied by a woven Aztec sunburst. I preferred the sunburst. One of Pete's kids answered the phone and yelled for her father. He might have been scuba diving somewhere off the Yucatan and heard her.

"I think I have something for you, Wells," he told me.

"A new ear drum?"

"Sorry, we're trying to teach her. She doesn't realize. . . ."

"The Maitland girl?"

"No, and it's a good thing. You remember La Merced?"

"Sure, the old market district. Lots of charm, the cops used to work in threes as I recall."

"That's the place. Yesterday afternoon, we had a report of a body there. An old man investigating a smell found it in one of the condemned buildings. The rats had gotten to it pretty badly. . . ."

"You think it's Berry?"

"We can't be sure. Even if the rats had not fed on the flesh, whoever killed the man wasn't taking any chances—the head and hands had been cut off. From what's there, the coroner thinks he's been dead a week or two, so the time is about right for it to be Berry. The size, also, is about right, but what convinces me is that the man had had a hip replacement. We called Berry's former wife and she confirmed that he had the surgery in 1973. His walking had gotten very bad—some sort of war injury in Korea years earlier."

"I kind of wish you'd caught him banging some sun bunny at Club Med."

"I know."

"Any other evidence? Cause of death?"

"There was no evidence of recent injuries other than those I mentioned. There are blood stains going from a side entrance of the building to where the body was found so we assume he was killed elsewhere and taken there."

"Clothes?"

"None. But that's not unusual."

"Taken by scavengers?"

"Probably. It appeared that the body had been turned and moved a short distance from the position in which it was originally left."

"I hope they know a good dry cleaner."

"I'm sorry it isn't better news. Have you learned anything?"

"That Ramon Aguirre was not the ideal son. Other than that, not much. I'm going to try to arrange a meeting with Bobby Barron."

"How can he help you?"

"I won't know till I ask him. Maybe not at all. Ramon was a sleaze. Barron is a sleaze. Ramon was trying to get Bobby to take an interest in him. Maybe he was successful, maybe too successful."

"Señor Barron is not very approachable from what I understand. He may not see you. He might be insulted by the suggestion that he even knew a man like Ramon Aguirre."

"I know someone who can get me the meeting. There are other ways I can go if it doesn't produce anything, but seeing Barron is an easy and obvious place to start. What are your people doing about Ramon?"

"The usual. . . ."

"Nothing?"

"Have you not heard that we Mexican police are notori-

ous for locking up innocent visitors to our country and
making them pay huge fines—after they've rotted in one
of our jails for a month or two?''

"In other words, nothing.''

"I'm sure Lieutenant Portillo is checking for witnesses
and interrogating sources in the drug trade.''

"So as far as you know, there are no real leads or special
angles. It's a straightforward investigation based on the
circumstantial evidence.''

"That's right. If there's anything more to it, Portillo
didn't confide in me. You think there is?''

"There might be. Ramon has no history as a drug
dealer; neither does Melanie.''

"You said she was a user; they have to pay for it.''

"I was with her forty-eight hours ago. If she's doing
drugs now, it's not heavy. Did you see the autopsy on
Ramon.''

"Just alcohol in his system. But Wells, none of this
proves they weren't dealing.''

"I didn't like Portillo's description of the hotel room. It
sounded like it had snowed cocaine in there.''

"A fight. The place was a mess.''

"And there's nothing in the autopsy to confirm that
Ramon had been in a fight, right?''

"As a matter of fact, no, but that doesn't mean he
wasn't in a fight, and it says nothing at all about the girl.
She could have been in the fight.''

"What can I say? It reads like a fake to me. If Melanie
would sell her own kid, why wouldn't she tell these guys
what they wanted to know to save her ass? And if they'd
wanted to rape her, they could have gagged her easily
enough and done it there. Portillo's on a dead-end street.''

"If so, it will be familiar territory for my friend the
lieutenant. But you are not on familiar territory. Melvin
Berry was not on familiar territory, either. There are six

million rats in La Merced, Gardner. They're always hungry."

"I'll be careful, Pete."

"See that you are. Adios."

"Adios."

I was tired. I asked room service to dispatch some Glenfiddich, undressed, and climbed into the shower. It had been a long day, a complicating day. Ramon was dead; Melanie had disappeared and was possibly dead as well. And little Ben. Little Ben was not where he belonged. Twenty-four hours earlier, the situation had appeared stable. I wondered what had happened to the equilibrium. I wondered if the what had been me.

It wasn't Glenfiddich, but whatever they sent had the rich, smoky taste of good Scotch. With my trusty white robe wrapped around me, I stretched out on the king-size bed and sipped, and looked at the closed dresser drawers across the room from me. I had left the second drawer from the bottom open a quarter of an inch as a security precaution. It was closed tight. The suitcase I'd left hard against the right rear corner of my closet was an inch off the back wall and three inches to the left of where I'd put it. In the suitcase, I keep my little black box. It looks sort of mysterious and high tech, yet when the curious intruder flips it open, he sees nothing more interesting than a Hewlett Packard scientific calculator. When he closes it, he signs my guest book. If pressure is not applied to a concealed touchpad below the left hinge when the latch makes contact, an LED under the calculator is switched on. I swung the suitcase onto the bed, opened it, and took out the little black box. Whoever visited me had not been a thief. I pulled the calculator from its Velcro moorings; beneath it glowed the red eye.

Less than six hours had passed since I'd dropped my bag in the closet and cracked open the drawer. Pete Velasquez, José Portillo, Chaco Aguirre, and Doe Aguilar all knew I was in town and where I was staying. Pete hadn't ordered my room searched. Chaco seemed like a real longshot. Either Lt. Portillo or my friend the reporter might have been curious enough about me to have a search done. I would have liked to think I'd won Doe's confidence. But that was presumptuous. I dug my bug buster from under the false panel in the bottom of my Hartmann and checked the room for transmitters. Nothing. Someone had missed a golden opportunity to hear me do *Pagliacci* in the shower. I reset the black box; turned off the lights and got into bed.

There's something lonely about sleeping by yourself in a king-size bed. If Doe had had the room searched, and if she'd told them to leave a bug, I could have invited her to join me, just by saying a few words to the walls. Then, in an hour, there might have been a gentle knocking, followed by a sheepish smile, as she climbed into the bed.

If we had some ham, we could have ham and eggs, if we had some eggs.

·· Chapter Six ··

A pot of coffee arrived from room service while I was shaving. As the aroma from the steaming pot spread through the room, I hit the deck for some physical maintenance: pushups, situps, stretches, and deep knee bends. I like what exercising does for me, but I've never learned to enjoy it.

When the workout was over, I poured myself a cup and put in a call to Frank Cutter's home in Las Vegas. It was an hour earlier there, but I remembered Frank as an early riser. Cutter had parlayed the small fortune he made producing movies for the drive-in circuit into pieces of two big casinos. We met because Frank thought he had an embezzler on his payroll. A guy I'd worked for who sold Frank electronic gaming equipment told him I could help. I tagged the crook and Frank said he owed me.

In his world, Cutter is a powerful man, enshrined in a grandiose office, surrounded by people panting for his approval. But a block away beneath the flashing blue light,

Frank is just another K mart shopper. I thought I'd do better with Frank if I caught him away from the trappings of power, preferably standing in his underwear.

" 'Lo," he said. My former client was gasping.

"Frank, it's Gardner Wells. How are you?" He sounded like he was having a coronary.

"Nev' bet'. Who'd you say this is?"

"Gardner Wells, Frank. Did I catch you at a bad time?"

"Oh, Wells, hey, s'okay. I was just riding the exercise bike. You know, fifteen minutes a day."

"Good for you, Frank." I imagined his round, freckled face, flushed like a tomato. "I won't keep you, Frank. I need a favor. I'd like you to arrange a meeting for me with Bobby Barron. I'm in Mexico City; so's he, at the El Dorado."

"Shit, Wells, whaddya wanna fuck with him for?" Breathing and vocabulary returning to normal, Doctor.

"My client's daughter and grandson have disappeared. The daughter's boyfriend worked for Barron. He was murdered two days ago."

"Great. You want me to set up a meet for you with Barron so you can accuse him of murder. Call him yourself."

"We both know I wouldn't get past the steno pool."

"I can't see it, Wells." I could hear him lighting one of his seven-inch cigars. "Barron's a wild man. You know, they call him the 'Lord of Las Vegas'? He believes it. He'd shit bricks if you come on to him about something like this."

"Frank, I'm not going to accuse Bobby. He's a humanitarian. There's a child involved. I'm sure he'll want to help." I tried to sound sincere.

"Makes sense, what you say; the only thing is, I'm not gonna call him. Barron and I have some of the same business associates. I got an investment to protect. I said I owed you, but I never had nothing like this in mind."

"What did you have in mind, Frank? Use of the place in Tahoe for a weekend? I'm talking about a five-dollar phone call; you're getting off cheap. You wanted your embezzler and I handed him to you. Our understanding was that you'd fire him, recover what you could, and make sure he never worked in Nevada again except washing dishes. No publicity, no scandal. Everybody knows all the casinos are squeaky clean these days. Well, that was okay with me. What wasn't okay with me is that you had old Freddie Tarbell mashed by a truck before I'd even left town."

"I don't have any idea what you're talking about and you better shut up."

"Phone bugged, Frank?"

"You son of a bitch."

"I'm going out for a couple of hours, Frank. When I get back, I'll expect to be able to call Barron's office and hear them ask what color limousine they should send around."

"Bastard."

"I'll take that as a yes, Frank." He hung up, but he'd make the call.

The hotel pool was directly below my window. In it, a long-legged brunette with a deep tan and a pale blue stretch bikini was swimming slow laps. There was no one else around. I felt a sudden desire to get wet. I pulled on the swim trunks that live in my suitcase, grabbed my robe, and headed her way. It was eight-ten when I left my watch and other belongings on a chair beside the pool. The pool was on the shady side of the hotel; the air was cool enough to make goose bumps. If the brunette had noticed me, she was doing a great job of not showing it. I walked to the end of the pool. She was swimming away from me, same easy cadence. Her well-muscled arms barely rippled the oily smooth surface of the pool as they dug into the water and pulled her forward. The kick appeared almost effort-less, scissor smooth, but powerful; like the stroke, leaving the surrounding water nearly undisturbed. Her buttocks and shoulders rolled in a gentle reciprocating rhythm as sheets of water washed over her.

I crouched at the edge and made my dive. She was just pushing off the far end when I hit the water. My entry was respectable: not too much splash, deep enough for an efficient trajectory. The water was warm, near body temperature. Just prior to surfacing, I opened my eyes and saw the submerged half of her swimming toward me in the neighboring lane. Each of her strokes filled the water under her with tiny bubbles. Her full breasts, barely contained by her bikini, rocked gently as she worked her torso. Her pelvis remained almost motionless despite her kick. I surfaced as we passed each other, about mid-pool. It took me several strokes to find my beat. I swam easily to the end, and then pushed off, using the full strength of my legs to propel me in the opposite direction.

Lap after lap, she held the same intoxicating, almost languid, cadence I'd admired from my room. When the sun found us, she was only a stroke or two ahead of me. I slowed down to admire the view. Her lower back made a powerful arch, up and under the bottom of her bikini. Her buns shifted deliciously under the expanse of stretch fabric, which glistened now in the light. Her hair flowed in glorious mahogany tresses over her back. I felt the sun's heat on my shoulders and began to imagine us coupled in heated passion under a palm. Just then, she kicked out. Flank speed, Admiral. My mind was not on swimming. She moved quickly ahead of me. I'd almost matched her at the turn. I pulled ahead in the next lap, pushed off, and passed her, still swimming for the wall. I gave it everything I had. At the end, I turned to wait for her. But she was gone. Breathing hard, I looked in every direction. A big steel and glass door leading to the side lobby hissed closed. I saw her through it, wearing a towel, tall legs and magnificent haunches receding into the shadows.

I rolled over and did an indifferent backstroke to the far end, where I lifted myself out. A trail of wet footprints, female variety, crossed the concrete from the pool to the chair where I had left my things. I followed them, and there, among my belongings, was a key to room 919, which did not happen to be the room in which I was staying. I looked up at the acre of glass above me and wondered if she was up there somewhere, watching the large wet man with the sudden, silly grin all over his face.

I had only a few minutes to shave and dress. No time for breakfast with the swimmer. No taste for the anonymous screw. To the gray suit and blue shirt, I added a red Paisley tie. I needed to look responsible. I gave myself the once-over in the mirror and decided I would have happily lent me large sums of money.

I had two quick items of business to take care of in the lobby. One was breakfast: a candy bar. I took care of the other item in the resort shop, where I bought what I thought was a rather snappy little string bikini, diagonal multicolor neon striping, on a black background. I asked the salesclerk to gift wrap it with the key and send the package to Room 919, along with a note. "Enjoyed our swim. You make a lovely wake. —Gardner Wells." This was safe sex in the extreme.

The Mendez Adoption Agency had no inventory, I discovered. No sparkling glass counters full of babies cooing at excited couples. It was just another office on the third floor of a tired low rise in the Federal District. I'd taken the name from Melanie's relinquishment papers and called for an appointment after my session with Lieutenant Portillo. Mendez was certainly not trying to impress anyone. The suite was small, dark, and smelled faintly of disinfectant. There were two private offices behind a reception area. The door was opened to one: closed to the other. Through the open door, I could see a sixties-style wooden executive desk with a high-back swivel chair. There was a window behind the desk covered by a closed Venetian blind. There were no lights on. According to the name plate in front of her, the receptionist was L. Griego. She made a point of telling me she was born in the U.S. Immigrant parents, I guessed; probably grew up in the Corpus Christi–Brownsville region. She spoke Texan as well as J.R.

"Señora Guzman will be with you shortly," L. informed me. "You-all can just have a seat right here and keep me company till she's ready. I'd offer you coffee but the maker's busted; wouldn't you know it?"

"Happens every time," I agreed. She was plump, about thirty. The sleeveless yellow sun dress was an unfortunate choice for a woman whose upper arms looked like loaves of unbaked bread.

"You and Missus Wells . . ." She pronounced it "whales." ". . . interested in any special sort of child? We do have the most lovely children. I can say that for a fact."

"I think I'd like a rich one," I said. "You know, heir to an oil fortune. Working is such a bore. And a girl; she'd be less likely to disown me when she comes of age than a boy."

"Oh, Mr. Wells, you're a scream." L. laughed hard enough to flutter the fins of flab below her arms. "But you know," she leaned over to confide in me, "Señora Guzman takes her job very seriously. I wouldn't joke with her."

"Wouldn't think of it," I promised.

The stern matron I expected to confront in Señora Guzman's office turned out to be five feet ten inches of handsome strawberry blonde; vintage 1947, I guessed. The fine, glossy hair was pulled behind her head in a French braid. She had high cheekbones and pale, pink lipstick that complimented her lavender suit. She rose as I entered and extended her hand.

"How do you do, Mr. Wells?" The grip was warm and sure.

"Very well, thank you." I followed her lead and sat in one of the pair of Queen Anne chairs facing her desk. The whole office was done in English antiques. Except for the skyline framed in the window behind her, it might have been the office of a Vassar dean.

"I'm from Sneden's Landing, originally," she said, anticipating my question. "It's . . ."

"On the Hudson, just above New York." I couldn't help showing off.

"Correct." She sat back and folded her hands in front of her chest.

"I guess I'm not the first to be surprised."

"It's perfectly natural. No one expects Señora Guzman to be someone like me. My husband was born in this country, you see." There was a hint of embarrassment in the way she said it, but none in the way she wore his ring—a four-carat-plus, marquise-shaped diamond on a split gold ring. Señor Guzman, I guessed, was not a sharecropper. "Well," she said, gaveling the meeting to order, "Lucinda tells me you're interested in adopting. Perhaps I should tell you about our agency. . . ." I wanted to hear her spiel, but she would not appreciate my allowing her to proceed under a misapprehension.

"Excuse me, Señora. . . ."

"Please call me Adrienne."

"Thank you. When I made the appointment, I said that I was interested in *an* adoption."

"Yes?" The bright smile slumped a sixteenth of a inch.

"Your agency recently handled the relinquishment of a little boy named Ben Maitland by his mother, Melanie." Her smile faded into an impassive stare.

"All of our services are confidential, Mr. Wells, without exception."

"I understand. Two nights ago, Melanie's boyfriend was murdered. Melanie has disappeared. Her parents are very concerned."

"I'm sure."

"I thought you might be able to shed some light on her situation in Mexico City . . . friends, contacts, whoever referred her here."

"Just what is your capacity in all this?"

"I'm acting for her father."

"As a lawyer, investigator?"

"As a friend with more time and talent for such matters than he has."

"I'm sure you understand why I can't help you." She pressed her palms against the edge of her desk. She wasn't going to budge.

"The agency is represented by legal counsel, I assume. Perhaps you'd be kind enough to tell me who your lawyer is."

"Of course, Mr. Wells," She produced his card from a side drawer of her desk as efficiently as she might have her own. It said, "Tio Romero" in raised gold letters on heavy, cream-colored stock. The address and telephone information were printed in flowing script along the bottom. I was impressed.

"Thank you," I said. We rose together. "Who has the office next to yours?" I asked as she rounded the end of her desk.

"Mr. Albert," she answered pleasantly. "He's out of town. I'm the director. Mr. Albert is our associate director."

"Another American?" I asked as cordially as I could.

"I'm sure Mr. Albert's nationality is a private matter, Mr. Wells. Good day." She opened the door and stood aside to let me pass.

"Good day, Adrienne, Lucinda," I said as we stepped into the reception area. "Thank you for your time."

·· Chapter Seven ··

One did not call Bobby Barron at his hotel room. One called The Barron Group, Limited, and talked to Mr. Barron's personal secretary, Glenda, who was, of all things, English. There was a time, I remembered, when it was very "in" in show biz to have an English secretary. Maybe it still was. Glenda informed me with hushed urgency that Mr. Cutter had indeed called on my behalf and that Mr. Barron would, of course, be delighted to see me. She had taken the liberty of scheduling me for four that afternoon, and said she hoped I could transact all of my business with Mr. Barron in two minutes because that was all the time he could possibly spare. I hardly knew what to say.

For lunch, the hotel chef was pushing shrimp in red sauce over rice, served with a big, green salad. I decided not to risk the salad. In Mexico, the wrong lettuce leaf can have you shackled to the john for three days. I settled for warm, crusty bread and an ice-cold bottle of Dos Equis.

Despite sheer curtains, the brilliant glare of midday flooded the big dining room with light. My sunglasses were upstairs. I allowed the waiter to twist my arm and ordered another beer to keep me company while I tended to the last of my shellfish. I was thinking siesta when I heard the maitre d' asking a group of men nearby if any of them was "Dr. Gardner Wells." I identified myself and got directions to a house phone.

"Gardner?" An anxious female voice. "I had them page you that way because I wasn't sure they'd look for you otherwise. I'm glad I found you."

"I am, too, Doe, unless you're about to tell me you can't make it tonight."

"No. We're all set. But something's happened. The orphanage I visited this morning? One of the women who works there told me something. We're going to meet in about an hour, when she goes home. I want you to be there. Can you make it?" She was excited.

"Yes. What did she tell you?"

"I'm calling from a store around the corner. . . ."

"Too public?"

"Yes. I don't mean to be mysterious, but you'll understand when you hear."

"Just tell me where we meet." I could hear an old-fashioned, mechanical cash register in the background and customers chatting with the woman running it.

"I feel kind of funny asking you, but the more I thought about it . . . You're really ideal."

"I'll take that as a compliment."

"Please do. I think I should have a witness, preferably someone hard to get to and with some experience in matters of . . ."

"Villainy?"

"That's close enough. . . . Oh, someone else needs to use the phone. Let me give you the address. The park is at the intersection of Gallisteo and Agua Fria in Iztapalapa."

She spoke the words of her native tongue beautifully, creating rich, rolling sounds that made me want to hear more.

"It will be tight, all the way down there, but I'll leave now."

"Thanks, Gardner."

"See you."

There was no monument in Monument Park, at least none that I could see. It was an open block in an area that was primarily residential, although there were a few small shops and a couple of cantinas on the square. Three large cottonwoods made shade and served as community bulletin boards. What little grass there'd been had turned to straw. Half a dozen concrete benches offered creature comfort to an assortment of young lovers and senior citizens. A noisy gang of ten-year-olds were kicking a croquet ball in the dust. Someone's mutt was trying to referee. It was a couple of minutes after two when I arrived. Doe wasn't there. I parked myself under the largest tree and started reading the posters. There were numerous ads for local candidates of Mexico's ruling political party. Mexico is one of the world's great one-party democracies. For those interested in a contest in which there is some doubt as to the outcome, there were going to be boxing matches, lots of them. From their pictures, some of the pugilists looked like they belonged in diapers instead of boxing trunks.

I'd changed into a short-sleeved shirt and cotton slacks, but I was warm, despite an intermittent breeze that kicked up dust devils and circulated trash among the benches. After ten minutes, Doe appeared. There were two people with her, a long-haired kid about seven in a pale blue dress and a stocky girl of nineteen or twenty. Doe had on a sleeveless pink dress that held her body in all the right places and let it move seductively under the fabric everywhere else. She stopped to buy a chunk of pineapple for the kid from a vendor. I waved. They headed my way.

Doe handled the introductions very efficiently. The stocky woman, Maria Estevez, was one of the aides at the orphanage Doe had visited. She was perspiring so profusely that it had soaked through her dress, a long-sleeved print with pink and orange flowers on a yellow background. There was a lot of tension among the three females standing in front of me. The child was Juanita Gutierrez, a skinny but pretty little waif who lived at Casa Barron. I ripped down four outdated posters and offered them as seats. I should have given a larger one to Maria.

While we arranged ourselves on the ground, little Juanita stared at me as if she could not believe a normal human being could grow so tall. "Vitaminas," I whispered to her, "vitaminas." She giggled and I counted her missing teeth, "uno, dos, tres," pointing my big finger at the holes. She laughed and covered her mouth.

"Gardner," Doe said, "when I was at Casa Barron this morning, Maria handed me a note after I had interviewed a group of the children. She had heard there was a reporter in the building." Doe spoke Spanish. Her inflection and choice of words gave the impression she wanted Maria and Juanita to track every detail of what she was saying. "The note asked me to meet her a few minutes later in one of the bathrooms. She was waiting for me there. She told me she is very upset about something that happened at the orphanage. She is afraid that if she goes to her superiors or to the police, she will lose her job, or worse." Doe looked to Maria, who nodded. Juanita was staring at the ground and sucking on a corner of her pineapple. "She asked me to promise not to tell anyone she had talked to me before she would tell me what was on her mind. I gave my word. Now I must ask you to do the same." Maria looked at me apprehensively. "I've told Maria and Juanita who you are and that I trust you. They understand that for my protection, I need a witness and that you may be able to help me later, if things become difficult. Do you agree not to tell anyone about this meeting with Maria and Juanita?''

In Spanish, I said, ''I promise not to say or do anything that would hurt or endanger either of them.'' Doe looked to Maria, who nodded.

''Juanita?'' The little girl studied me for a second, smiled, and said okay. Doe continued, ''One morning a few weeks ago, a friend of Juanita's named Helena did not come to breakfast with the other children. They found her a little while later in one of the showers. She had taken poison. There was nothing they could do for her. Maria believes she knows why Helena took her life. She says there will be much trouble when the truth is known, but for the sake of the other children, she can't keep it a secret. That's as much as Maria told me. We arranged this meeting so she can tell the rest. Maria, why don't you do that now?'' Doe pulled a notepad and pen from her purse. ''It's okay, Maria,'' Doe assured her. ''I just need to write down all the facts. I don't want to make any mistakes.'' Maria reached out to Juanita and pulled her close.

''I . . .'' Maria's voice and hands were shaking. ''Juanita and I are cousins. They don't know that at Casa Barron, but it's true. Juanita and I look out for each other. We tell each other our secrets. We trust each other. I wish I had enough money to take care of her.'' Maria took her little relative's hand and went on. ''Nita and Helena, they had beds next to each other. They were good friends, very close, like sisters. One night, Helena was having a nightmare. Nita woke up. Helena was screaming and tossing in her bed. Nita went to her. She comforted her. It happened again the next night, and the night after that. Helena wouldn't talk to Nita about what was wrong. She started staying away from Nita and the other children. She acted very sad all the time. Nita asked me what to do for her friend. I said, 'Just be nice to her, be her friend. Walk with her. Say a prayer with her.'

"The afternoon before Helena died, she told Nita she was going to hell. Her soul was damned. She started crying; she couldn't stop. Nita held her until the crying stopped. She begged Helena to tell her what was wrong. . . ." Nita had started trembling; tears traced the delicate curves of her cheeks. Maria gave her a squeeze. I dug in my pocket and handed her a handkerchief. "Nita had a little money I had given her," Maria continued, "she invited Helena to go with her for a cold drink. On the way to the store, Helena told everything. . . . You okay, Nita? Okay for me to go on?"

"I'm okay," Nita said, staring at the ground.

"There had been a contest at each of the three orphanages of Señor Barron. The children were supposed to make up a story about why it was important for people to help the orphanages with money. Helena was one of the winners; one girl and one boy from each orphanage. For a prize, they got to eat dinner and see Señor Barron's show at the Hotel El Dorado. All the children were excited, not just the winners. One of the other girls lent Helena her special dress. Helena told Nita that the children thought the show was so wonderful, they begged Señor Barron to let them stay and see his next performance. He said that would be okay. Am I telling it right, Nita?" Nita looked up, her young eyes wide and full of rage. She spoke.

"Helena, she told me he came close to the children and sang to them, one by one." The little girl's voice was tight and low, as if she had put a weight on her emotions to keep from screaming. "He stayed the longest with Helena. He put his arms around her. Helena said she felt like Cinderella. It was so late when the show was over, he got rooms at the hotel for all the children, one for each. After Helena was in her bed, he came to her room and locked the door. Then, he got in the bed with her and started putting his tongue into her mouth. . . ." Tears reappeared in Nita's eyes. Doe's hand covered her mouth; she'd stopped writing. "Then he made her do something bad. He put his penis in her. He hurt her, inside." As Nita's tears led to sobs, Maria slowly rubbed her cousin's back. "Later he made her promise not to tell. He said he was her friend and would take care of her, but if she told, she would have no home and bad things would happen to her."

"Who are you talking about?" Doe asked. "Who did this to Helena?" It was a necessary question.

Nita looked confused. "Señor Barron," she said. "Bobby Barron. He did it."

"The next morning," Maria said, "Señor Barron took everyone to a carnival." Her eyes were hard now, her voice singed with contempt. "A man with a TV camera took pictures of him hugging and kissing Helena. . . ."

"Helena prayed about it every night," Nita said, as if trying to excuse her friend. "But the nightmares wouldn't go away. She was scared she would have them the rest of her life, and she was only seven, like me."

"She drank what they use to open drains," Maria said. "The doctor said it burned her and she bled to death inside."

Nita added, "I think Helena was afraid someone might kill her if Señor Barron found out she had told."

"Are you afraid?" I asked Nita.

She nodded. "But he shouldn't have done that to Helena. He made her kill herself." Nita and her cousin fell silent. Doe assured them they'd done the right thing by coming forward and thanked them for trusting her. She said she'd do everything she could to expose Barron so he could be punished for what he'd done to Helena. I watched Doe watch them leave. Her expression made me want to put my arms around her, but I wasn't sure she'd welcome it, not yet. Nita and Maria crossed the street that bordered the park on the west and disappeared behind a corner where a woman was selling lingerie from a cart.

"Jesus," Doe said as she turned toward me, "I knew it

was something like that; but still, just hearing it, it makes me want to hand in my membership in the human race. That bastard. . . . He's probably forgotten her name.''

"What will you do?" I asked. "You can't print what Nita said without proof.'' We started walking slowly in the direction from which she'd come. She sighed.

"I know," she said. "I'll have to find another victim, a live one. You know Helena wasn't the first. Who knows how many little girls he's used? That great champion of the poor!''

"It will be tricky. You never would have gotten in the orphanage if Barron or his people thought the children would say anything that could threaten or embarrass him.''

"It will take time to find her, but I will. I should have told Maria and Nita not to expect anything right away. I'll have to call them. . . . There are agencies. . . . Maybe I could get an investigation started, but . . .''

"He could get it fixed. And you, too.''

"Probably, depending on how much I knew by then.''

"How do you feel about unsolicited advice?''

"Okay, so long as it doesn't insult my intelligence.''

"Work it from Barron's end. Find someone in his organization who hates him. Maybe the guy we saw the other night with the pudgy girlfriend. Or the guy with the video camera. Deviates get a thrill out of seeing themselves perform. Maybe the Chairman of the Boardwalk is no exception. If you can get tapes of him with kids, you'll never need anything more.''

We crossed the street. Half a dozen teenaged boys on skateboards were getting a free tow from a city bus. "I wish I were more patient,'' she said as we stepped up on the curb. "I want to do something now. I want him stopped. He shouldn't be allowed anywhere near children. This certainly explains why he's so interested in them.''

"It's probably more complicated than it seems.''

"Please don't try to justify him.''

"I wouldn't, Doe. I just doubt that his philanthropy toward children is motivated exclusively by a desire for sexual opportunities. With his resources, there are more efficient and discreet means of procurement available to him."

"I suppose." We walked in heavy silence to her car, another block and a half. I could see the orphanage from where she had parked, a three-story white brick building. A banner with Barron's likeness hung from a window above the front door.

"I know this is hard for you, Doe. But you're going to help a lot of people."

"I hope so." She was looking at the orphanage. "What should have been one of the happiest experiences of that little girl's life turned into something so ugly that she killed herself. What are we supposed to make of that? Can you imagine how she suffered because he wanted to indulge himself? It's so cruel."

"I'll help if I can. Let me know. Will I see you later?"

"Sure." A smile. "Life goes on. I should warn you, I may be thirsty."

"You pick the medicine. I'll make sure you get it in therapeutic quantities."

She took my hand and said, "Thanks for being here today, Gardner. I'll see you later." Then she drove off into the yellow haze in her gray Prelude. Nice car. Nice lady.

It was going to rain again. I'd meant to ask Doe for a ride, but the session with Maria and Nita had taken my mind off the practical stuff. I turned my back on the self-satisfied countenance of Bobby Barron and began walking. I had the strange, disconnected feeling I sometimes get after hearing rotten news. I didn't know where or how to file it. A child's life seemed like a very high price to pay for Bobby Barron's orgasm. I suppose young children commit suicide every day; I don't plan to get used to it.

Steam rose as long drops began pelting the pavement. Cabs, generally, are as common in Mexico City as teenage pregnancies, but there were none in sight. I started to run. The Metro station was a block and a half in front of me. When I reached the intersection, wipers were being switched on and Glenda's voice was on my internal P.A. system announcing that "Mr. Barron does not see anyone soaking wet, not even for two minutes."

When I was halfway across the street, a horn honked behind me and a familiar voice yelled, "Hey, Gardner, I'd gone five blocks when I realized you needed a ride. Hop in." It was a pretty lady in a gray Prelude.

·· Chapter Eight ··

It was a small, upscale office building near the El Dorado. The tenants were all professionals, accountants, lawyers, investment advisers, an ad agency, and a couple of theatrical agents. The Barron Group, Limited, occupied the entire fourth floor. I stepped off the elevator into their reception area. The walls were varying shades of lavender, pink, and violet. The receptionist's huge, French Provincial desk was white, as was the woodwork. There were three low-slung chairs and a loveseat for waiting, all gray like the nubby carpet. I announced myself to the young Mexican receptionist and took a seat with a couple of people who looked anxious to sell someone something.

It was the beginning of a forty-minute wait. Twenty times the length of the meeting I'd been offered with Barron. I try not to be offended by such rudeness, but it doesn't work. From the nature and volume of the incoming phone calls, I gathered that The Barron Group office employed at least half a dozen people who managed ventures in real estate and entertainment for the corporation. It struck me as odd that there was not a single likeness of Bobby Barron on display, not even one of those clever Hirschfeld cartoons or an old poster. The end table next to me offered not dog-eared issues of *Variety,* but very current copies of *Fortune, Forbes,* and a couple of Mexican business weeklies. I got the feeling that "the real" Bobby Barron, astute businessman, did not want visitors to confuse him with the leering idol of millions.

Glenda was tall, slim, and wore her black hair in a boyish style. Her lipstick and smartly tailored business suite were maroon. She was full of soft-spoken apologies. "Mr. Barron is so sorry to have kept you waiting," I was assured. "The day has just been mad. He's just now finished his two o'clock, if you can believe, and hasn't had a bite of lunch." She pointed me toward a door and led the way. "You will be brief?" The door led to four busy-looking secretaries and another door. Beyond the second door was a hallway that passed several individual offices. It was very quiet; all the doors were closed. At the end of the hall was another open area, Glenda's space. Here, the French Provincial motif came into its own. It was reminiscent of the other waiting area, but more elegant. Good prints of the great French masters Monet and Seurat graced the off-white, paneled walls in gilded frames. A twenty-five-inch TV was disguised as an armoire. A bronze bust on a marble pedestal kept vigil beside the arched doorway that led to the inner sanctum. The subject, apparently, was Malcom X, the late Black Muslim leader, whose stern visage seemed ludicrously out of place in Barron's glitzy headquarters. Glenda flashed me an unconvincing smile as we approached the door. "He's so looking forward to meeting you," she said, knocking. "I'll buzz in two minutes. He wishes he could spend more time. . . ."

"Hey there, Gardner. Come on in." The familiar voice

spoke to me as the richly polished mahogany door swung away, as if by magic, from Glenda's knock. Mr. Enchantment stood on the far side of the room, partially silhouetted by the glare from a full-wall plate-glass window. In front of him was a massive desk. He waved me on. We hadn't met and already we were old friends. I made it across the expanse of mauve carpeting just in time to shake the soft hand as he extended it. "It's great to meet an actual friend of Frank Cutter's," he said, smiling mischievously. "I didn't know he had any." I laughed appreciatively.

"It's good of you to see me on such short notice," I said.

"Hey, no problem." Barron looked older and shorter than I expected. He was wearing a yellow turtleneck and white slacks. The trademark narrow waist and broad shoulders seemed to have been left in a drawer. "Coffee?" he said. "A drink?"

"No thanks, I'm fine." We sat.

"Thanks, Glenda," he said, motioning her to leave. "Oh, hey, get me an egg salad on a bagel, huh? And a cherry coke?" She left. Behind us, the guy who had opened the door, slowly lowered his great bulk into a white leather wing chair, which was part of a grouping of furniture that formed a sitting area in a corner of the large office. Barron was sizing me up. "Hey, you don't mind if Luis joins us, do you, Gardner? He doesn't speak a word of English. Isn't that right, Luis?"

"Not a word, Bobby, that's right," Luis answered, in English. Again, I laughed on cue. They liked that.

"I saw you looking at the statue when you came in. What do you think?"

"Good likeness," I said.

"Thanks," he said. "Of course, I got my start on the Sullivan show. When he died, it was like I lost my own father. That's when I did the statue. I figured, if Tony Bennett can paint, why not, right?"

"Right," I agreed. It seemed that Barron's talent for

sculpture matched his Shavian wit. He settled back in his high-backed swivel chair, his pudgy fingertips pressed together above his lap. The glare from the window behind him made it difficult to see his face.

"So. Frank says you're looking for a girl." He leaned back farther and put his small feet up on the desk. His patent leather shoes looked like they were built to add a couple of inches to his height.

"Melanie Maitland. Her boyfriend, Ramon Aguirre, was a gopher on the film crew doing the documentary about you. He was murdered Wednesday night in their suite at the Camino Real. Melanie's missing. She has a son, Ben. He's four. The family's very anxious to know he's safe." I handed Barron the picture Ben Maitland had given me of his grandson. He shook his head.

"Why do you think I'd know anything about it?" Barron asked as he flipped the snapshot back across the desk.

"I understand Ramon was trying to ingratiate himself to you, to attract your attention."

"I have a lousy memory for people, Gardner. It's a real handicap. I meet so many people, in so many places. . . . You just can't remember everyone. Frankly, a lot of them are ass kissers. I turn off on them right away. It sounds like this kid you're talking about was like that. I wish I could help you out." He swiveled around and lowered his feet to the floor. Interview concluded.

"Melanie comes from a very prominent family," I said. "They won't let go of this until she and the boy are located. I'm sure you understand how they feel." Barron leaned forward to hunt for something in his top desk drawer. The desk was white with gold trim. From my perspective, it looked like a coffin for a bimbo with a thyroid condition. I went on, "I know Melanie's parents would be very grateful for your cooperation. Perhaps if you authorized your people to discuss the matter with me, I might be able to turn something up."

"I'll have my head guy down here personally interview

everyone who might know anything about the girl you're looking for and we'll get back to you. Tell her folks not to worry, okay? If we can help, we will.''

''Would you have any objection to my talking to your staff?''

''What are they going to tell a stranger, Gardner? They trust Steve; they'll open up to him. If there's anything they know that could help you, he'll find it.'' A light lit up on his desk.

''I'll take that as a 'no.' ''

''It's in the eye of the beholder, Gardner.'' He rose. I could hear Luis's chair sigh with relief behind me as he followed the lead of his boss. ''Look, here's a couple tickets to my show. They're full comps. Food, booze, everything. You be my guest, and we'll get back to you. Glenda knows where you're staying, right?'' He waited a second for me to take the tickets from him; then tossed them on the desk in front of me. I rose. Barron's oily confidence annoyed me.

''You've been very generous with your time,'' I said.

''Don't forget the tickets,'' he said as we shook hands. I could almost hear him laughing at me. I fought off an urge to test Doe's theory, to see if he remembered the name of his seven-year-old victim. I looked hard into his eyes; there was nothing there.

''Thanks anyway,'' I said. ''I've seen your show.'' Luis was standing close enough that I could feel his body heat. I could smell him, too; it wasn't Old Spice.

''Hey, Gardner,'' Barron said, ''you know why they put the string on a tampon? So you can floss your teeth after you eat.'' Luis laughed hard enough for both of us, so I didn't bother. Barron smirked. ''Real pleasure to meet you, Gardner. I'll get with Steve about the girl first thing.''

''I know you will, Bobby. And I'll stay glued to the phone.''

·· Chapter Nine ··

Doe lived in Bosques de las Lomas, a chic neighborhood carved out of a hillside. Auto access to her building was by a narrow road on the uphill side at about the level of the sixth floor. The middle floors of the building were actually a parking garage with apartments above and offices, a health club, and two restaurants below. Signs near the main entrance indicated that the half-dozen tennis courts and swimming pool I'd seen from the street were also part of the property.

Doe welcomed me with a big smile and merry, mischievous eyes that told me it was going to be a good night. She had on a teal blue strapless dress. It was made to order for her deep tan. We exchanged hi's and nervous laughter. I gave her a still-cold bottle of Moet Chandon I'd picked up in the course of a pit stop at my hotel.

"What are we celebrating?" she said.

"We'll have to figure that out."

"A stimulating intellectual challenge? That's wonderful! I'll get some glasses."

Doe seemed to have a fondness for big seascapes. Several of them, apparently by the same artist, occupied walls around the apartment. The subject matter was reminiscent of Winslow Homer, but the treatment was much lighter. The rich blues and greens of the tropical sea dominated each piece with the rest of the scene merely suggested in simple lines and washes of color. The room was large and expensively furnished, yet simple, uncluttered. A comfortable sitting area looked through a glass wall to a generous balcony and the opposing hillside, which was lined with similar upscale midrises. The furnishings and accessories in the room looked Danish: lots of natural wood; rich but plain fabrics in pale blues and grays. I heard the cork blast off from the champagne bottle. A minute later, she returned carrying the bottle and a couple of glasses on a tray, which she set down on the teak coffee table in front of the sofa. She took the end of the sofa. I sat in a chair facing her. She handed me a glass of the bubbly. "To chance encounters," I said. We touched glasses.

"Chance encounters," she agreed. We drank. "Mmmm that's nice. Thank you."

"I decided we might both need some cheering up."

"You were right. Maybe I should ask you while there's still plenty of champagne: How did it go with Barron?" Her perfume was nothing Maggie had ever worn. It reminded me of gardenias.

"He tried to give me tickets to his show." She laughed. "Full comps."

"This *is* your lucky day!"

"I think my contact in Las Vegas may have told Barron to play me for a lightweight. He acted like he drew a blank on Melanie's boyfriend, Ramon. I don't believe it, but I don't know what it means. Maybe nothing more than the fact that Barron can't be bothered with something as petty as the murder of one of his employees. He wouldn't let me talk directly to his people."

"So do you think he knows something about Ramon's death or not?" She refilled our glasses as she spoke.

"Thanks. I honestly don't know. Denying that he knew Ramon could simply be his style. He has a lot to hide. Maybe he hides things whether he needs to or not."

"Why did he agree to see you at all?"

"A favor to Frank Cutter, the guy I called in Las Vegas. Or curiosity. If Barron's dirty in this, it makes sense that he'd want to check me out. He had one of his goons in the room with him the entire time. I don't think he'll lose any sleep over our meeting."

"But do you think you're in any danger?"

"If I am, we'll know Ramon was no stranger to Bobby Barron."

"I couldn't have faced him today, not after listening to Juanita. The temptation to hit him with something would have been too great."

"Have you decided what you're going to do?"

"A wise man suggested I try to get at Barron via his enemies. Tomorrow, I start looking. I'd like to find someone who used to work for him; someone who'd know the organization but not be depending on it for a living."

"Where do you start?"

"Our morgue. I hate staring into those screens, but at least this time I'll have a real sense of purpose."

"I know a couple of people in Las Vegas. One's a cop. Let me know if you need a contact up there."

"Thanks, I will. It's going to be hard for me to be patient. I keep thinking about who he's hurting now or who he'll hurt next."

She took my hand and led me into her kitchen. The scent of gardenias bloomed behind her. The kitchen was a galley layout with natural finish birch cabinets and pale blue countertops, small but functional. She seated me on a stool facing a large, built-in cutting board and went around to the other side. I love gardenias. "I'm learning to make sushi," she said. "Do you like it?"

"Most of it, yes." I poured us another round.

"You sound so apprehensive. Actually, I was being modest. I know how to do sushi and I'm pretty good. I dated a Japanese guy for a couple of months. He owns the best sushi bar in town. He taught me all the trade secrets." She was piling all the makings on the cutting board in front of me.

"Before he died mysteriously of food poisoning?"

"Before I found out the creep was married. Are you?" She stopped piling and waited for an answer.

"No. I was living with someone. She moved out a couple of days before I came down here. I think it's over."

" 'Think?' "

"Know. I'm just trying to accept it. We were together a long time. The move was her idea. She'd been thinking about it. We agreed it was the right thing for her to do."

"Would you like to start with tuna or octopus?"

"Tuna."

"Chicken!"

Doe's skillful fingers transformed the seaweed, rice, and fish into eye-catching edibles that would have done credit to a pro. In addition to the tuna and octopus, she'd bought salmon, crab, eel, and an assortment of veggies, which she shaved into colorful ornaments for her creations. When the champagne was gone, she poured glasses of chilled rice wine, which flowed as freely as the conversation between us and the laughter.

"When we first met," she said as we polished off the salmon, "I got the feeling that you're embarrassed about being a detective. Is it true?"

"It's a marketing thing. I try to distinguish myself from the guys who take pictures of people coming out of motel rooms. I charge a lot more and have to deal with more complex situations."

"Do you like your work?"

"For the most part"—I sensed the question in her mind—"although it's difficult to maintain a personal life."

"I guess we're both workaholics. I love what I do. I can't imagine giving it up to wash a man's underwear."

"You certainly live well."

"I couldn't rent a linen closet in this place on what I make at the paper. Fortunately, I learn a lot of things about people that they don't want publicized, so I'm able to generate a nice second income from blackmail."

"*Intensely private* workaholics. Your finances are none of my business."

"I don't mean to be coy. . . ."

"How are you able to live like a regional sales manager on a reporter's salary will remain part of your inscrutable mystique."

"I wouldn't want to interfere with that. . . . Come on, I want to show you my view." We went out on her balcony. The sun was down. The western sky was bright orange. Lights glowed in the jam of buildings around us. A steady breeze brought tidings of a cool evening. Fifteen stories below us, a couple were playing tennis. A man was swimming lazy laps in the pool. On a bench near the office building across the way, a fat man sat taking it all in.

"Nice," I said. "I'll bet when you rented this place, you imagined yourself spending all sorts of time out here and down at the pool, but it hasn't turned out that way, right?"

"I guess not. I'm always so busy. . . ." She was looking at the couple playing tennis. There were goosebumps on her forearms.

"Do you need a sweater?"

"No, I'm fine." She turned toward me. "How long do you think you'll stay down here? Until you find Melanie?"

"I haven't thought that far ahead." I wanted to evade the question. "I'd like to have something solid for her father, a direction at least. I can't stay very long." She moved closer to me. I was blocking the wind.

"What's your next step?"

"Another session with Ramon's brother. I'm sure he can point me toward other people to talk to. This morning, I went to the adoption agency that handled Melanie's relinquishment of her son. Mendez, ever heard of it?" She shook her head. "Predictably fruitless. The boss lady is very slick. I thought they might have some information about Melanie that would be useful. I'm going to see if I can find some string to pull; then visit their lawyer, a guy named Tio Romero."

"On Miguel Aleman?"

"Just a minute, I have his card." I pulled out my wallet and found the card Adrienne Guzman had given me. I handed it to Doe. Her expression brightened.

"It may be just a coincidence," she said, "but this guy is Bobby Barron's lawyer, one of them. He was at that party in the dressing room the other night."

"Small World Department." I put the card back in my wallet. "I don't like the feeling I'm getting about this."

"You're thinking of the little boy."

"Ben. The people who buy Caucasian kids in the States are usually affluent couples who don't want to wait the five years it can take through a traditional agency or who don't think they'll get approved for some reason—age, physical handicaps, interracial marriage, whatever. In the majority of cases, they do all right by the children—better than a lot of natural parents. I don't believe in selling human life, but maybe no great harm is done when an unwanted kid is matched with people who want him and can afford the expense. But there are people who buy kids—usually Ben's age and older—whose interest in them is definitely not parental."

"Pedophiles."

"The people who sell to them usually set up shop in countries where children can be made to disappear very easily. They advertise in sex magazines. . . ."

"People are so damn clever about finding new ways to abuse each other. . . . I'm going to put on something warmer. Some more sake, or would you like to switch?"

"Only the topic of conversation."

"Agreed."

"What time do we leave?"

"We've got plenty of time. You know we Mexicans are late eaters."

She closed the sliding glass door behind her. It was still in the high sixties, but I suppose the evening breeze on bare arms made it feel cooler. The furniture grouping on the balcony was white wire mesh with bright yellow canvas cushions. Along the low concrete wall were half a dozen blooming bougainvilleas in barrel planters. Their blossoms were a mix of pinks and purples. Doe's apartment was on the top floor, so, instead of the bottom of another balcony, what I saw when I looked up was a sky turning black. The tennis players were gone; the swimmer was climbing out of the pool. The fat guy on the bench was still there, watching. In my business, there's a tendency to assume that every fat guy sitting on a bench watching is watching you. Most of them aren't. Most of them are killing time. If you give in to the tendency often enough, it's called paranoia and you're a candidate for another occupation.

Doe returned after a few minutes wrapped in a white shawl. She had the bottle of sake and fresh glasses. We sat next to each other on the loveseat.

"I hope you're not uncomfortable, Gardner," she said. "I just love it out here. I'm stuck in office buildings all day."

"I'm very happy," I said. She poured the wine.

"Can you see okay? I think it spoils it if there's light coming from inside."

"I have a hammock strung between two cedars behind my house. I've been known to lie out there in total darkness for hours."

"Sounds nice."

"The evening star is Venus," I said. "Shall we toast her?"

"To Venus," she said, and we drank.

"I want to know more about you," I said. "You like seascapes, sushi, your work—when you're not writing puff pieces about slimy celebrities. You live well. You're exceptionally bright and attractive. . . ."

"Don't forget the inscrutable mystique," she laughed.

"Of course, what else would you like me to know?"

"Well, let's see, I have two brothers. One's a lawyer and the other is going to graduate school in the U.S. like I did."

"Another journalist?"

"A businessman, I'm afraid. My sister is married to a politician and has two children."

"How about your parents?"

"My mother died two years ago. Cancer. It was very hard on my father but he's still pretty active. He is a deputy in the Ministry of Finance now."

"Tough job."

"I don't know. We're a hundred billion dollars in debt. We were going to pay it off by selling oil. The situation is impossible for now. There isn't much my father or anyone else can do about it."

"I'll bet you and he have some lively discussions."

"You're right about that. Naturally, I'm too liberal for him. I think it would be nice if his party let the other guys win an election from time to time. I don't think he approves of me."

"Disagree, maybe. Disapprove, that's hard to believe.

Somebody did a hell of a job raising you. He's got good reason to be proud.''

''Am I blushing?''

''I couldn't tell in this light if you had measles.''

''Good, then I won't have to worry about my makeup.'' Our eyes locked for a second. It was becoming difficult to perceive nuances of facial expression, but I felt a growing physical awareness of the woman beside me. She poured the last of the wine into our glasses. The phone rang. She went in to answer it. I stood up to stretch my legs. There was just enough light from inside the building facing Doe's to see that the bench where the fat man had been sitting was empty.

''There was no one on the line,'' she said, sliding the door shut behind her. ''I hate it when that happens.'' We sat down at the same time, a little closer. I could feel the warm touch of her thigh against mine. She handed me my wine glass. ''I have two confessions to make,'' she said. ''Whether I make the second one will be determined by how you react to the first.''

''You have my complete attention,'' I assured her.

''There's no way to say this, except directly. First, please understand that many things are different in Mexico, especially in the city. There is less sensitivity about personal privacy because there is less personal privacy. There is a tendency to take liberties. The government does very little to honor individual rights and that rubs off on the people.''

''To be blunt about it . . . ,'' I said.

She laughed. ''Sorry, Gardner. Speaking directly, I had your hotel room searched. When you came to see me that afternoon at the paper, I realized there was a possibility that we would become more . . . involved. I don't mean necessarily personally, but professionally. It wasn't that we were working on exactly the same thing, but there were connections. I wanted to be sure you were who you said you were.''

''Am I?''

''The person I sent didn't find anything to indicate that you aren't.''

''Does that clear me in your eyes?''

''What do you think? Would I be sitting here in the dark with you if I didn't trust you? Do you forgive me?''

''Sure. I'm glad I've won your confidence. It's certainly not the first time I've been searched. It had to be you or the cops. I decided that cops wouldn't have taken as much trouble not to mess the place up.''

''I feel foolish. You knew all along.''

''And here I am sitting with you in the dark. Do you think I'd risk that with a beautiful woman I didn't trust?''

''You're very brave,'' she said. I took her hand.

''What's the other thing you want to confess?''

''Well, when I went in for the shawl, I canceled our dinner reservations. Do you mind?'' Our eyes met again, and then our lips. I kissed her lightly, exploring her lips softly with mine. I felt the gentle press of her hand against my back.

''I have another confession,'' she said.

''Three?''

''Yes. I've been looking forward to kissing you all evening. Now, thanks to the sake and champagne, I even have the nerve to tell you.'' She stood up and went to the wall. The breeze caught her hair briefly and lifted it from the back of her slender neck. I rose to join her. I stood close and put my arm around her. She turned and presented her lips. As I was about to kiss her, something in my peripheral vision made me turn. Doe pulled away. The fat guy was back, with binoculars. He hadn't been there when Doe's phone rang. In the darkness, it may have become too difficult for him to tell whether we were still in the apartment. So he had called to find out, and grabbed his binoculars while he was at it. He could see us now, as long as we stayed outside. I reminded myself of the possibility that he was a voyeur or a suspicious husband watching someone else in Doe's building. If Doe and I were not the focus of his interest, he was watching one of her closest neighbors because his binoculars appeared to be pointed straight at us. I felt self-conscious; it seemed strange that the chubby spy had made no effort to hide himself. I wondered if the explanation was incompetence or something else; I wondered if he was alone.

"What's wrong?" Doe asked. "Do you see something?"

I had avoided looking directly at the fat man. "Let's go inside," I said and put my arm around her. Doe turned on a table lamp as we entered. I closed the drapes. I debated whether to tell her what I'd seen and risk destroying whatever romantic mood we had created. "I saw a guy out there. He may be watching us; he may not be. I'm not particularly concerned about it, but I didn't want to include him in a romantic moment between us."

"What did he look like?" She seemed only mildly concerned. She approached the drapes as if to peek between the two panels but then stepped back. "I guess I shouldn't let him realize we know he's there."

"No," I agreed. "He's a fat man, probably in his thirties. Dark hair, white, short-sleeved shirt, dark slacks. He's on a bench at the base of the office building beyond the tennis courts."

"He doesn't sound like anyone I've seen out there before, but there are only a couple of people I'd recognize, I suppose. Why would he be watching us? Do you think he works for Barron?"

"No one else would have a reason to watch me. What about you? Any other possibilities?"

"The only reason Barron would have for starting to watch me now is if he found out somehow about my meeting with Maria and Juanita."

"How much chance is there of that?" We sat together on her couch.

"They're scared to death someone will find out what they've done. I can't believe they would have told anyone about our meeting."

"It seems unlikely. Which leaves us with the possibility that Barron has told someone to keep an eye on me, or that someone else is having you watched."

"I don't know who. Everything I'm working on 'officially' right now is very routine."

"Would anyone be having you watched for personal reasons?"

"No."

"Sorry. I thought I should ask."

"Do you think we should do anything about him?"

"Like confronting him, or calling the police? No. The most logical explanation seems to be that he's watching me. If I'm not followed when I leave, we can rule out that possibility. If I am followed, we may be able to work it to our advantage. The tail wagging the dog, if you will. Sorry."

"You're forgiven," she said. Her expression soured suddenly. "I really resent this, you know?"

I took both of her hands and held them, resting the backs of my hands on my knees. "Doe," I said, "I have been followed, watched, spied upon, and generally had my privacy invaded in more ways than Rambo has brain cells. Just the other day, a beautiful woman about whom I had been having romantic fantasies for days had my hotel room searched. I have never gotten used to it; I never will, but I have learned to live with it. Life cannot come to a halt because somebody wants to know where you ate lunch. I think we should have a liqueur, turn down the lights, and pick up where we left off a few minutes ago."

"I guess I don't have anything to fear with a big,

handsome man here,'' she said with mock girlishness.
''Do you like sambuca?''

''With three coffee beans,'' I said.

''I'll be right back,'' she said, rising. ''Why don't you
put on some music? There are some cassettes in that
wooden box beside the deck. Nothing too fast!'' I pawed
through the big box of tapes and found a cassette of very
mellow-looking traditional dance pieces performed on acous-
tic guitar by a guy I thought I'd heard of. It looked like a
safe bet. I adjusted the volume: low enough for conversation, high enough for listening.

The sake and champagne were having their way with
me, not unpleasantly, but definitely. I found the rheostat
that controlled a pair of recessed lights that shone on two
of Doe's seascapes and turned them to a faint glow. I was
about to switch off the table lamp by the drapes when my
hostess came back into the room with our drinks.

''Ah haa! What mischief do you have on your mind,
Mr. Wells?''

''I have romance on my mind, Ms. Aguilar. Shall I turn
it off?''

''As long as you leave me enough light to gaze into
those strange amber eyes of yours.'' I turned off the light;
Doe handed me a glass. The pungent licorice scent of
sambuca enveloped my nostrils. ''My compliments on the
choice of music,'' she said. ''Do you know who that is?''

''I thought I recognized the name. . . .''

''It's Jorge Santos. I met him after a concert a couple of
years ago. They say he's the next Segovia.''

''You should buy a digital tape deck,'' I said.

''I want one,'' she said.

''Let's dance,'' I said. We put our drinks on the coffee
table and began turning slowly around the room. We
moved easily together. Whatever accounted for her unusual height, I was grateful for it. She was half a head
taller than most women in her country. Our bodies were

well matched. We danced wordlessly. I'm not sure how long. The room resonated with Señor Santos's guitar. Doe's head rested on my shoulder. My right hand nearly spanned her narrow waist. Occasionally, one of us would shift slightly to enhance the contact of our bodies. I felt the gentle movement of her breasts against my torso; her warm breath and the sweet touch of her lips against my neck. Her thigh slipped like silk between my legs. My hand floated on the juncture of her back and buttocks.

In the middle of a piece by Fauré, Doe pressed me with her lower body and turned her head upward toward mine, as she caressed my face. "What are we doing out here with all these clothes on?" she asked. Her eyes were devilish and ripe with yearning.

"You'd do anything to avoid having dinner with me," I said, and I kissed her hungry mouth. We held each other for a long moment and then went into the bedroom.

·· Chapter Ten ··

I awoke at two-fifty. The glowing red numerals in the clock on Doe's side of the bed were the only light source in the room. She was sleeping soundly, her head resting on the left side of my chest where I had last seen it hours earlier. The hair on my chest seemed to capture the warmth from each of her slow, deep breaths and hold it until the next one. As I lay there, my senses became more acute and I began to see the gentle, curving shape of her beneath the sheets. Her left arm was outstretched across my pelvis; one of her knees was touching my left leg. This woman who had been so ferocious in sex now seemed vulnerable and childlike lying beside me. I felt a rush of affection and kissed her lightly on the forehead.

I wasn't sure why I woke up . . . a noise, the unfamiliar surroundings. . . . Maybe it was because I needed to use the bathroom. I lay there wondering how I was going to extricate myself from bed, grope my way into the bath-room, use it, and complete the return trip without disturb-

ing Doe. Then I heard the subfloor creak in the next room.
My nervous system responded to the sound with a jolt of
adrenalin. I slipped out of bed with as much care as I
could. By now, a light, dim but searching, was visible
through the gaps around the bedroom door. I crept toward
it on all fours. I wished for clothes. A reflection helped me
spot a small table in my path. The light had stopped
moving. It was brightest near the knob. I hoped Doe
would not wake up and alert whoever was out there. The
flashlight went out. I heard the knob turn. I was directly in
front of the door. It began to swing open. I had wanted to
get to one side. My breathing was rapid and shallow. I
wondered if there were two of them. I hunkered down.
The door was wide open. I could see only the black shape
of him. Doe called out from behind me, "Gardner . . . ?"
Her voice was weighted by sleep. As she spoke, he swung
his gun to fire; a machine pistol, silenced and braced. I
heard the brace tighten in its fittings as he pulled the
weapon against his waist. I lunged. Both hands found the
silencer. I pushed it up under his chin and held it there as
he squeezed the trigger. It happened before he could react.
We went over together. The full clip was in his skull
before he hit the floor. My hands burned from holding the
silencer. Doe turned on the light on her night table. She
was sobbing. There was a twenty-two automatic on the
bed beside her. The man on the floor looked like something from hell.

I grabbed Doe's pistol and moved cautiously into the
hall beyond the bedroom. "Gardner, don't leave me," she
cried. I kept moving. The front door of the apartment was
wide open. I checked the kitchen, closets, the balcony, the
office Doe had made of her second bedroom. If there had
been anyone with the dead man, he was gone. I closed the
front door, locked it, and jammed a chair under the knob.
Back in the bedroom, I used newspaper to cover what was
left of the fat man's skull. The wall, ceiling, and carpet

nearest him were splattered with blood. I asked Doe if she was okay; she nodded. After I'd wiped the blood off myself, I pulled on my clothes and sat on the bed beside her. I took one of her hands.

"I'm pretty sure it's the guy I saw watching us," I said. "Same clothes, build. I can't be positive." She looked at me with wide, sad eyes. There seemed to be no color in her face. "I think he was alone." I put my arms around her. I wondered if she could feel my heart pounding. "I must have heard him out there when I was sleeping. . . ."

"I was so scared. . . ."

"It's over now."

"Is it? Somebody wants to kill us." She sounded in control again. I released her and stood. I wanted to take a closer look at our visitor. "What do you think we ought to do?" she asked.

"I'm thinking about it," I said. "It depends: How sure are we it's Barron and how many more good citizen awards do we want him to collect?" Doe had gone to her closet and was pulling on a white robe.

"I can't imagine why Bobby Barron would want to have you killed for asking about your friend's daughter and her little boy."

Fatso's pockets produced a key ring, half a Snickers bar, two sticks of Juicy Fruit gum, about three dollars' worth of pesos, a used kleenex, a pair of dark glasses, a Bic pen, and a piece of paper with Doe's phone number and one other written on it. On his left wrist was a *Time* magazine digital watch, the kind they give away with new subscriptions. I read Doe the other telephone number.

"Does it mean anything to you?"

"No. He doesn't have any kind of identification at all?"

"Nothing."

"What do you make of that?" She stayed in the corner, hands gripping her elbows. I don't think she could see the corpse from where she stood.

"I doubt if it's very significant. He may have ID in his car; he may use aliases. Who knows?" I stood beside the body. "We have to decide what we're going to do with him." She looked perplexed. "You raised the question of why Barron would want to have me killed. Maybe it's because he regards someone looking for Melanie Maitland and/or her son as a personal threat. My friend sent a private investigator down here a week before I came. The cops found what they think is his body in the Merced two days ago. Does Barron have Melanie and the boy? Are they dead? I don't know. Has Barron abused Melanie's son? I'm trying not to think about it. What I am thinking about at the moment is that Micro Uzi our friend was carrying. Here you have a three-thousand-dollar gun on a dollar-fifty man. Somebody with deep pockets and no management ability set this up. This isn't organized crime; this is personal. Draw your own conclusions."

"You're saying it's Barron acting alone."

"Either alone or in conjunction with people very close to him. If I had to report to management, that's what I'd say." I moved closer to her. "I'm going to leave this up to you," I said. "We can call the police. They'll interrogate us endlessly. They'll be all over your apartment for a day. We can't mention Helena without endangering Juanita and Maria; therefore we have no evidence against Barron. My guess is that the police will decide the guy on the floor was your ex-boyfriend and we're trying to cover something up with insane allegations about Mexico City's favorite son." She was frowning.

"But he worked for Barron. . . ."

"Do you know that for a fact? Did you see him with Barron?" She shook her head. "Do you think the cops will take our word over Barron's—you the muckraking reporter; me, the gringo who's down here meddling in their business?"

"If there's an investigation, Barron will have his guard

up. He might leave town. They stop traffic for him when he goes to the airport." She laughed. "That would be just like our little village: stop traffic for Bobby Barron the murderer and child molester so he can escape."

"I think you see the dilemma. As I said, I'll leave the decision up to you. You have to live here."

"There's no dilemma, Gardner. There are some Hefty bags, the big ones, in my kitchen closet. I'm going to take a shower. You better work quickly. It will be light soon."

I had the guy, his weapon, and pocket junk, except for the money and telephone numbers, bagged, taped, and ready to travel in about ten minutes. It took three bags, one with the bottom cut off around his middle. While Doe put on a tan dress and clogs, I went to work on her carpet with Perrier and paper towels. When she'd finished dressing, she left the room briefly and returned with a small box, which she handed me.

"Here, try this," she said.

"Cornstarch?"

"It will absorb the blood. Use more soda; then sprinkle it on."

"I thought I was doing pretty well," I said.

"You were and I appreciate it. Humor me, okay? This carpet cost three months' salary."

The hall outside Doe's apartment was as one would expect it to be at almost four in the morning. We'd decided not to risk being seen by taking him downstairs so we headed for the roof. She went ahead to catch the door to the fire stairs while I dragged. It was one of those occasions when the drudgery of exercising yields unexpected benefits. I was able to move all two hundred-fifty pounds of him at a smart clip along the vermilion carpet. Doe looked worried when I caught up to her.

"The door to the roof is locked," she whispered. I keep my lock pick, a rake design, in my wallet between my Master Card and American Express. After a few seconds of fiddling, we were on our way up the stairs. The dead man needed a breather when we got to the top. I left him just inside the door to the outside, which was unlocked, while Doe and I looked for a hiding place among the outcroppings of her building's circulatory systems. Not knowing how much sound insulation there was between us and the apartments below, we kept our movements to a minimum.

The sky was cottony gray, overcast but brightening in the east. There was enough light to see adequately but not enough to show the color of anything. A breeze was making up its mind which way to blow. It was as quiet as Mexico City gets. As we prowled among a cluster of ducts near the elevator shaft, the compressor for the air-conditioning system kicked on behind us. Doe gave a little yelp, and said, "I hate this. Let's get it over with." I took her hand and we walked the perimeter of the roof. Midway along the south wall, I looked down and saw what we were looking for: a dumpster, nearly two hundred feet straight down, adjacent to a lighted service entrance to the building. Some considerate soul had left the cover panels open. I raised my voice to be heard above the air conditioner.

"I played a little basketball in college," I said, and pointed down. I felt Doe's grip tighten as she leaned over the knee wall to look.

"Do you think you can do it?"

"I think it's too good to pass up." While Doe waited, I returned to the stairwell doorway. Dragging the dead man across the gravel under our feet seemed like an excellent way of attracting the attention of any light sleepers below us, so I stepped over him and, standing on the third step down, I pulled him onto my back. Doe looked away as I turned and off-loaded him onto the top of the knee wall.

"I'll meet you at the stairs," Doe said. "I don't want to watch." I had to move the body a couple of feet east to center it over the dumpster. When I thought it was in the best position for launching, I shoved my hands under it, and got a good grip. With a deep breath in me, I pulled upward and pushed at the same time, rolling him off the edge, hoping no one below me picked that instant to look out the window. The plastic bags flapped noisily as he dropped. There was a loud THUNK as one end of him hit the edge of the dumpster, but he landed inside.

Thirty years earlier, the contents of that potato-shaped bundle half buried in garbage had been someone's little boy. I could not help feeling sad and a little sick.

For nearly two hours, as the sky went from gray to white outside her bedroom windows, Doe Aguilar and I scrubbed, wiped, blotted, sprinkled, and scrubbed some more. There wasn't much conversation; she went out on the balcony a couple of times when it really got to her. I found twenty-eight bullet holes. All appeared to be singles. If the would-be killer had started with a full clip, four slugs were still in his head.

Using flour and water, we concocted a paste of the right consistency to fill the holes and hold an appropriate texture. When I'd filled and textured, Doe used her hair dryer to dry the paste. She still had some of the paint that had been used in the room, about an inch of it in the bottom of a gallon can. It was heavily skinned and had turned the consistency of peanut butter, but we were able to revive it with warm water, a strainer, and a wire whisk. Doe was anxious to complete the cover-up operation when the paint was ready, so while she went to work with the one paint brush on the premises, I put on coffee and stepped into the shower to flush the rest of the fat man's blood from my skin. By the time I'd dried off, Doe's bedroom looked virtually as it had the day before.

We needed to get out of there. We needed time by ourselves to think through the events of the preceding twelve hours. We needed distraction. A white water rafting trip would have suited me perfectly. I was headed instead to Ramon Aguirre's funeral. Doe was luckier. She got to spend the day in her paper's morgue looking for the names of people who had reason to strike Bobby Barron's name from their Christmas card lists.

It was a little after eight when we pulled up in front of my hotel. Doe didn't want me to get out of the car. She was trembling. "I wish we'd called the police," she said. "I'm no good at this sort of intrigue."

"It's not too late," I said.

"Yes it is. We've incriminated ourselves . . . covering up the bullet holes, hiding the body. How could we explain that?"

"The truth. It would be awkward, but I think we could persuade them. The problem is that unless we go into hiding, we're still targets for whoever sent the guy in the dumpster; and if it's Barron, with one whiff of the police, he'll activate all of his defenses and we'll lose him. For whatever it's worth, I don't think we have anything to be concerned about before tonight at the earliest." I put my left arm around her shoulders and took her damp right hand in mine. "We weren't followed here; I was watching. You'll be fine at the paper. I'll meet you there later."

"I feel so . . . exposed." She turned to me with wide eyes and heavy lips. When we kissed, my plans for the next hour changed. Nothing needed to be said. We exchanged the knowing smile of lovers and got out. In my room, we immediately shed our clothes. It was unmannered this time, unself-conscious. On the bed, we tangled joyfully, a jumble of eager arms and legs. Her lips took me and pulled while her tongue probed and I enjoyed the sweet, wet feel of her mouth. A moment later, we rolled and turned. I entered her. Her body shuddered as she wrapped her legs around me, locking us together. We danced to primordial rhythms, slowly at first, then with all the fire and frenzy of our passion. I met her moan with my mouth.

As we lay together afterward, I wondered what the future held in store for us. I wantéd to tell her that everything was going to be all right, that we'd slay the dragon and sail off happily into the sunset. But I wasn't sure it was true. I knew neither the breed nor the strength of this dragon. It could be tough, if not impossible, to kill. I wanted to tell her that I had only the highest hopes for us. But I wondered if there could be an "us" at all. So I said nothing, and we lay together, and in time, we kissed and said good-bye and she was gone.

· · Chapter Eleven · ·

The cab got me to St. Therese in Cuauhtémoc a little after ten-thirty. I had the driver park across the street. We waited. The church was a small, stucco building, traditional architecture, with a red tile roof. In front of it was parked a Cadillac hearse, which must have had a year or two on Ramon.

After fifteen minutes, the big wooden doors in the front of the church opened. Ramon had not endeared himself to me during our brief meeting, but I couldn't help feeling sorry for his mother and brother as the funeral party emerged from St. Therese. Grieving for Ramon looked like lonely work. The pallbearers were the priest, the funeral director, the hearse driver, and Chaco. In black veils and a long-sleeved black dress, the mother was striking. She looked about five-foot-four, with a good figure and bearing that reminded me that she was an actress before she married. At her arm was a younger woman accompanied by twin boys about seven years old, and that was it. No aunts. No neighbors. No Melanie. If life is a popularity contest, Ramon blew it.

The priest and the funeral director waited in the hearse while the family arranged themselves in a ten-year-old Plymouth Duster parked down the block. It seemed wrong that I had a cab to myself.

It was a huge Catholic cemetery. Endless rows of white markers were punctuated with garish clumps of plastic flowers that bloomed incongruously above the parched brown sod. I stayed in the cab while the priest spoke. From the rise where we parked I could see two other burials going on. It was typically bright overcast, but cooler than the other days had been. Two workmen from the cemetery stood at a respectful distance from Ramon's grave waiting for their cue. It was over in a few minutes. Ramon's mother had to sit down. Chaco tossed earth onto his brother's casket.

I caught up with Chaco near his car and expressed my sympathy. Though he looked a little shell-shocked, he greeted me like a rich relative and told his family I was a good friend of Ramon's from the United States. I guess he thought it would make them feel better. From under her veils, the mother smiled at me with sweet, sad eyes. I told her Ramon had many friends in the United States who would miss him. She embraced me; then climbed into the back seat of the pale-blue car. The younger woman, Alicia, was Ramon's cousin. She was attractive in a domestic way; her boys, Hector and Humberto, looked like they couldn't wait to wriggle out of the dark suits I suspect had been borrowed for the occasion. As Chaco was introducing me to Father Fuentes, Señora Aguirre summoned her surviving son and asked him to invite me to join the family at her house. It was an invitation I was hoping for. I had a hunch about Ramon's unexplained second visit to his mother's house and I wanted to check it out.

There were forty-four houses in the block where Chaco

and Ramon grew up. All one-story, stuccoed brick construction with common side walls. Hard to tell apart except
for the few that had paint jobs. Yellow, orange, and green
were popular. The Aguirre house was turquoise, badly
faded, with a crimson garage door in the front wall. The
garage door did not open onto a garage but rather a tiny
open space with just enough room for the Duster, a couple
of folding chairs, and some potted plants.

The tiny rooms inside were packed with hulking, old
pieces of furniture that were not only the wrong scale but
jammed in so tightly that all traffic was one way, sideways
in my case. Despite the clutter and stress, Señora Aguirre,
"Aunt Grandma" to Hector and Humberto, moved through
her poor house with regal grace. Minutes after we arrived,
she began setting out coffee, little cakes, sandwiches, and
a platter of fruit and cheese. While she organized the food
and the rest of the family kibitzed, I browsed a wall of the
sitting room, which was virtually covered with clippings
attesting to the Señora's artistic and social accomplish-
ments during the nineteen forties. It seemed that for a
season or two, she was the most sought-after starlet in
town.

Despite her generous provisions, Señora Aguirre did not
join us. Once the food was set out, she left the room
without speaking to anyone. For several minutes, we stood
in expectant silence. Finally, Chaco dispatched Alicia who
reported a moment later that Señora Aguirre had locked
herself in her room. Chaco shook his head, and poured
two slugs of tequila. While Alicia nibbled on a sandwich
and the boys dove in to a pile of sweet rolls, I followed
Chaco and the drinks outside, pausing en route to park my
suit coat on a peg near the door.

The tubular aluminum chair with its frayed webbing was
too short in the seat for me, but once I satisfied myself that
it wasn't going to collapse, I was fairly comfortable. A
wire milk crate made a fair footstool. After we'd been

sitting a few minutes, Chaco realized a planning error and
went to fetch the bottle. My eyes played over his mother's
tiny yard while he was gone. In a space that amounted to
less than two hundred square feet, the señora's battle-
scarred Plymouth Duster made one hell of a conspicuous
lawn ornament. There was little else to see: parched plants
potted in coffee cans, some rusty gardening implements, a
wheel rim, an empty pet dish, and a foot-high pile of dead
birds. The birds were partially concealed by a bushy thistle
plant, but the noise from the cloud of flies they'd attracted
caught my attention. I'd gone for a closer look when
Chaco came back with the bottle.

"They fall out of the sky, dead," Chaco explained,
"and my mother collects them. In a week or two, there
will be many more. Today we have another inversion, and
the cooler weather is just beginning. The inversion holds
the bad air like a gas chamber. The birds fly into it and
they die. The worst air is only a few hundred feet up. The
scientists worry that someday it will sink to the ground and
people will die. People are collecting the birds all over the
city. In a few weeks, they will take them to the office of
the Secretariat of Ecology to protest." Chaco handed me
the bottle as we both sat down.

"What will happen?" I poured each of us a drink.

My question made Chaco laugh. "They will have a hell
of a lot of dead birds to clean up. The corpses will smell
worse than the air."

"No official response? No action?"

"Words. Just words." Chaco tossed back his drink.
"My mother has a passion for lost causes, like my father
and brother." Chaco leaned forward and studied the backs
of his hands, then the palm side, then he poured himself
another drink.

"You told me your brother was very slow about coming
to see your mother after he came down here to work on the
Barron film. Then, a day or two after he finally visited

her, he returned to the house and practically ignored her. Is that right?"

"Yes. I think he stole something to sell. I think it's how he supported himself in your country."

"I have another theory," I said. "I think he left something here. I think whatever it was got him killed."

"You mean drugs?" Chaco said. He looked anxiously at his mother's house. "They told us there was cocaine around the hotel room—you knew that."

"Yes."

"That bastard. He would risk our mother's life to hide his shit in her home. What if they come here looking for it? What do you think he told them?"

"If he had told them anything, they would have been here by now."

"You're right."

"Last night, someone sent a man with a machine pistol to kill me. The detective who came down here before me to check on the son of your brother's girlfriend was killed. Ramon is dead. Let's suppose that these events are related. . . ."

"You don't think it's drugs in there . . . ?"

"It was generally known among the people you worked with that you and Ramon were brothers, correct?"

"Yes."

"And no one has shown an unwelcome interest in you recently? You haven't noticed anyone following you? Your home hasn't been searched?"

"No, but like I told you, no one who knew we were brothers would have thought we were close. We weren't. Ramon's choice."

"It doesn't feel like drugs to me, Chaco. I know the timing couldn't be much worse, but we need to find out what, if anything, your brother hid in there. I'd be happy to help."

He ran his fingertip around the lip of his glass. "What if

it's something valuable—money, drugs, whatever—what happens to it? You expect me just to give it to you?"

"Unless it's a four-year-old boy named Ben Maitland, no. What you do with it is up to you. I'm interested in what it is and what it means. If it's something someone is willing to kill for, I'd consider the matter very carefully if I were you."

"I suppose if you had anything to do with Ramon's death, you wouldn't be sitting here talking about all this with me, would you?"

"It would be a radical departure in tactics. Can we start now?"

"You wait out here." He stood. "I know the house. I know where Ramon and I used to hide things when we were boys. If I find anything, I want to think about what to do with it. I want to be able to tell you your theory was wrong, even if that's not the truth."

"Sounds reasonable to me," I said, because it did and because there didn't seem to be a hell of a lot else I could say.

Chaco's expression simmered somewhere between anger and sadness when he emerged from the house ten minutes later. He had found something; I could see it in his eyes. I followed him to the corner of the tiny yard farthest from the front door. He spoke in a whisper.

"You were right. It's movie film, a hundred feet of sixteen millimeter. I unspooled enough of it in front of the window to see what it is, but whatever got Ramon killed must be farther in. He hid it in the light fixture in the room we used to share. There were still a few cards in there from a deck he had when we were boys. You know, the kind where every card has a different woman with big tits on it."

"So he was trying to blackmail someone. Barron?"

"It must be. The film was shot at a surprise party some of Barron's business partners gave for him a couple of weeks ago. They all own this big cattle ranch together outside the city. That's where the party was. I was there. I didn't see anything you could blackmail Barron for, but they made the crew leave about eight o'clock. Everyone had been drinking. They must have forgotten Ramon was there. What happened, that afternoon, we had been shooting at the zoo. Barron had left and we were getting ready to go, too, when this guy from Barron's office shows up and tells the director about the surprise party. They decide we should film it so everybody on the crew who was still there got drafted. When we got to the ranch, they handed Ramon a little Arriflex and some high-speed film and told him to go up on the roof and get overhead shots of Barron arriving and the party on the patio. The sound man had already left, so I got stuck with that. They didn't let us use lights at the party," Chaco added. "Most of the stuff that's come back from the lab is grainy and full of shadows. They had to shoot wide open. It looks like shit."

"When can we look at Ramon's film?" I asked.

Chaco showed me his find, an aluminum can about four inches in diameter. "It's got to be private," he said. "I don't have a projector, and I don't want anyone to know I have this."

"How about a viewer. Can you borrow one?"

"Wait a minute. I know somebody. Toney Ortega. That bastard has a projector. He gets these porno films and charges people to see them. He wanted me to help him make one a couple of years ago. I told him no, but he and Ramon were friends growing up."

"Where is he?"

"His house is only three blocks from here. He never left the neighborhood."

We started walking. At the corner, a squinty-eyed drunk stumbled out of a pulqueria, followed by sounds of radio music and a boozy argument. He found us on radar as we passed and strained valiantly for words that wouldn't come.

"That was my father's office when he wasn't working," Chaco said as we crossed the street. "When I was
fifteen, he got me drunk in there. At first, I enjoyed it,
then I got sick. He wanted me to keep drinking. His
friends were all watching us. He said he was teaching me a
lesson. I think he wanted to prove he was a better man
than I was. For a long time after that, I couldn't walk past
the place without feeling a little sick in my stomach. My
father was a very unhappy man."

In the middle of the next block, a pile of rubble marked
the place where three houses had been bulldozed. As we
passed a four-story tenement beyond the empty lot, Chaco
started walking faster and warned me to watch my step.
There was human waste on the street and sidewalk in front
of the building. "Fecal rain," Chaco laughed. "A big part
of the city has no sewers. You take a hell of a chance
walking near one of these old buildings after dark."

"It must have been tough growing up here," I said.

"We didn't know that," Chaco said, "but I guess it
was. My mother had a little money. She made sure Ramon
and I got as much education as we would absorb. If it
hadn't been for her, I would probably be back there in the
pulqueria right now, like my father."

"You said he was going to direct a feature when he
died."

"He told us some investors were putting together their
own production company and wanted him to direct their
first film. We never found out if it was true. I wanted to
believe it then: I still do."

Toney Ortega's home was one of the shabbiest in a
block of shabby, one-story dwellings. The foul air left no
doubt that we were still in an area without sewers. I
yearned for the sweet smell of sulfur dioxide outside my
hotel. A five-count after Chaco knocked on it, the corru-
gated metal door swung forward. We stepped back. The
young woman wore leopard skin stretch pants, high heels,

a ruffled, black see-through top, teardrop rhinestone ear-
rings, lavender eye shadow, plum-colored lipstick, and a
predatory smile. It was perhaps the only time in my life
I've been glad a woman went overboard with the perfume.
In her neighborhood, she might have earned a nice living
as an air freshener. I had her figured for an exchange
student from Radcliffe, but she turned out to be Toney's
wife, Rosa. Her smile slumped as Chaco introduced us.
Her husband, Rosa said, was away on important business.

Between anxious looks down the block, Señora Ortega,
who seemed to be expecting someone, rejected every reason Chaco could think of to persuade her to let us use the
projector. I contributed a twenty to the conversation, and
suddenly, as if by magic, we had projector time and the
place to ourselves. I just wish Rosa hadn't winked at us
and laughed as she went out the door.

A mussed bed and a cluster of mismatched wooden
chairs surrounding a black and white TV occupied the first
room in the house. In the second, a metal dinette table was
crowded by more chairs facing a beaded glass projection
screen, which practically filled the opposing wall. While
Chaco threaded his brother's legacy into Toney's old Bell
and Howell projector, I stood ready to position the dis-
jointed cardboard box, which, Rosa had told us, they used
to block the window during daylight screenings.

There was no countdown leader on the reel; no previews
either. As the projector chattered into action, we went
directly to the feature presentation. Ramon's overhead vantage point looked down on an expanse of flagstone-covered
patio lit by floodlights mounted on the house and trees. A
pair of long serving tables were covered with a clutter of
booze bottles and the remains of a buffet. A paper napkin
blew across the frame past the feet of Bobby Barron who
was standing in the middle of the patio talking with a
couple in their fifties. There was no sound on the film, but
the woman's occasional twists and dips gave the impres-

sion there was music playing. Barron wore yellow cowboy boots, red jeans, and a loose white shirt. He seemed to be in a good mood, laughing and joking with the couple. Chaco had been right about the film quality. Not only was it grainy, the low level of available light had caused the color to go blue.

By turning the cluster of turret-mounted lenses on his camera, Ramon was able to go from a wide shot in which the full width of the patio was visible to a much tighter view that isolated the three people talking and made me wish I could lip read in Spanish. A whip pan to the right caught three men walking onto the patio toward Barron. A man in his thirties with a white shirt open in the front, dark slacks, and the body of a flamenco dancer was leading a pair of drunks, one about forty and the other considerably older. When the groups merged, there was much handshaking, kissing, and backslapping. By his body English alone, I could tell that the guy with the dancer's body was trying to herd the couple and the two drunks toward the exits.

The next shot convinced me that Ramon knew he was onto something. I could think of no other reason why he would film a scene so inherently uninteresting under lighting conditions so poor that even he must have known that the footage would never make it into the documentary. Barron, whose back was toward the camera, and two other men were standing under a tree. I could just make out a drink in Barron's left hand and a cigarette in his right. He was swaying slightly in the manner of someone mildly smashed. The man to his left was the flamenco character. I could see only the large torso of the third man; Barron's head blocked sight of his face. The flamenco was chattering away at Barron. Every few seconds, one or both of them looked off camera in the direction of something behind Barron. No indication what or who. About fifteen seconds into the shot, the flamenco whispered in Barron's ear. Barron began laughing and threw an arm around his companion's shoulders. This movement exposed the third man's face to the camera. I could see now that he was standing at a deferential distance from the other two and was definitely not included in the merriment. I recognized him despite the lousy lighting, and although I didn't know his name, I knew that the last time I had seen him, he'd just made a hard landing in the dumpster beside Doe's building. When Barron finished laughing, he spoke to the man, gesturing in the direction of the camera. The shot ended as the fat man walked off frame. I glanced at Ramon's reel. There were only a dozen feet of film we hadn't seen.

Those twelve feet were made up of about four hundred and eighty individual pictures, practically any one of which could have finished off Bobby Barron personally and professionally. Still, I could imagine Ramon's frustration at running out of film when he did. To make the most of the footage he had left, he squeezed off the frames sparingly in bursts of a few seconds each.

The setting was a kidney-shaped pool next to the house. Ramon shot down at it through the limbs of a craggy cottonwood whose smaller branches invaded some of the shots. If he was unlucky in the amount of film available to him, he was fortunate in another respect. The concrete apron surrounding the pool was awash in light and the underwater floods were on full.

In the beginning of the sequence, Barron and the flamenco were alone in the pool, naked, drinking, and sloshing around in the shallow end, pretending to dance, exchanging theatrical kisses. The flamenco played Scarlett O'Hara to Barron's Rhett Butler, then they reversed roles. In the next series of shots, a woman in a robe escorted two Hispanic children, a boy and a girl, each about ten years old, to the edge of the pool. They were naked and appeared to be afraid. Barron took the boy by the waist and swung him into the pool. In the next shot, they were

cavorting; beyond them, the flamenco was dancing with
the little girl. Ramon switched to a longer lens. The woman
had joined them. It was a sexual free-for-all. Three adults
and two children mouthing, groping, and screwing in a
tangle of bodies that spilled from the concrete apron into
the water. I wondered how it had made Ramon feel to see
Melanie in the middle of it.

Chaco let out a big sigh as the tail of the film whipped
through the gate of the projector and the screen went
white. I pulled the sheet of cardboard out of the window
frame and let in the afternoon glare. After several seconds
of silence, we made eye contact as Chaco shut down the
projector; he spoke first.

"I should have known it was something like that," he
said in a low, sad voice, "but I don't know, I wasn't ready
for it. I feel so bad for those kids."

"You didn't recognize them?" I asked.

"No. Barron's always got kids around, the bastard.
From one of the clinics, an orphanage, some school. It
makes me want to puke to think about it. I've heard
rumors for years he was queer, but this is something else.
Someone ought to chop his balls off. Jesus!"

"Who is the other guy?"

"Luis Montoya. He's Barron's art director. He designs
costumes, sets, things like that. Conceited asshole, he is,
too. Always has all the answers, knows more than anyone
else. I should have known he was some kind of pervert."

"Do you think Ramon knew what was going to happen?
Do you think Melanie tipped him off?"

"No. She wouldn't dare do that shit in front of Ramon.
He'd kill her. My brother was very old-fashioned that
way. Not that he didn't know how she was with men. I
heard them fighting once. He called her 'Thirty-one Flav-
ors' for all the different guys' jit in her when they met. But
he told me he made her straighten out. I guess not. I guess
he had a few things to say to her about this."

"Were you surprised to see her in the film?"

"I don't know. Maybe I'm getting too old to be surprised. You could tell she was a little crazy. She wore strange clothes sometimes when she came around. One time, she colored her hair all blue and orange. She was worse than Ramon about kissing Barron's ass. Hey, you saw her; I guess she was willing to do more than that."

"When Melanie had little Ben with her, how was that? Did she act differently?"

"Yes, in a way. Instead of her flirting with Barron, she used the kid to get to him. Like a dog, you know, trying to get him to do his tricks. I remember one time, Barron had given the boy something, a little radio, like a Walkman. The boy thanked Barron but then that crazy Melanie broad, she tried to get him to say, 'I love you, Uncle Bobby.' Well, the kid wouldn't say it. It was kind of funny. Everybody started watching the three of them. The harder she would try to get him to say it, the more stubborn he got. After a while, he started to cry. I could tell she wanted to give him a whack right there, but she was afraid to in front of Barron. Barron just wanted to end it; you could see that. He was embarrassed and kind of pissed; so he said, 'Well, I love you!' and gave the kid a big kiss. Everybody clapped. Barron loved it. Shit." Chaco wiped a nervous hand across his mouth. "I wonder if that bastard Toney has anything to drink around here." I followed Chaco into the back of the house where he found two bottles of tequila in the bottom of a metal cabinet. He said it was a peasants' brand, but took a long pull from one of the bottles, then offered it to me.

"I guess not, Chaco," I said, "but have another one for me." He did, a big one. It encouraged me to push the Q and A. "A couple of weeks ago, Melanie's father sent a detective named Mel Berry down here to check on his grandson. When Berry disappeared, the father called me. The police found Berry's body in La Merced a few days ago. Someone had chopped off the head and hands to make it hard to identify, but whoever it was didn't go far enough. Berry had an artificial hip; so did the corpse. Everything else fit, too. This was no random street crime, Chaco. Someone wanted Berry dead. Your brother and Melanie come to mind." Chaco turned away from me and took another drink.

"Ramon was a coward. I don't think he had enough nerve to shoot a sleeping man in the back. I know he couldn't cut somebody up. . . ."

"The cops told me Melanie and Ramon had alibis for the day Berry disappeared. That doesn't mean they weren't responsible." Chaco still had his back toward me. He was evading. I put a heavy hand on his left shoulder. "Chaco," I said, "my gut tells me that Bobby Barron bought the little Maitland boy from his mother. You saw the movie; I don't have to tell you what Barron likes to do with little boys. The one I'm looking for is only four, Chaco. I need to find him and I'm impatient. If you know something about Berry's death, I want you to tell me. There's nothing anyone can do to your brother." Chaco pulled away from me and went to the projector. He flipped the spindle to release the take-up reel and slid it off. As he spoke, I could see that there were tears in his eyes.

"My brother was shit. A scheming, lazy shit. He wanted everything to be easy. He cared only about himself. I guess I hated him; yet I wanted us to be close. I don't know what I wanted. He's dead, and what I'm sorry about is that I'll never have a real brother. I don't miss him at all.

"I think you're right; I think he had Berry killed. They had a big fight, Ramon and Berry, one day when we were on location. Not physical, just yelling. It was about the kid you're looking for. When the director started to get pissed about them holding up the shoot, Berry left. But he warned Ramon he'd be back every day until he saw the kid. I think Ramon and the girl were hiding him. It was before they moved to the Camino Real. Later on, when we were packing up, Ramon asked me if I knew how to find Tito Melendez. I said no. Tito is a vicious animal, a mad dog. He used to terrorize this neighborhood when we were younger. Now he's all over the place. When he was about sixteen, he and some other boys tied up a twelve-year-old girl in a shed and raped her over and over again for almost a week. When she got sick, they burned the shack down. I always thought Ramon was in on it. I didn't tell Ramon how to find Tito, but he probably did. Tito isn't hard to find if you know where to ask. For fifty dollars American, he would have killed the detective, and enjoyed it.''

"You never saw Berry again after he and Ramon fought that day?"

"No. Here, take this. Maybe it will help you get the boy back." Chaco tore a foot of film from the end of the reel and handed it to me.

"Thanks, Chaco. If I'm right about little Ben, you've just done him a big favor."

"I won't do anything with the rest of the film until I hear from you. It should be worth a few bucks, don't you think?"

"With proper management, you're probably holding a lifetime endowment for the next several generations of your family. If you jump the gun, all you'll get is dead."

"I won't do anything."

"Good. This would probably be a smart time for you and your mother to visit relatives out of town. As for Barron, he's circling the drain as far as I'm concerned. My job is to make sure he goes down. When it happens, I'll be in touch with the name of someone in the States for you to call. It's going to give me a lot of pleasure to see you get rich at his expense."

"Thanks. I hope the little boy is okay." Chaco gave me the name and telephone number of a priest and said he'd check with him regularly for messages. Our business was finished. We said good-bye. I left Chaco Aguirre with his dead brother's film in one hand and one of Toney Ortega's bottles in the other. At the avenue, while I waited for a cab, I watched the drunks stumbling out of the pulqueria and hoped that somewhere Chaco Aguirre had a friend.

·· Chapter Twelve ··

Doe looked great, much better than she had any right to after two days of the sort we'd been through. She logged off her work station as I sat down beside her desk. I sensed that she, also, had news. She put her hand on my forearm and gave me a squeeze. Her eyes made me forget we were in the middle of a busy newsroom.

"Hi," she said. "How has your day been?"

"Long, but productive. Ramon Aguirre filmed Barron and another man having sex with a couple of kids. Melanie Maitland was in on it. Ramon stashed the film at his mother's house. I have a foot of it in my pocket to use as leverage if the need arises. I expect it to. I think Barron bought Melanie's son. Chaco told me Ramon asked him how to get in touch with some goon from their old neighborhood after Ramon had a blowout with Mel Berry. Chaco thinks his brother had Berry killed."

"And you think Ramon was killed for the film?"

"Seems likely. He tried to blackmail Barron. Barron had him destroyed."

"You've got him, Gardner!" She seemed delighted, almost.

"I want to meet with my friend on the cops, Pete Velasquez, and see what he thinks we should do." Now she was frowning.

"Damnit, Gardner, Barron's left town. After we talked to Maria and Juanita, I hired a paparazzo to record all of Barron's movements. He was waiting for me this morning when I came in. These shots were taken at 2:00 A.M. today. Look." She handed me a pair of contact sheets marked with grease pencil, and a series of eight-by-tens that corresponded to the marked shots. Our forearms touched as we studied the pictures together. She flashed me a little smile and said, "I think the photographer was hoping for more than two days' work." The prints showed Barron and some other people boarding a tri-engine Falcon 50, *The Rising Star.* "That's Barron's plane, of course," Doe added.

"And that's Melanie Maitland," I said, "There, the blonde, and that's her son."

"I thought it might be," Doe said. "See in the next shot, she's turned away and she's trying to hide the little boy with her coat."

"Your paparazzo did a hell of a job. Barron looks furious."

"Some of Barron's men chased him all around the airport, but he was faster than they were, obviously. I paid him for an extra day."

"He earned it. Did you get a flight plan?"

"Mexico City to Denver. They went through customs at Stapleton Airport and flew on to Aspen. Barron has a huge ranch near there, *Castillo Colorado.* He's running, Gardner. He wasn't supposed to leave Mexico City for four more days."

"No shackles on Miss Maitland as far as I can see; no sign of duress."

"Just the opposite. Look at this contact sheet. First column, third shot down. The faces aren't very clear so I didn't have him print it, but look at the three of them. She's trying to get Barron to take her hand."

"I'm going to have to go up there, Doe. Next flight."

"Nine forty-five tomorrow morning was the best I could do. We get to Stapleton at two-twenty. It's an hour earlier there. I assumed a big boy like you would like first class. I told my editor I had a hell of a time persuading you to let me come along."

"How much did you tell him?"

"Just that we had an exclusive lead on a story that would be bigger than the Rock Hudson–AIDS thing. He knows enough to trust me. And I know he'll try to take all the credit, but it will be my byline over the copy and there isn't a thing he can do about it. I told him we could break within seventy-two hours. Do you think that's realistic?"

"It's got to be. If you're right, that Barron's spooked, and I think you are, things will come to a boil very quickly once he learns that you and I and Ramon's film have turned up like the proverbial bad penny. The guy who tried to kill us has a featured part as a Barron flunky in Ramon's film."

She shivered. "So at the same time Barron was leaving town with Melanie and the little boy, someone working for him was trying to kill us. . . ."

"It looks that way."

"I may not buy his next record."

"There won't be a next record, I hope, and thanks for getting the tickets. You dazzle me with your competence. If you ever tire of journalism, Wells, Inc., would welcome an opportunity to discuss your professional future. We have an excellent benefit package. Just get in touch with our personnel department."

"Haven't I already been in touch with your personnel department?"

"We're great believers in the follow-up interview."

"So am I. I have some beautiful mahi mahi fillets in my freezer, if you'd care to combine pleasure with pleasure."

"May I suggest that you pack for the trip while we're at your place and then join me at my hotel for dessert? We can leave from there in the morning. I think the arrangement has certain advantages from a security standpoint. Barron may have appointed another goodwill ambassador to pay us a call."

"You're not going to ask me to pack the Hefty bags, are you?"

"No, but if you've got some naughty underwear, you might bring it along."

It was dusk when we pulled into the sixth-floor parking garage at Doe's building. From her look as we got out of the car, I knew we'd both had the same thought. She waited while I went to the south end of the building and looked below. The dumpster was empty.

Doe held the elevator when we got to her floor; I went ahead to check the apartment. I knew we hadn't been followed, but there was a possibility someone was waiting inside. I rang the bell a couple of times and mumbled the Spanish word for plumber. There was no response. As I let myself in, I thought about which of the pistols in my collection would have felt best in my right hand. Any of them would have made me feel more secure than Doe's doorkey. Inside the apartment, the air was pungent with the smell of fresh paint. So far as I could tell, no one had been there since we left. I went back to the door and beckoned to Doe. The look of apprehension lifted from her face as she released the elevator and started down the hall toward me. I took her hand as we went in.

"I don't like this," she said. "Will I ever be able to

walk in here again without remembering, without feeling afraid?'' She looked at her home as if it were contaminated.

''Within a week, there will be headlines about Bobby Barron in every major newspaper in the free world. Hundreds of millions of people will know what only a few know now. He can't kill all of us.''

''You cook, I pack?''

''Agreed.''

Between attempts to answer the questions, Doe called to me from the bedroom about fashion and temperatures in late September Aspen. I stir-fried most of the fresh produce in her kitchen and broiled a pair of large mahi mahi fillets, which I basted periodically with an improvised sweet-and-sour sauce. The results, accompanied by a respectable chardonnay, were very gratifying.

The cab came for us soon after we finished cleaning up. It was neither good luck nor good service. The cab was an hour late, but we'd anticipated that and called for it to arrive long before we expected to be ready.

No one in the hotel lobby seemed particularly interested in our arrival. I paid my bill and asked for a six-thirty wake-up call. We took the same precautions at my room that we'd taken at Doe's apartment: She held the elevator while I checked for unfriendly visitors. The room was clear.

Doe went first in the bathroom. While she did her ablutions, I hung a motion-sensitive alarm on the doorknob and packed everything except what I planned to wear in the morning. Given the prospect of Doe's company, I was even happier to be leaving Mexico City than I'd been two days before.

When it was my turn in the bathroom, I took a shower under the hottest water I could stand. The pleasure of settling in between clean sheets when the body is newly washed and the pores are open wide is one of life's most underappreciated experiences. In the shower, I noticed that

my beard felt twice as long as it usually does twelve hours
after a shave, so I tended to that when I got out. Once the
teeth were brushed, I wrapped a big towel around myself
and stepped into the cool darkness of the room, my mind
set on a nice, slow screw to end the day. But, alas, the
lady was dead asleep. Even the contact of our hips as I lay
beside her had no effect. I had no choice but to lie there
and remind myself over and over that settling in between
clean sheets is one of life's most underappreciated experiences.

I was in deep sleep when the red light flashed on in my
head. Soon there were more, a wall of them; then a great
dome-full. And a siren, but I couldn't wake up. Then
the domes went black and I was at the bottom of a
Vaseline lake, crushed and unable to breathe. A brick
grew in my throat. My arms weighed a thousand pounds.
My voice made no sound. Then, with terrible slowness, I
rose toward the light; the world rolled back into focus.
Doe was shaking me. Tears fell from her eyes onto my
shoulder. I heard a blistering wail and pounding. I shook
myself.

"Someone's there," she said. Her whisper was wound
like a scream. Whoever was on the other side of the door
was knocking hard enough to have set off my alarm. I sat
up. She was holding the phone to her ear. "The switchboard won't answer," she said. I cupped a hand on her
shoulder.

"Stay on the line," I said. "Give the room number
first, 1011." I went to a position beside the door, reached
out, and shut off the alarm. He saved me the trouble of
deciding what to say.

"Goddamnit, Wells, let me in!" I stepped into the
slacks I'd laid out for morning and opened the door. Doe
was still pulling on her robe as Ben Maitland barged in
like a wounded beast. I don't think he noticed her until I
flipped on the overhead light; even so, the discovery had
no effect on his manners. "I've been calling you for two

days. Where in hell have you been? I thought you were coming back.''

"Ben," I said in a voice intended to show less irritation than I felt, "this is my friend Doe Aguilar."

"Hi, how are you? Wells, look, I'm sorry I hung up on you the other night. The more I thought about what you said, the more I realized I hung up because you were right and I couldn't face it. Then, when you didn't come back, and I couldn't reach you, I started worrying that the same thing happened to you that happened to Berry."

"And here you are."

"That's right." He gave each of us a half smile. "Look, I'm sorry to intrude like this, Miss . . ."

"Aguilar. It's okay."

"You look terrible, Ben."

"That's how I feel. The plane landed an hour ago. I'm checked in here, but I haven't been to the room yet."

"Don't unpack," I said.

It was four-thirty when I finished telling Ben most of what had happened since our last conversation. I didn't tell him I'd learned that Bobby Barron had a strong sexual appetite for little boys and girls. Whether to spare him, or myself, I'm not sure. I said that Ramon had filmed a sexual episode between Barron and another man, and let it go at that. Ben showed little interest. He was grateful that his daughter and grandson were okay.

"Freddie Gordon's company has a big condo in Aspen," Ben said when I stopped talking. He was sitting in the straight-back by the writing desk. Doe was curled up in the easy chair by the window; I was on the edge of the bed. "I'm sure he'll let us use it, fabulous place. I'll call him as soon as it's late enough."

"Two people are dead, Ben. They're not going to invite us in for dinner and send us home with your grandson and what's left of the pie."

"Please don't patronize me, Wells. I'm going with you.

If I understand you correctly, Ramon had Berry killed and now Ramon is dead for trying to blackmail Barron. We're not going to try to blackmail Barron, and that gutter trash Ramon is out of the picture, so what are you so worried about?''

"I'm worried because between the two of them, Barron and your daughter have enough psychopathology to start their own funny farm. I'm worried because Barron may have legally adopted little Ben and if he wants to keep him, there may not be a hell of a lot you can do legally to get him back. I'm also worried because it looks like our favorite entertainer had Ramon killed because of the film, but they didn't recover it, and it may have occurred to them that we have it. And we do, a foot of it anyway. I expect to use it to pry loose little Ben.''

"I have friends in Denver. We'll slap Barron with so many writs and restraining orders, he'll need our permission to fart. Excuse me, Doe.''

"Ben,'' I said, "Barron can hire the kind of lawyers who come equipped with a judge in each pocket. If it weren't so late and I weren't so tired, I would find a more diplomatic way of telling you you're being naive.''

"I've given this a lot of thought, Wells. I want one night with Melanie and Ben; that's all. I'm going to ask her to forgive me. I'm going to tell her I'll help her any way I can. Money, psychiatrists, a job, it doesn't matter. I hope if I admit my mistakes and tell her how much I love her, maybe she'll give me a chance to be a father to her.''

"Maybe.'' I stood. "Good night, Ben. Get a seat on Mexicana Flight 916 and ask for a wake up at six-thirty.'' I opened the door for him. "If you hurry, you can get almost two hours in the sack.'' He rose wearily, stretched, and gave a mighty yawn. He was about to say good night to Doe when he saw that she'd fallen asleep.

"What do you think, Wells?'' he whispered to me in the doorway. "Do you think I've got a prayer with her?''

"How long has it been since you and Melanie spent as much as an hour together?"

"I don't know, seven, eight years, sometime before the divorce."

"She's a woman, Ben, all grown up, an adult with adult problems. She thinks she hates you. It may be the right time for you to reconnect with your daughter, but it may not be the right time for her. She may want to hurt you some more. She may see your apology as an opportunity to cut deeper. I wouldn't count on immediate success. My guess is that if you're going to build a relationship with her, you're going to need a lot of patience and a very thick skin. I'm sorry." He smiled feebly at me and started down the hall toward the elevator. His shoulders were stooped, his gray suit badly wrinkled, his feet barely cleared the nap of the carpet as he plodded along. I'd never thought of Ben as old before that moment. It saddened me to watch him, all the more so because I had a strong sense that he was going to get badly hurt; and there didn't seem to be a single, reasonable thing that I could do to stop it.

· · Chapter Thirteen · ·

We landed in Aspen at four-thirty. As the little De Havilland we'd boarded in Denver taxied toward the terminal, I noticed *The Rising Star* parked amid a bevy of lesser aircraft near the aviation building. It was a golden afternoon, as clear and crisp as it had been smoggy and malodorous when we left Mexico City. Aspen's miniature airport was snoozing through the doldrums of Indian summer. The hikers and bikers were gone; the skiers wouldn't arrive until Thanksgiving.

The car-rental lady hated to set aside her paperback copy of *Hollywood Husbands,* but she was very sweet and with a little diplomatic guidance eventually presented us with the keys to a dark red Dodge Aries and a local map.

Aspen sits at the southeastern end of the Roaring Fork River Valley, 7,900 feet above the sea. South and west of the town, foothills skirting fourteen-thousand-foot peaks have been systematically shaved of vegetation and strung with lifts to create the ski slopes for which, among other things, the place is currently famous. A hundred years ago, silver made Aspen go. Twelve thousand people lived there, and the mines were so rich they ran out of places to store the ore.

By the 1930s, Aspen was a dying agricultural town of five hundred. Skiing and, later, glitz fueled an incredible boom from shortly after World War II until the early eighties. Prices for property were jumping 5 percent a month; Aspen was the center of the universe; John Denver was going to save the world; and it was all going to go on forever. Or at least until OPEC collapsed; and inflation fizzled; and the town's mob of baby-faced real estate moguls found that buyers had become as scarce in their town as sincerity.

I first skied Aspen as a high school senior. The Gucci set hadn't arrived; I don't think there was a Gucci set. I fell in love with Aspen. I fell in love in Aspen. Like many others before and since, I fantasized about how great it would be to live there and ski all winter and climb the "Fourteens" all summer. A local girl told me that Ph.D.'s lined up for jobs to teach kindergarten.

By the time I gave up on Aspen, the town was suffering from acute narcissism. It was a new era: The big hustle was on. Every corner had a bad restaurant selling trendy, overpriced food. Stuffy boutiquism, which previously was contained in its own ghetto, had metastasized. Within practically any block you could buy an espresso maker from Italy; pseudoart from Taos; or drop five hundred bucks for a leather bikini bottom from the Costa Brava. Ersatz Victoriana had engulfed the real thing. The disaffected talked about finding "a new Aspen," but there was as much chance of that as there is of finding "a new McDonald's" that sells fat, juicy hamburgers, cooked to order, for fifty cents. Aspen was the prototype. What had taken twenty years to happen there was happening elsewhere in two or three. If a town had plans for a ski area, a first-annual film festival, and someone in residence who'd once played rhythm guitar in a rock band, it was a safe bet that three-room shacks were going for six figures.

Though it was the off-season, I couldn't find a place to park in town. I wasn't surprised. The difference in-season is that in addition to there being no place to park, there's no place to drive either. While Ben went into Lars Lindstrom's real estate office to pick up the key to his friend's condo, Doe and I looped into the downtown business district.

I was only half an hour off the plane and cocooned inside a Dodge Aries, yet I could feel the anticipation. Like squirrels with the scent of an early snow in their nostrils, the locals were scurrying about on foot and in their Saabs and BMWs making ready for the forthcoming avalanche of ski money. Someone's art gallery was getting a new facade; window displays were in transition. Behind the serious faces of the bright and expensively dressed, allegiances were being weighed; deals evaluated.

"They all look so healthy," Doe exclaimed.

"You were expecting maybe a leper colony?" I asked. We swung down Galena toward Main. I noticed two sushi places within a block.

"I don't know, I've heard they do a lot of big cocaine deals here. I guess I was expecting a different class of people."

"Black limos; guys named 'Tony the Nose?' "

"That's right."

"Really!" I said. "Does every Mexican wear a sombrero and sleep all day?"

"Have I offended you?"

"No, but many of our finest crime families have spent many years and a lot of money cultivating an Ivy League image. They have feelings, too, you know."

"Naturally."

"I have heard that the Italian restaurants in Aspen all have bulletproof windows, but I wouldn't blab it around."

"I'll keep it under my sombrero."

Ben, who had slept most of the day after having a brace of screwdrivers on the plane instead of breakfast, seemed raring to go as he greeted us in the middle of the street outside the real estate office.

"Good news, guys," he said as he piled into the back seat. "Freddie's swapped the condo for a big place on Red Mountain. I don't know why he didn't tell me on the phone this morning. Probably thought I knew. Son of a bitch made a ton of money on some venture capital deals just before the new issues market dried up a couple of years ago. He probably stole this place. Hang a U, Wells. Go back to Mill; turn left; bear left past Gibson; and keep going. What do you think, Doc? Hell of a town, isn't it?"

"I'm impressed," she said. "I really am. It's quite attractive." The narrow road switchbacked through groves of aspen up the side of a hill immediately north of downtown. The trees, their leaves bright yellow against a cobalt sky, shivered in the fading light. Both house and lot sizes increased as we gained elevation. About a third of the properties were for sale. Most were mountain contemporaries—natural-stained cedar siding, shake roofs, decks, stone accents, and lots of glass. Configurations varied with size, roof treatment, and setting. They were probably asking $800,000 for the cheap stuff.

Freddie Gordon's hideaway was not the cheap stuff. It was as high on Red Mountain as mortal man in an ordinary road car could go. It was a big rust-colored place ringed on three sides by thirty-five-foot pines and mature aspen. We parked on gravel in front of the three-car garage and trotted up two flights of wood steps, carrying bags, to the broad redwood deck that led to the front door. I think it embarrassed Ben that he was so winded. While he worked on his oxygen deficit and played with the touchpad for the security system, I walked Doe around the deck.

I don't think the term ''scenic climax'' ordinarily has sexual overtones, but it was not hard for me to imagine a Sierra Club zealot becoming physically aroused by the sight before us. We stood nearly a thousand feet above Aspen, which, nestled in the valley below, looked every inch the innocent hamlet. Due south, the Aspen Mountain Ski Area rose dramatically above the town. Already, its upper reaches were dusted with an early snow. Down the valley to the west, we could see the rugged Fourteens, where, above timberline, it was already winter and the wind whipped snow plumes before the setting sun.

I put an arm around Doe as she snuggled against me. With the combined effects of sunset and the elevation gain, it was probably somewhere in the low fifties, fifteen degrees colder than it had been in town. Above us, the tall pines whispered in a sweet-scented breeze that carried the promise of evening. I kissed the lady on impulse and remembered what it was like to fall in love.

The house had two master suites. Doe and I took one; Ben the other. There appeared to be at least three other bedrooms, plus servants' quarters on the ground floor, and, scattered throughout the house, virtually every hedonistic luxury imaginable. The place was grand, yet rustic. Hard to pull off, but they clearly weren't hamstrung by money. Under a twenty-foot exposed beam ceiling in the living room, massive red leather chairs and a sofa surrounded a walk-in mossrock fireplace. There was popular sentiment in our group for a leisurely tour with drinks in hand, but we yielded to a higher calling. Faces were washed, clothes changed, and we were off again in our little Aries. I wondered if the homeowners' association would complain if we parked it outside.

The graying hippie working the register at a gas station near the bottom of the hill plainly hadn't memorized direc-

tions to the stars' homes, but he did tell me that John
Denver and others lived in a guarded enclave called
Starwood, which he pronounced as if it were the punchline
to a dirty joke. I had better luck with the bartender at the
Hotel Jerome. He gave me not only complete directions to
Castillo Colorado, but also to Jimmy Buffett's and Goldie
Hawn's places, which he said were closer and easier to
see. From town, we headed northwest on 82, a good
two-lane highway that follows the Roaring Fork River to
the Colorado. As the valley descends and widens, forested
mountains yield to a gaunt landscape of red hills and
ridges, dotted with scrub pine.

About a dozen miles from town, the asphalt under us
gave way to gravel as we passed through an area of road
reconstruction, which, fortunately, was shut down for the
weekend. The dust cloud that rose behind our car on the
temporary roadway drifted into a small trailer park, one of
several in the upper valley where the people who wash
Aspen's dishes go to at the end of the day.

A couple of miles past the construction, we turned south
onto a county road that teased us with a mile or so of
pavement before going native. Our route followed the
valley formed by Capital Creek. The lower end was wide-
open horse country with a few clusters of houses that
looked like Aspen on a budget. Ahead, snowcapped peaks
and ridges stood cotton-candy pink in the sun's last light.
The sight of blue woodsmoke rising in a delicate column
from the chimney of a small ranch house west of the road
seemed to prompt Doe to switch on the car's heater.
Crossing the last great open space in the valley, we saw a
Benedictine monastery tucked hard against the darkening
mountains.

Past the monastery turnoff, the road began to deteriorate
as it passed through a thick stand of aspen. I turned on the
headlights to help me navigate the rocks and ruts and
began to wonder if it might have been wiser for us to

check out Goldie Hawn's place as the bartender at the Jerome had recommended.

"How far are we from town, Wells?" Ben demanded from the back seat.

"Thirty miles," I said.

"What is Barron hiding from out here? I mean, it's not like I know the guy, but he doesn't exactly come over like the back-to-nature type, would you say?"

"Not exactly. . . ." Doe gasped as the car's back bumper slammed down on a rock. "Sorry," I said.

We went on, climbing. The road got as bad as it could without being beyond the capability of a Dodge Aries. I was in the midst of replaying my mental tape of the bartender's directions when our high beams lit up the signs: "No Trespassing," "Keep Out," "Private," and, for good measure, "Violators Will Be Prosecuted." They straddled the west branch of a fork in the road. "Welcome to *Castillo Colorado*," I said.

A triple switchback beyond the signs brought us to the top of a ridge and some relatively easy going as the road followed the crest northward through a series of small clearings surrounded by stands of pine and spruce. Snow-caps began to appear on fallen trees and in other places insulated from the warmth of earth and sun. Atop the valley's far ridge, a harvest moon sat like Humpty-Dumpty in a nest of silhouetted evergreens.

We had begun to lose elevation when the road turned west, across the width of the ridge. The moon flashed through my rearview mirror as our little car crunched through a puddle crusted with ice. Ahead of us, in the blackness, a red, eye-shaped thing suddenly appeared. "It's a reflector," I said out loud, as if they couldn't see so for themselves. The twelve-inch hexagonal panel was mounted on a steel and aluminum gate that blocked the road.

"Shit," Maitland muttered in the back seat.

Doe expressed Ben's feeling more eloquently, "I can't believe we've come all this way for nothing," she said. An eight-foot chain-link fence topped with three strands of barbed wire ran from both sides of the gate into the forest. I stopped short of the gate's swing marks, but close enough to tell that it was locked. Through the fence, I could see a metal building with two single garage doors and what looked like a small office at one end. I gave the car horn a couple of honks. There was a light on in the office. "You think there's anybody in there?" Doe asked.

"We'll find out," I said.

"What are you going to say to them?"

"Just the truth, that we want to see Melanie and little Ben. They won't let us in, but it'll give old Bobby something to think about." I was about to honk again when the office door opened. A big bearded guy in his thirties sauntered toward us. He carried his shotgun with the butt under his armpit and the barrel over his forearm. "He needs the serape and the flattop hat," I said, "and some guy whistling in the background."

"Don't joke," Doe scolded. "I think we should get out of here."

"In a minute," I said. "Ben, when I get out, you take the driver's seat. Study the area while you're out of the car. The moon's bright enough that you can see behind us. Now, you remember all that trick driving stuff they taught you in Tucson?"

"Sure."

"Well, forget it. This guy has no idea who we are and I have no reason to think there'll be any trouble once he finds out, but if there is, kill your lights, back around to the left—in there, and get the hell out of here. I'll take care of myself. If you play the hero at this range, everybody loses. Okay?"

"Okay," Ben answered. "Just be careful, will you?"

I got out of the car. "Leave the motor running and the

lights on," I said. I left the door open for Ben and started walking. I gave Mr. Hospitality a big wave. "Hi," I said. "I'm Gardner Wells. My friend's daughter and grandson are visiting Mr. Barron. He'd like to say hello to them. Will you let us through?" I stopped as far back from the gate on my side as he was from it on his and stayed across the headlights from him so I was harder to see.

"Friend," he said, "I'm afraid somebody gave you some bad information. There's nobody stayin' at the ranch just now." I glimpsed another man as he moved across the office window, holding a radio transceiver below his chin. "And you're trespassing on private property. The owner don't like that. What say you head on back where you came from? Right now." He raised the shotgun a few degrees. The light in the office went out.

"I'm ready to leave," I said. I took the envelope out of my jacket pocket. "But I'd like you to give this note to Mr. Barron after I go. Now don't bother to tell me again that he isn't here. Let's just pretend he is, and let's just pretend you do something really stupid like decide not to bother him with this. Well, that would be too bad, because this note requires a response, and if there's no response, some things are going to happen that will make Mr. Barron very unhappy. In fact, friend, he'll be so unhappy, you'll probably spend Christmas in a shallow grave out here on the Ponderosa." I approached the nearest section of chain link with the envelope and pushed it halfway through one of the open spaces. The backup man was standing in shadow off the end of the building. I could only guess that the large shape hanging from his right hand was a pistol. "You guys have a nice night," I said. They looked at each other. The guy with the beard shrugged his shoulders. As I walked back to the car, I noticed that I could see my breath.

"What was in the envelope?" Doe asked as I got in the back seat.

"The phone number where we're staying and two frames from Ramon's film," I said. Ben started backing the car around.

"Succinct," she said.

"Thanks," I said. "You could sue me for reckless endangerment but this ought to get things moving."

"It's the right move as far as I'm concerned," Ben said as we drove away. "The way that character with the gun acted, you could blow a week trying to get someone to admit Barron's not in Mexico or a hundred other places. . . . I want to see that film when we get back to Gordon's."

"I don't think so, Ben."

"Bull. I'm flattered you think I'm so innocent. In the Navy, we had these . . ."

"Ben, I've got about a second and a half of film. Melanie's in it. Seeing it isn't going to improve the quality of your life, and it won't help us accomplish our objective here. Forget it." He let out a big sigh. For a minute or so, I think he debated whether to press the matter, but he let it go. I was sorry to hit him with the news about Melanie, but I didn't want him to see Barron with those two kids. I knew where his mind would go next: the same place mine had. My friend deserved to be able to think about his grandson without feeling sick or angry, and I was determined to protect that right as long as I could. If the worst had happened, Ben would never wish for more time to mull it over.

We ate Italian at a place called Abalone on East Hyman. They gave us a hard time about not having reservations. There were six other customers. The prices were New York; the food was Chef Boy-ar-dee. We should have known better.

After dinner, we gassed up the car and bought breakfast fixings at the local market. The town had gone to bed for the night. Barron's people had had plenty of time to match an address with the telephone number I'd left. So, on our

return to Red Mountain, I parked car, Doc, and Ben a
hundred feet short of the driveway and went in on foot.
The moon shone brilliantly overhead. I passed the drive
and approached the house under cover of a clump of scrub
oak. In the valley below, Aspen sparkled like a postcard
fantasy. The house got a clean bill of health, but the
diagnostic process left me determined to acquire warmer
clothes and a gun. Both were available inside.

Freddie Gordon's gun collection was locked in a small,
windowless room adjoining his study. Ordinarily, I'm not
the kind of houseguest who rewards his host's hospitality
by breaking into locked rooms and locked gun cabinets,
but in a way it was his fault. I needed a gun, and there
were animal heads staring from almost every wall in the
house; hunting trophies with Freddie's name, a date, and
location on each one. If my host had not chosen to flaunt
the carnage he'd inflicted on the animal kingdom, I would
never have gone looking for his arsenal. It was a nice,
little arsenal; not huge, but obviously the collection of
someone discriminating and well-funded. I was glad to see
he'd left me plenty of ammunition.

There were a dozen long guns, from a twenty-two to a
pair of Perazzi shotguns, and an assortment of pistols,
including a matched set of World War I vintage forty-
fives. The Glock surprised me: relatively new and exotic
compared to the rest of the collection. It's a 9mm, semiau-
tomatic pistol made in Austria and used by police there.
All major parts except for the slide, barrel, springs, and
other key firing components are made of a supertough
plastic. A comparable conventional weapon, fully loaded,
weighs three times as much. They hold eighteen rounds
including one in the chamber, and they're ugly. I loaded
two clips from a box of silver-tipped, hollow point shells,
and wondered why Freddie felt the need of ammunition
that will punch a nickel-sized hole through the vital or-
gans. By the time I emerged from the ordnance depot, a

Remington .308 bolt-action rifle in one hand, the Glock in the other, Ms. Aguilar and Mr. Maitland, fortified with snifters of brandy, had taken seats in a pair of red leather chairs before a blazing hearth. They looked like characters in a *New Yorker* cartoon. The only thing missing was the bored Afghan.

I could see that Doe would have preferred to see me bearing flowers and a violin. "Sorry," I said. "I'm thinking about our friend with the Micro Uzi." I leaned the rifle against a tall bookcase and put the Glock on a table beside it. "Is the brandy self-serve or is there a St. Bernard?"

"I'll get you some," Doe said. She started to get up.

"You look too comfortable. Just tell me where."

"There are three crystal decanters on the bar. It's the middle one. The snifters are in the far left cabinet, bottom shelf."

"Anybody else?" I said.

While I refilled Ben's glass and poured one for myself, I heard him telling her about the antiterrorist training he'd had in Tucson a couple of years earlier. He didn't want to go, but the insurance company from which Data Matrix was trying to buy a ten-million-dollar policy on his life was insisting, and Ben's board of directors felt the company owed the coverage to their public stockholders. I told him I thought he should go. He went, and came back swaggering like General Patton. For a while, he was never more than an arm's length from a pistol.

"Ben, you still take that Beretta everywhere you go?" I asked as I handed him his drink.

"No," he said, "I kept forgetting not to wear it when I had to fly somewhere. I'd trip the damn security alarm, then miss the plane while I tried to explain myself to the marshals. The third time, that was it. The damn thing was uncomfortable, anyway. Oh, I've worn it at a couple of big conventions since then. I didn't think I'd need it this trip. Things are bad between me and Melanie, but, hell, they're not that bad. . . ." He laughed. I sat on an armrest at the end of the sofa nearest Doe. Ben's chair was a few feet beyond.

"I think we should take watches tonight," I said. "Eleven to two, two to four, four to six. If Barron sends anyone, he'll be expecting to kill us in our sleep. There's no way he'll fight except to defend himself, so we'll scare him off before he's committed. Okay?" They nodded. "I'll take two to four. Who wants to go first?"

"I can," Doe said. "Two cups of espresso and a strange bed, I probably wouldn't get to sleep before two, anyway."

"I'll try not to take that personally," I said. She smirked. "Four to six okay with you, Ben?"

"Sure. What about tomorrow? What's the plan?"

I said, "I'm expecting them to tell us. But if we haven't heard anything by eleven, we hire a plane and check out the place by air. If it looks like they're still in there, we'll try to spot an alternate route to his house, one that bypasses his security. After we land, I'll rent a jeep and go in. That guy with the shotgun had a crazy kind of crooked look in his eyes. Maybe he threw my note in the woodstove. Maybe he doesn't believe in Santa Claus. Who knows?"

"You're asking to get shot at, Wells," Ben said.

"I'm impatient," I said. "Jimmy Tanaka wants to send me to Tokyo; Doe's Pulitzer is starting to rust; and you and your grandson are neglecting the 49ers."

"What about the police?" Doe asked.

"Is the expression 'Keystone Kops' familiar to you?" I said.

"Mack Sennett. Silent movies, slapstick comedy. I saw a couple of their things when I was at Columbia. Are you making a comparison?"

"I'm not, but when I skied here, that's what the locals called their men in blue, although I think the uniforms are beige in this case. They were a laughingstock."

"Maybe they've changed," Doe said.

"Maybe not," I said. "In any case, I'm sure we'll find out, unless Barron and his entourage take off on us. In the meantime, I suspect Barron throws as much weight around here as he does in Mexico City. Maybe more. It might be dumb to involve the local cops before we—" The sharp ring of the telephone startled all of us. It was a chocolate brown desk set on the table where I'd left the Glock. I took a swig of brandy and answered.

"Mr. Wilson?" Cultured male voice, raspy from smoking, booze, or both.

"There's no Wilson here," I said.

"I'm looking for the individual who delivered two frames of film and a telephone number this afternoon. Might you be he?"

"I might. Who might you be?"

"Perhaps it's Mr. Gordon I'm speaking to. I've rung Mr. Gordon's house, haven't I?"

"You've rung Gardner Wells, connoisseur of the erotic and bizarre, currently featuring in my collection an extraordinary piece of film in which the legendary Mr. Enchantment demonstrates unexpected talents heretofore hidden from his devoted fans. Now can we cut the crap?"

"Yes." The lilt was gone. Ben had left his seat and was standing at my side. "What do you want?"

"Melanie Maitland and her son. You get the film."

"Money?"

"Thanks, we have enough."

"We'll need to meet. No sense in making it unpleasant. How about lunch?"

"With Melanie and the boy?"

"Impossible. Whatever gave you the idea we know these people?"

"Photographs of them boarding *The Rising Star* yesterday morning."

"The individuals you speak of are quite safe—and content, I might add. Now let's be reasonable. You have something of great interest to us, and we, as you may know, have certain resources that we could employ to take possession of it. You can hurt us, and we can hurt you. It's a stalemate, so why not be cóoperative? I'm sure we can work this out to everyone's satisfaction once we've had a chance to talk. No one needs be harmed, Mr. Wells.''

"People have already been harmed, Mr. . . . ?''

"Snyder. Jim Snyder.''

"Shall we review the body count, Jim?''

"The Ute City Banque does a nice lunch. Then, of course, there's the Wienerstube. Or how about the AlpenGlo? That's always fun.''

"The depth of my indifference would astonish you.''

"The AlpenGlo, then, on the Mill Street Mall?''

"I'll find it.''

"One o'clock?''

"I can't wait." I hung up. "They know where we are,'' I said. "He asked if he was speaking to Mr. Gordon.''

"What did he say about my grandson?''

"That he and Melanie are okay. 'Content,' he said.''

"They're out there then. He admitted it?''

"He didn't specifically deny it,'' I said.

"Who did you talk to?'' Doe asked. She was jollying a hefty chunk of piñon onto the fire.

"Jim Snyder. Know him?'' I picked up my snifter and gave the contents a swirl.

"I've never met him, but he's way up there in Barron's organization. Personal manager, I think. I found a column in which his role was compared to Colonel Parker's with Elvis.''

"The malevolent puppeteer?'' I said.

"Exactly,'' Doe agreed. She picked up her drink and sat on the end of the sofa, where I'd been.

"Comforting to know we're not dealing with lackeys,''

I said between sips of brandy. The nicotine demon was screaming for a cigar.

"If what I've heard is true," Doe went on, "in some ways, Snyder is closer to Barron than Barron. What was his tone?"

"Artificially friendly, conciliatory in the same way. He seemed irritated when I mentioned Melanie and little Ben. I think he'd rather pay us off. . . ."

"Screw him," Ben said.

"We're going to have lunch tomorrow."

"LUNCH?" Ben roared.

"We've got one card to play, Ben. I don't want to spook these people by acting like we're out of control. I'll try to set up an exchange tomorrow night."

"What time do we meet?"

"You don't. You're going to take Doe on a walking tour of the town. I don't want you here by yourselves, or rolling around the countryside, either. Get your heart and mind ready for your family. Let me negotiate with the bad guys." His sigh signaled acceptance.

"Which gun do I get?" Doe asked. "The big one or the little one? I have a feeling I should start my watch."

While Ben shopped Freddie's arsenal, I gave Doe the little one and showed her how to use it. When the lesson was over, we bundled her up like a Laplander in January and stationed her on a folding chair on the deck outside our bedroom with a box of Triscuits and a thermos of hot tea. She looked cute. Except for the Glock. The black barrel protruding from layers of colorful Indian blankets was all wrong, like razor blades in Halloween candy.

I told her not to shoot except to defend herself. I told her to listen. On a crisp, clear night in the mountains, when the air is still, you can hear forever. A car approaching. Gravel crunching underfoot. I told her to get me if anything aroused her suspicions. I told her to close her eyes and prepare to be kissed.

I built a fire in the bedroom fireplace and stretched out on the bed, fully dressed. Maybe we wouldn't have visitors, but the Uzi man had made an impression. I lay there for a while, just watching . . . the flames, their orange light dancing on the ceiling; Doe sipping tea under moonlight beyond the glass; slate gray foothills overseen by snowcapped peaks; twinkling lights, scattered like stars across the landscape. The fire crackled. I couldn't sleep. Doe jumped when I opened the door to tell her I was going to look around. I put on a navy blue wool jacket I'd found earlier in a downstairs closet. It was short in the sleeves and tight in the shoulders but a better fit than anyone my size could reasonably expect under the circumstances.

Rifle in hand, I stepped into the hallway outside the bedroom. Maitland was snoring. Moonlight filled the rooms below. Coals glowed red in the great fireplace. A mouse scampered ahead of me as I entered the kitchen. A thermometer outside the back door said it was twenty-six. Sparks from the bedroom fireplace rose like Tinkerbell's offspring from the chimney. I walked down to the road and circled back around the house by the opposite side to the back door. An unseen semi accelerated reluctantly on the highway below. Nothing to report, General. All quiet.

I made Doe fresh tea in the microwave. We shared an orange and some chocolate chip cookies I'd bought earlier. I got back in bed.

It was three-ten when I woke. Doe was hunkered down outside the glass door, tapping on it lightly with the barrel of the Glock. My eyes went immediately to the security system control panel beside the bed. Everything looked okay. Doe saw me approaching and motioned to me to stay down. I squatted beside the door and opened it slightly.

"There's someone out there," she whispered. "I heard something in those bushes. I thought it might be an animal, but then I saw a reflection. The movement was coming this way."

"How long since you've seen or heard anything?"

"No more than a minute."

"Why didn't you get me at two?"

"I didn't want to wake you. I was doing okay."

I put my finger to my lips. "I thought I heard something." We listened. I took her hand and brought her in. "I'm going downstairs," I said. "Stay away from the glass."

Halfway down the staircase, I heard the noise again, but the sound of my own footfalls obscured it. I stood still. Nothing. I checked my grip on the Remington. At the bottom of the stairs, I heard it again. In dead silence, it was easy to identify. Someone was on the roof. Doe called to me in a hushed voice from the top of the stairs. I bounded upward and reached our bedroom just as his legs descended from the eave toward the deck rail. I raised the Remington, pointed it at his left knee, and fired. In the same instant the glass shattered, he cried out. His legs disappeared upward in a single motion. He had help. I heard cursing. They were making their way up the roof. I went out on the deck. They had crossed the peak of the roof and were starting down the other side. The deck and rail where I'd shot him were splattered with blood. While I waited for them to appear below, I spotted a pickup parked a couple of hundred yards down the road. There was no point asking Doe why she hadn't heard it drive up. They made only a halfhearted effort to hide themselves as they did a three-legged race down the driveway. The one whose knee I destroyed was wearing a bill cap. He'd be sitting out the ski season this year. When they got to the street, I lost sight of them, but picked them up again when they reached the truck. As the able-bodied one was helping his pal into the passenger seat, I shot out the windshield. It fractured in countless pieces and collapsed inside the cab. I heard more cursing punctuated by yowls of pain as the truck swung around and drove off. It was going to be a breezy ride back to the *castillo*.

Ben was standing at Doe's side, a few feet from the door, when I walked in. He was in his pajamas, barefoot, one of Freddie's forty-five automatics in his right hand. She'd shed her mantle of blankets, but not the Glock.

"You guys look like Bonnie and Clyde," I said.

"Are they gone?" Ben asked.

"Yeah, I think so," I said.

"Gardner, I'm sorry," Doe said. "I must have fallen asleep. I don't know how they could have gotten so close otherwise."

"Forget it. There's a guy out there with no left knee who's a hell of a lot sorrier you fell asleep than I am. . . ." Cold air poured in through the gaping hole where the thermopane had been.

"Why'd you let them go?" Ben asked.

"They were cannon fodder. Grabbing them would have complicated things. I wouldn't have shot to hit the guy if I'd seen him sooner."

"How did they get up there?" Doe asked sheepishly.

"Probably jumped from the high ground behind the house."

"I'll call the real estate guy in the morning and get him to send someone to fix this," Ben said. "What do you think in the meantime, a sheet?" I looked at Doe and smiled.

"Hefty bags," she said.

"I saw some in the kitchen," I said.

"I'll take care of it."

By the time she returned with the bags, tape, and a dustpan and brush, Ben had gone back to his room to catch a few more Z's before his watch. After we cut the bags into sheets, I held them against the molding while she taped. "What are my chances of having lunch with you and Snyder tomorrow?" she asked.

"Nil," I said.

"That doesn't sound like there's much room for negotiation."

"There isn't. The organization knows you, even if Snyder doesn't. They may have someone stationed in the restaurant who'd recognize you. Maitland and I don't have a prayer of dealing with these people if they think we're traveling with the press."

She laughed. "Are you mad at me?"

"No. What makes you think so?"

"I don't know." She started sweeping glass fragments into the dustpan while I finished taping.

"I guess I'm tired. Sorry." I kissed her ear.

"I'm really sorry about falling asleep. I should have come for you at two."

"Any one of us might have done the same thing."

She smiled at me. We finished cleaning up. While she brushed her teeth and conducted the other rituals of presleep, I rebuilt the fire. When it was blazing nicely, I turned off the room lights. A moment later, a cop car U-turned in front of the house. I wondered if someone had called in about the gunshots. If so, the response time was thirty minutes plus.

Maitland's alarm went off. I heard him yawn. It was almost four. The moon was setting. I decided to assume a horizontal position and see if the covered window blocked the view from the head of the bed. It didn't. The setting moon was plainly visible through the neighboring window, about one diameter, now, above the mountains. The door from Ben's bedroom to his deck opened and closed. Doe's slinky nightgown shimmered in the mixture of fire and moonlight as she entered the room.

"You still here?" she said.

"Just checking out the view," I said. She sat on the bed beside me. I could not tell the exact color of her nightgown, but it was a light color, and it was sleeveless, and the fabric looked like satin and clung to her breasts like a kiss.

"You think they'll come back?" she asked.

"No," I said. Moonlight flashed in her eyes and glazed her lips with a soft sheen. She was wearing that incredible perfume. "You smell like gardenias," I said.

"You smell like sex," she said, and proceeded to unbuckle my belt.

·· Chapter Fourteen ··

Doe was showering when I got back from a run to the Aspen Club at about ten. She welcomed my company and I was grateful for the opportunity to conserve water. After shaving, I put on Levis and a dark-blue shirt. Doe, with her hair up, wore designer jeans and a lavender blouse. It was the first time I'd seen her dressed American. She looked great, but I'd gotten fond of the dressier, more feminine things she wore at home.

Breakfast was a joint effort. While Ben talked to his office, Doe made a huge pan of cornbread and I put together a monster ham and cheese omelet using the biggest skillet in Freddie Gordon's kitchen. Later, Ben got to clean up.

When we'd eaten, I refilled my coffee mug and repaired to Freddie's office to make a phone call. I had met Dave Sachs at my health club. His schedule and mine seemed to permit workouts at similar times. When he told me he was an analyst, I guessed he meant people because he had a habit of asking me how things made me feel, and whatever I said, he tended to nod as though it was profoundly significant. I liked him in spite of it. He had a hearty laugh, and he looked like a balding teddy bear.

Directory Assistance gave me the number of a group practice in Palo Alto. The woman who answered the phone said Dave was with a patient. I introduced myself and arranged to try again in fifteen minutes. She put me right through when I called back.

"How are you, Gardner?" he said.

I could visualize the little knot of concern on his brow.

"I'm fine. I'm in Colorado. I need your help on something."

"Of course. I missed you at the club last week. Anything wrong?"

I stood up and quietly closed the door to Freddie's office. "I'm in Aspen with a friend," I said. "His grandson and daughter are here, too. The daughter has a history of psychiatric problems and is potentially dangerous given the right circumstances. She's attached herself to a man who's also dangerous, very wealthy, and a pedophile. She's staying with him. The boy is there, too. My friend wants to take his grandson back to San Francisco. We have film of the pedophile in action to use to pry the kid loose. I want to know how we should approach this guy. Which buttons to push, which ones to stay away from."

"I've read case histories. I treated one briefly several years ago, but I'm not an expert. I deal mostly with family problems."

"I appreciate your honesty."

"You said he's dangerous. What makes you think so?"

"On two occasions, he's sent people to kill us."

"Knowing you have the film of him?"

"Yes."

"The fear of discovery is a powerful influence. Most of these people are very clever about not getting caught, and most of them never are. It's quite common for them to threaten to kill their victims if the child reports the activity to anyone. Is your man homosexual?''

''In the film, he's with a boy. A few weeks ago in Mexico City, a seven-year-old girl swallowed drain opener after he forced himself on her.''

''The sexually indiscriminate pedophile tends to be quite detached from his victims. The thought processes are quite primitive. There's no guilt, at least not in any lasting sense. It's a compulsion. They go to prison for a few years and start right up again when they get out. The violent ones tend to have been abused violently.

''The one I treated was a Sunday school teacher. He loved children—generally, not just in a sexual sense. He'd never grown up. He was an empty, yearning human being. Quite pathetic, really.''

''Someone had abused him as a kid?'' I asked.

''A camp counselor, as I recall. He came to me because of an incident at the church. The child said he was going to report my patient to his parents. The man wanted to be able to say he'd sought treatment on his own. The child evidently never said anything to his parents and the man stopped coming to me. The cure rate with pedophiles is extremely low once they reach their mid-twenties, and it gets worse as they get older. If they get treatment in their teens, there's a fair chance for success. Is any of this helping?''

''If he's violent and remorseless, I suppose we should be sympathetic—never mention the pedophilia.''

''I agree. Don't confront him.''

''What else?'' I asked.

''Impossible to say,'' Sachs sighed.

''I don't know whether this man has abused my friend's grandson. The kid's only four. . . .''

''He's old enough, Gardner. There have been cases involving babies.''

"If he has been abused, what are the odds of his becoming a pedophile himself later on?"

Sachs couldn't completely suppress a little laugh. "Well, it's not the same as vampires," he said. "If the boy is reasonably well-adjusted otherwise and the pedophile isn't a significant person in his life, a parent or teacher for example, and the abuse doesn't go on for a particularly long time, then there's a good chance he'll develop in a normal way sexually. It depends on the individual."

"The first three years of his life, he and his mother bounced around like gypsies. She parked him with his grandmother last year; then after months of having nothing to do with him, she showed up and took him to Mexico without slowing down to kiss grandma good-bye. In Mexico, she sold him, at least that's what she told me. I think the pedophile is the new owner. If there's anything well-adjusted about this kid, it's the eighth wonder of the world."

"Get him, Gardner. It sounds like time is working against you."

I thanked Dave for his time and reported back to the main company. We'd talked about walking into town, but by the time the men the real estate company sent over to replace the broken window had finished their work, it was too late. Ben won the car keys and the fun of finding a place to park. When he dropped me near the Mill Street Mall, he was making noises about taking Doe to lunch at the Red Onion. I made them promise to stay where there were plenty of witnesses, and pick me up at two.

As a saloon, the AlpenGlo was more Halston than John Wayne: high ceilings, hanging plants, a greenhouse roof, and lots of art deco stained glass back-lit by fluorescent tubes. The crowd was mostly young, chic, and chattery. Snyder was trying to act the part, but he was too old. I spotted him posing next to a Bloody Mary at the bar. He was about fifty, six feet tall, slender, with graying good looks. He was dressed like a refugee from a brunch-theme layout in *GQ:* camel's hair blazer, mauve turtleneck with a matching pocket square, wool slacks in a wine plaid, and brown tassel loafers. I'm not sure how I knew he was Snyder; I just knew. The package fit the voice on the phone. He checked me out like a side of beef when I introduced myself. The way his eyes widened when he looked up at me made me think he was expecting someone short and shifty, the type that sells hot watches on Times Square. He was nervous. We didn't shake hands.

As soon as Snyder caught the eye of the maître d', we were shown to a corner booth in the back of the restaurant. He ordered another Bloody Mary. I asked for coffee. As the cocktail waitress left us, Snyder managed a half-smile. "I hope you're hungry," he said. "The food here is marvelous, and the portions are immense." He lit a Benson and Hedges menthol, and buried his head in the bill of fare.

It was one of those grandiloquent menus in flowing script where French fries sound like something Princess Di would wear on her ears and the coffee—specially imported, roasted, blended, ground, and brewed—seemed bargain-priced at two bucks a cup considering all they had to do to it. I found something that I thought might turn out to be a roast-beef sandwich and started people watching. Snyder didn't look up until the waiter, Ken, reappeared to take our orders. Snyder ordered lobster ravioli, with a straight face.

When we were alone, I said, "I want the exchange to take place today: Melanie and little Ben for the film. We meet on neutral ground, somewhere in or near town. Any problem with that?"

He set his cigarette aside and studied me for a few seconds across the top of his Bloody Mary. "I wish it were as simple as that, Mr. Wells," he said. "You see, certain bonds have been established. You can't treat people as if they were livestock."

"Please, Mr. Snyder, you'll spoil my lunch."

"Beg pardon?" He put down the drink and sat back in his chair, tossing a quick glance to the bar.

"Twice you have sent people to shoot me in my sleep. Now you insult my intelligence by pretending to be a humanitarian."

"I gave no such order, Mr. Wells."

"It's irrelevant, Snyder. They came from the organization you represent. Do we make the exchange or not?"

"You speak as if we're holding them prisoner. It's actually quite the contrary. I, for one, would be delighted to see Melanie leave."

"Enlighten me," I said. Ken delivered bread and a salad to Snyder. I accepted his offer of more coffee.

"As I understand it, you represent her father, is that correct?"

"Yes," I said.

"And we both understand that the young lady has the morals of a hyena? Well, of course you do; you've seen the film of the party, haven't you? They tell me she was part of the fun."

"You're not enlightening me, Mr. Snyder," I said.

"She first appeared a couple of months ago, when they began filming the documentary. Her boyfriend, Ramon, was working on the crew in some capacity. She hung around. After a few days, she began trying to ingratiate herself with Bobby. The pattern is very familiar. When she saw that he was fond of children, she began telling him stories about her son. Bobby eventually became intrigued with the boy's antics and invited her to bring him to see the filming. As he tells it, she became tearful and said she hadn't the money to bring him with her to Mexico. She said that if he would lend her the cost of the plane tickets, Ramon would pay Bobby back from his salary. Regrettably, Bobby agreed.

"A few days later, she reappeared with the boy. As luck

would have it," Snyder reported grimly, "they hit it off right away—Bobby and the boy, like brothers, or father and son. Bobby invited the child to go with him and a group of his orphans to a carnival. After that, they were inseparable."

Snyder leaned toward me. "Just two weeks after Bobby lent them the money," he said, "Ramon repaid his kindness by attempting blackmail. Now I want you to understand in the clearest possible way that what the young man caught on film was a once-in-a-lifetime incident, a case of too much tension, temptation, and tequila. Bobby was actually in tears about it the next day. He was sick, really."

I wanted to ask Snyder in what lifetime Bobby had forced himself on Helena, but it would have broken my agreement with Maria and Juanita, so I went with a less inflammatory question. "Is that why he had Ramon killed?"

"He didn't."

"Come on, Snyder."

"It's true. Melanie called Bobby as soon as she discovered the body. She was hysterical, terrified of what might happen to her. He offered to take her in."

"You'll have me believing your boss is the reincarnation of Albert Schweitzer."

"Believe what you like. But let me ask you, have you never done anything under the influence of too much alcohol that you sincerely regretted later on, and never repeated?"

"On the order of criminal child abuse? No."

"My 'boss,' as you call him, is a mortal man, with strengths and weaknesses, good points and bad. He is also a public figure—the idol, the entertainer, the philanthropist. You seem to be a reasonable man; surely you can see that this film you have would not only destroy Bobby Barron personally, it would also destroy the faith of millions of people around the world. It would shatter a dream. . . ." Ken arrived with our lunches and Snyder cut short his spiel.

When the waiter was out of earshot, I said, "I don't want to show the film, Snyder; I want to turn it over to you."

He finished chewing one of the plump blobs of pasta from his plate and said, "Melanie was desperately worried about her son's future. She knew she couldn't raise him properly. She saw him with Bobby—happier than he'd ever been, and she thought about all the advantages a man in Bobby's position could give him. She said the idea to have Bobby adopt Ben came to her like the word of God. . . ." I stopped clearing the mound of alfalfa sprouts from my sandwich. Snyder had finished off my appetite.

"Barron has adopted the boy?" I said.

Snyder smiled down a sip of Bloody Mary. "With the help of some excellent legal people and the Mexican government, yes. It's quite official. Mr. Wells, you're asking the man to give up his own son."

"I had some inkling of this, Snyder, but I must tell you, as reality, it's infinitely more vile."

He shrugged. "As I mentioned, the girl is free to go anytime, but she wants very much to stay on. In fact, she's asked us to find a job for her so she can become a permanent member of the family. I think that might become awkward, but Bobby wants to mull it over.

"As you can see, the whole matter is far more complex than you imagined."

"I disagree," I said. "It's really quite simple: You deliver Melanie and her son or every scandal sheet in the country gets its own, exclusive blowup from the film. That's the deal. It's not negotiable."

Snyder started to speak a couple of times, but came up short on words. After a minute, he said, "We have resources, Wells, as you're aware. We are capable of inflicting great harm on our enemies. . . ."

"Please don't threaten me," I said. "It's laughable coming from you, anyway. And tonight, when you say your prayers, thank God those two guys you sent to kill us were unsuccessful. If they'd performed as directed, you'd be watching Mr. B's poolside peccadillo on the news tonight.

"You should know," I went on, "there are twelve feet of film altogether. I have one of them. The rest of it has been hidden by a guy who is himself in hiding. You may hear from him later on; he'll want money. All I want is the two Maitlands. In the meantime, if anything happens to me, he goes directly to the press; Mr. Enchantment isn't even invited to submit a bid."

"You miserable bastard. . . ."

"The party's over, Jim," I said. "I hope you have an IRA."

"That little whore accepted a substantial gift," he said. "The adoption is perfectly legal, dammit. That kid is damn well off!"

"With the Chairman of the Boardwalk teaching him the fine points of anal sex? I don't think so."

The impact of Snyder's fist barely shook his water glass as he pounded discreetly on the table. "Can you give me one good reason," he demanded, "why we should negotiate for this film one piece at a time?"

"Yes," I said, "you don't have any choice." I stood up. "Tonight. The parking lot in front of the Aspen Highlands Ski Area. Seven o'clock. And remember what I said about the rest of the film. Oh, and thank Bobby for the lunch, will you?" On the way out, I got hard eyes from Snyder's backup, a young guy at a table by himself near the bar.

While they cooked a hamburger for me at the Red Onion, I reported the results of the meeting with Snyder to Ben and Doe, leaving out the part about the adoption. The prospect of a reunion with his grandson at seven that evening so excited old Ben that he ordered us a pitcher of margaritas to celebrate. Doe was less jubilant.

"I don't trust them," she said. "It sounds like he gave in too easily."

"He bought time," I said, "and it won't cost the organization a nickel. Barron will be upset, if you can believe anything Snyder said, but they can hold out the prospect of getting Melanie and little Ben back. . . ."

"What are you saying?" Ben asked.

"I guess I'm just agreeing with Doe. I don't trust them either. They'll come through tonight; I'm not worried about that, but later on, if they think they have all the film and a fix on each of the people who used it against them, they'll want to tidy up."

"Kill us?" Doe asked.

"Over some damn fag incident?" Ben said. He sat back as the waitress arrived with our pitcher and three salted glasses. "No way. They'll forget about us once they have the film."

Doe looked at me apologetically. We'd both said too much. "What do we do about it?" she asked me.

"We do a marketing plan with our friend, Chaco," I said, pouring, "one that makes him rich and has trash collectors running extra trucks to handle the stacks of Bobby Barron records people have put out. We give them a mess so big they can't tidy up without nuclear weapons."

Ben shook his head as I handed him his drink. "You're overreacting," he said. "Do the deal and be done with it. Cheers!"

It took both Ben and the alarm to wake Doe and me from a nap at six. But once roused, we hustled our buns quickly into some clothes and out the door. I wanted to arrive at Aspen Highlands well before seven. We did. The chalet-style ski shop and, above it, the lift building overlook a rectangular parking area of about an acre. In a corner of the lot were parked a half-dozen whimsically decorated shuttle buses. We made a couple of very slow passes around the lot and a smaller one for the Highlands

Inn next door. The place was deserted. We parked in the Highlands Inn lot, from which we could observe the area where the meeting was to take place as well as the sparse traffic on Maroon Creek Road, which is the only way into or out of the valley where the ski area is located.

At six forty-five, I sent Doe, who was suitably dressed for outdoor duty in jeans and a red plaid wool jacket, up the hill to find a concealed vantage point for herself near the lift building. Ben joined me in the front seat. His nervousness had given way to anxiety. He was wearing a sort of safari jacket and periodically felt it under his left arm to reassure himself that his pistol hadn't vaporized since he'd last checked. I didn't like the idea of his coming to the party armed, but there had been no good chance to talk him out of it. I made small talk while we waited.

By seven, it was no longer possible to distinguish the colors on the shuttle buses. Everything had gone gray. The place where Doe was hiding, from which she'd waved when she first stationed herself, was now in deep shadow; we could only assume she was still there.

At seven minutes after seven, a Grand Wagoneer rolled into the parking lot below us, circled clockwise, and parked centrally, facing the road. They kept their lights on and their motor running. We watched it for a couple of minutes, long minutes for Ben. No one got out. It was impossible to see inside. As far as I could tell, there was still no one else in the immediate area. I started the Aries.

"Ben," I said, "I'm going to park parallel to them, about thirty feet away. Get in the driver's seat when I get out and stay there until I signal you. Do not leave the car unless I signal and be ready to head for the exits if it goes sour. Okay?"

"Sure," he said, "let's go." I threw it into gear and flipped on the highbeams. At Maroon Creek Road, I made a wide, slow turn, looking for anything above or below us that might be trouble. It looked clear. I swung into the big lot according to plan and stopped. The Glock was under my seat. Before I got out, I retrieved the pistol, cocked it, and stuck it under my belt above my right hip pocket. Though it was short on me, the blue wool jacket I had borrowed was long enough to cover the gun.

I walked slowly toward their car. The cool evening air was scented with woodsmoke. When I was midway between the two vehicles, the front, right door of the Wagoneer opened and Jim Snyder, in a green stadium coat, started to get out. The car's courtesy lighting was bright enough for me to see that the guy I'd spotted in the restaurant, still wearing the black sweater, was driving. Behind him was another soldier, less urbane: could have been old Festus, the gatekeeper. Beside Festus, staring straight ahead without expression was Melanie Maitland, and next to her, with his turned-up nose pressed against the window, looking at me, was little Ben. I felt an urge to run over and yank him out of there.

As Snyder stepped away from the car, he slammed his door and the lights inside went out, leaving only a dime-sized white spot in a window as evidence that there were people inside. "Okay, Wells," Snyder said in a voice with none of the convivial lilt, "let's get this over with. Give me the film."

I shook my head. He came closer. "Not until Ben and Melanie are out of the car and at least as far away from it as you and I. Have one of your boys escort them, if you like." He tilted his head at a funny angle as if I'd said something that made him suspicious. "Prove you have it," he said. I unbuttoned my shirt pocket and took out the film. He held a penlight behind a section of it, grimaced, then turned and walked back to the car.

After speaking briefly with the driver, he opened the right rear door to release the two Maitlands. Little Ben popped out as if he'd been sitting on springs. Snyder was barely able to grab the shoulder of the boy's jacket and reel him in. It was a different story with Melanie. Only after some animated dialogue with Snyder and a shove from Festus did her dainties descend to the asphalt.

"You see how desperate Melanie is for her freedom," Snyder said to me as they approached. The sullen shuffle and downturned stare in combination with tight, pastel jeans and a Talking Heads sweatshirt gave the boy's mother the look of a pouty fifteen-year-old who'd just been grounded for a year. Her son, by contrast, was fully tuned in and eagerly searching the darkness for his grandfather. Behind them, Festus was unloading bags from the Wagoneer.

"Hey, Ben," called the senior Maitland from behind me, "you ready to go home with your old granddaddy?"

"Hi, Granddaddy!" As little Ben yelled, he jumped excitedly and nearly broke free of Snyder's grip. "We got to ride on Bobby's very own plane, and I drove it!"

"Hey, that's great!" There wasn't much enthusiasm in Ben's response, but the kid seemed to buy it. I couldn't blame Snyder for snickering.

Snyder brought his troops to a halt three feet from me. Melanie was trying to sniff away tears. She didn't look up. She didn't act as if she knew her son was drawing breath beside her.

"Wells," Snyder said, "we know who you are, where you live, what you do. The same is true of your friend, Maitland, over there, and his ex-wife. In a few weeks, we'll have the names and addresses of everyone any of you gives a damn about. If you're into kinky sex, or dealing drugs, or even padding the expense account, we'll know that, too. We'll surround you. We have a terribly important investment to protect. Any threat to it is intolerable. If there is so much as a whisper in the press about this film, you will pay a terrible price. I hope you understand. I hope you realize that I'm deadly serious."

"I understand your desire to intimidate me," I said. "But everything you've just said about me, I could say about you. Do you have a family, a dog, a lover? Would you like to try running Bobby's business from a wheelchair? Here's the film. Take it, and get out.'' He checked a few frames with his flashlight.

"We will pay five hundred thousand for the rest,'' he said. "That's more than the photographer would have earned in several lifetimes. I'd like to do the transaction within a week.''

"You're talking to the wrong person.''

"You talk to the right one. Tell him that after a week, the price goes down a hundred thousand every day, until . . .''

"We're finished here, Snyder,'' I said. I took little Ben's hand and Melanie's arm and started walking them back to our car.

"You're a damn fool, Wells,'' Snyder called after me. I ignored him. Melanie tried to pull away from me. I squeezed her arm hard enough to make her stop.

Little Ben and his grandfather were chatting happily, as we covered the last few feet to the car. Ben looked at me expectantly. I turned and saw that Snyder was climbing into the Wagoneer. We stopped walking as they drove out of the lot, leaving behind a small pile of bags. When I nodded at Ben, he swung the car door wide open. Little Ben ran to him as soon as I let go and the two of them hugged. A moment later, as Ben emerged from the car to approach his daughter, a pickup appeared on the road, heading south. I held on to Melanie and started to reach for my pistol; but the truck passed the lot without slowing.

I saw tears in Ben's eyes as he drew close to his daughter. I released her. She went rigid at first, then drew away from him. "I love you, Melanie,'' he said, opening his arms. "I know I've screwed up, but I want to try to fix it. I'll do everything in my power, I swear.'' When he touched her, she spat in his face.

Ben stepped back, stunned—looking momentarily like an actor who'd memorized the wrong play. When he rehearsed this moment in his mind, I'm sure it had ended very differently. Little Ben shrank into the space behind the open car door. Ben wiped Melanie's saliva from his face with a Kleenex. "I hate you," she said to him, "and all your words and all your money can't change it. You can hit me. I don't care. I don't give a shit what you do to me. You've wrecked the only chance I ever had." He looked at me. Tears streamed down Melanie's face. I couldn't think of anything worth the breath to say it. "I had a chance for the real life with those people!" she shrieked. "A REAL LIFE! They cared about me. . . ."

"I care about you. . . ."

"The fuck you do!"

"Why do you think I'm here if I don't care about you?"

"For him! For little junior over there."

"And you."

"Bullshit."

"It's true, goddamn it, Melanie."

"Go to hell. You found out he likes kids and you freaked. Admit it!" The look of confusion on his face seemed to make her more angry. "You saw the film! You saw him with his thing in that Mexican boy! What are you playing dumb for?" He turned on her in a rage.

"Jesus Christ, Melanie," he yelled. "What are you saying?"

She smiled and folded her arms across her chest. "Bobby never touched him," she said, savoring her father's distress. "I made sure of that. They were like a kid and his dad. Nothing else. Bobby doesn't hurt anybody. He's just made different, that's all. He can't help himself. He's a wonderful person." Ben looked sadly at me. I think he was embarrassed. I couldn't tell whether Melanie meant what she said about Barron and little Ben, or if it was a lie. Ben slumped against the Aries. He covered his face with his hands. Melanie muttered something I couldn't make out. As I was trying to decide whether to say something to Ben or leave him alone, I saw a figure approaching us across the parking lot. My hand was on the Glock before I realized it was Doe.

Little Ben sat on his grandfather's lap as we drove back to the house. Doe was up front next to me, and Melanie was scrunched in the corner of the back seat behind me, as far away from her father, and everyone else, as she could get.

Ben broke the silence while we waited for the light to change at Main and Mill. "You could have told me, Wells," he said in a dead voice. I swung left past the Jerome and started the climb up Red Mountain.

"I thought it would make the waiting harder," I said. "You would have tortured yourself. As it turns out, for no reason."

"You don't believe her, do you? What do you expect her to say under the circumstances? She's protecting him."

Melanie laughed and started rummaging through her purse. "You can believe whatever you want about Bobby," she told her father. "I could care less. Even if he did it to babies, he'd still be a better man than you." I heard the spark wheel of her lighter and a moment later smelled her cigarette. "Anybody mind if I smoke?" she chuckled. "I hope so."

Doe put her hand, palm up, on the seat next to me. I took it in mine and gave a little squeeze. We were facing what looked like a long evening.

· · Chapter Fifteen · ·

On the way to Aspen Highlands, Doe and Ben and I had talked about throwing a welcoming party for Melanie and little Ben when we got back to the house—pizza, ice cream, champagne, and a good time was had by all. As it turned out, the four adults watched grimly as little Ben nibbled at a peanut butter sandwich and drank half a glass of milk. All of us then participated in putting him to bed.

I admired the senior Maitland for keeping his cool as Melanie needled him throughout the rites of bedtime. He had told me earlier that he was determined not to allow pride or anger to louse things up and, despite extreme pressure from his daughter, he pulled it off. When he blew his grandson a kiss as we left the room, I couldn't resist giving the old bastard a pat on the back just for trying so hard.

Melanie headed straight for her room as the door to little Ben's closed behind us. Ben flashed me a look that said he knew what he was about to do might seem foolish, and then called after her, "Hey, Mel, how about letting me buy you a beer?"

She turned at her door and said, "I'm going to bed."

"Please, I'd like a few minutes of your time. One beer?" She frowned at him and put her hand on the knob. Doe and I stayed back near our door as he moved on her like a trainer approaching a skittish animal. "I know you don't owe me anything," he said, "but there are some things I'd really like to say to you. Give me a chance to apologize, please. Let me try to explain myself." She shifted her stance impatiently as he reduced the distance between them to a safe four feet. I was beginning to have the same uncomfortable feeling I get when couples I know fight in front of me; yet I sensed that Ben wanted me on the sidelines for moral support.

"I don't think so," she said. "There's no point. It won't change anything."

"Maybe not, but look at it this way, it's certainly not going to hurt anything, either." He laughed. Her expression softened a little bit, but she cracked open the door to her room. "Look," he said pulling a wad of money out of his pocket, "I'll pay you a hundred dollars for ten minutes of your time. At the end of it, if you want to stay and talk some more, fine. If not, you're free to go to bed. No hassle. How about it?" She smirked and looked at the money. I could have argued with Ben as to whether his ploy demonstrated particularly good taste, or showed much respect for his daughter, but there was no debating its effectiveness. She pulled her door to, plucked the hundred from his hand, and led the way downstairs.

I woke at seven-twenty and felt the sweet press of Doe's arm and hip against my side. Without disturbing her, I slipped out of bed and pulled on my robe. Ben was in the kitchen, fiddling with the big Krups coffee maker. He was wearing badly wrinkled pale-green pajamas and dark-brown corduroy slippers, no robe. "Long night?" I asked. He looked it.

"You could say that," he said, stifling a yawn. "Want some?"

"As long as the number of the poison control center is handy." I got out a couple of mugs and handed them to him. As he started to pour, I noticed that his hands were shaking.

"I suppose you already know that deviate is the one who adopted my grandson." I picked up one of the mugs and went to a sunny place at one end of a big bay windowseat that flanked the kitchen table.

"I've been told that," I said. "Under the circumstances, Barron's not about to make an issue of it."

"She kept reminding me about, you know, how he is, and then she'd claim the bastard never touched him." He was pacing between the sink and a big, built in Sub-Zero refrigerator. "I don't know what to think. She wants to hurt me. She's done that. I told her so. Hell, she can't know for sure that Barron never touched the boy. . . ."

"He's safe now, Ben, and whether Barron abused him sexually or not, you need to get him to someone who works with kids. . . ."

"Melanie agreed to let him go back to his grandmother."

"That's good. You must have pushed some of the right buttons."

"I don't know. . . . I'm going to call Jack Millstein in a little while. That degenerate son of a bitch is going to find out he's not dealing with some two-bit store clerk. . . ."

"Ben, the film is going to do more harm to Barron in a day than your lawyer could if he spent the rest of his career on it." Ben put his mug down and came over to the table where I was sitting. He leaned toward me, pressing the heels of his hands on the table for support. He looked worse, more haggard, in the bright light. His eyes were red-rimmed. The stale smell of a night's boozing hung about him.

"Wells," he said, "she thinks I hate her because of

some damn incident that happened when she was thirteen.
There was a party in the neighborhood, older kids. The
parents were away. Melanie and a girlfriend wandered
over there. They were in over their heads. Some boy took
Mel into a bedroom. The girlfriend's mother found out.
Sonja got hysterical. . . . Now, seven years later, I find
out Melanie's convinced I hate her because of what happened. It was like a bad dream, listening to her. She
twisted everything around so it was all her fault: the
divorce; Sonja trying to kill herself; even my thing with
Bess. It's so crazy, so unnecessary. . . .'' Ben was losing
it; he turned away from me. I gave him a Kleenex and a
pat on the back.

"Thanks," he said. His eyes were apologetic. As soon
as he could, he went on, "Do you want to hear the kicker,
Wells?" he asked. "The thing I'm supposed to hate her
for, having sex with a boy at the party? I'd completely
forgotten about it. Oh, I'm sure I mouthed off about it at
the time, but until she brought it up last night, I hadn't
given it a thought since it happened. You remember how
things were for me seven years ago, with Bess and the
business. Who was I to play holier-than-thou with Melanie? I figured kids were doing it earlier all the time; it
wasn't such a big deal. How was I supposed to know what
was in her mind? I never meant to hurt her.''

"She invented your reaction to what happened all by
herself. You're guilty of neglect, selfishness, and insensi-
tivity, but you didn't make her crazy. The makings of that
may have been there when she was born. . . .''

"I always thought she knew I loved her, you know, that
it was understood, no matter what else happened. Maybe it
was just a cop-out; I don't know. Last night, I told her I
love her, to her face, over and over. I told her I never,
ever blamed her for what happened with the boy. But
nothing I said to her seemed to get through. Nothing. She
kept saying I thought she was dirty, that I was trying to

use her to get to Ben. Christ, I probably was. I don't know. He loves me." Ben suddenly turned away from me again and rubbed the back of his wrist across his mouth. "I keep seeing him with Barron, and Barron is making him do things. Little Ben is hurt and he's scared. Barron just keeps laughing and kissing him, and feeling him between the legs."

"Don't do this to yourself, Ben," I said. "You've got him back."

He shook his head. "It's not like a broken leg, you know? That can be fixed. You can't fix something like this. Whatever happened between him and Barron, it'll be with him the rest of his life. All the ice cream and ball games and bicycles in the world can't change it. Look at Melanie. She's spent seven years feeling miserable about something she made up." I stood and walked around to the far side of the island counter where I could face him.

"Ben, I'm sorry for your pain, but you're wallowing in it. What use are you to that little boy or Melanie if you can't stop feeling sorry for yourself?"

"Go to hell."

"He loves you. Forgive yourself and put this behind you."

"I'm responsible. I destroyed four lives for the sake of a little pussy. That's a lot of collateral damage, Wells."

"Maybe we should blame your parents for bringing you into the world, or their parents, or the girl in tenth grade who wouldn't let you feel her boobs." He sighed and drank the last of his coffee. I went on, "You have absolutely no evidence that your grandson was abused. If he was, Barron had access to him for what? A little over two weeks. Now it's over. You get him with a good child psychiatrist. You give him a lot of love. And you make damn sure the rest of his childhood bears no resemblance to the first four years. It's simplistic, but what the hell else can you do?"

"I'm going to go upstairs and have a nice, long shower, and then I'm going to take him out for breakfast, just the two of us."

"Make a day of it, if you want to."

"Maybe I'll take him to the hot springs later on, we'll see. Would it be beneath your dignity to get us some plane reservations for tomorrow? Include Doe if you like."

"Thanks. I'll talk to her. What about Melanie?"

"I don't know. I hope last night did her some good, but I doubt that it changed how she feels about me. I'll ask her if she'd like to come."

"You know, Ben, you're not a bad person. Human, maybe; imperfect. But men have cheated on their wives for as long as the institution of marriage has existed. If that doesn't make it right, it sure as hell takes it off the front page. When you joined the fraternity, you couldn't have foreseen the future and now you can't change the past."

I detected the glimmer of a smile on his face as he spoke to me from the doorway. "You know, Wells, the son of a bitch should have one last TV special. At the end of it, he's castrated and hanged. I'd sponsor it out of my own pocket."

"Hit the showers, Maitland," I said. "There's a little kid upstairs who's going to wake up hungry and I don't want him taking a bite out of my leg." He gave me a wave and left the room. By the time I'd poured juice and a fresh cup of coffee, I could hear the sound of water spilling through the waste pipe from his shower.

·· Chapter Sixteen ··

It was another brilliant day, the kind they savor on the East Coast and Coloradans take as their due. According to the thermometer in the kitchen window, the temperature outside had climbed to forty-two, but that was in the shade. The sun was good for another twenty. I strolled into the living room with my mug and picked up a copy of *A Day in the Life of America* from the coffee table. With the book under my arm, I went out on the front deck where I pulled a comfortable-looking chair around to the east side of the house.

I'd barely warmed the seat of the chair when I heard the sound. I didn't recognize it at first, but every nerve ending told me something was wrong. Below me and beyond, at the end of the house, the garage door was going up. There had been no voices from inside, no commotion, no good-byes. Ben would have checked with me before he left. I headed for the front steps. The Aries shot out of the garage before the door was fully up. Ben was at the wheel.

He was alone. I was off the steps and running toward him as he shifted from reverse to drive at the end of his swing into the turnaround. I don't know whether he saw me or heard me yelling at him, but he ripped out of the drive in a cloud of dust and flying gravel and nearly lost control of the car trying to make the sharp turn onto the road.

I took the front steps two at a time. I met Doe in the doorway. She was in her yellow robe; her eyes were wide with alarm. She said, "He just came into our room and took the keys from your bureau. I was brushing my hair; he never spoke to me."

"Melanie and little Ben?"

"I haven't seen them."

I gave her hands a quick squeeze and said, "Let's go."

I went up first. The door to Melanie's bedroom was wide open. The space looked as it had before she arrived. I noticed a crumpled up piece of paper near the foot of the bed. Doe watched anxiously as I unfolded it:

Dear Daddy,
        I *LIED!*
                Screw you,
                     Melanie

"About what?" Doe asked. "Barron and little Ben?"

"She told Ben last night that she was going to let the boy go back to his grandmother. Maybe she meant that." We went down the hall quickly to the next bedroom. Little Ben's bed was unmade; his things were gone. A cold, black feeling spread through my gut. I crossed the hall into our bedroom and started pulling on the Levis and blue shirt I'd worn the day before. "Doe, I can't say for sure that Melanie has gone back to Barron's place, but I'm certain Ben has, and I don't have to check his room to know he's got that forty-five with him. I'm going down the hill. Cutting across the switchbacks, I should be able to make

Main in ten minutes. There's a Jeep rental place there. We passed it yesterday, Charlie's, or Chuck's, maybe. Call them; say it's an emergency. Rent me anything with four-wheel drive and a full gas tank.''

"Is there anything else I can do?"

"You probably ought to get acquainted with the word processor in Freddie's study. I have a feeling your story's about to break.'' I hugged her.

"He'll be okay," she assured me.

I grabbed the Glock and the extra clip from the drawer where I'd stashed them. The gun was uncomfortable against the bare skin under my shirt, but I didn't want to be encumbered by a jacket.

I ran west on the road until I was directly above the Hotel Jerome; then started downhill through thickets, yards, driveways, gardens, and a garage, toward the floor of the valley. Dogs objected, but I managed to escape contact with irate property owners. I was on Main Street in twelve minutes, and at the wheel of a Jeep Wrangler in eighteen. By then, I figured Ben was past the turnoff and burning up the road along Capital Creek.

It was lose-lose for Maitland anyway I looked at it. If I called the cops, they would warn Barron, and Barron would feel he had no choice but to get to Ben first. I could only hope the gods would be merciful and give Ben a flat tire.

The traffic thinned past the Maroon Bells turnoff. I pushed the rented Jeep up to seventy and wondered whether Ben's driving had attracted the interest of the cops. I had to slow down again near the airport. I looked for *The Rising Star,* hoping it wasn't there, but it was, not where I'd spotted it when we arrived. It was in front of the hangar; two men with power nozzles were washing it off.

The engine noise and vibration at eighty miles an hour made it clear enough that I had pushed the little Wrangler to a speed faster than it was meant to be driven, but I had a

sense for the first time that I was gaining on Maitland. I
held the speed for several miles, passing a number of
people who I'm sure had never seen a Jeep moving so fast.
I was just beginning to allow the possibility that I would
arrive in time to do Ben some good when the end of a long
line of cars stopped in the road ahead of me appeared
suddenly in the shadows as I rounded a bend. I had no
room to stop safely behind them. The only uncertainty
involved the number of cars that would be knocked forward by the impact of the Jeep as it, and I, plowed into
them. I swung left and for a long instant I felt the Jeep
wanting to roll, but it settled down and we shot through
the construction zone that on Sunday evening had been
shut down. As I brought it down to sixty, I could begin to
hear the curses of the drivers who were waiting in line. At
fifty, all four tires remained in contact with the rocky
roadbed most of the time. I flipped on the high beams.
People were honking at me. In my rearview mirror, I saw
them engulfed by the great plume of dust that rose behind
me. Ahead, a line of cars coming in the opposite direction
snaked past the first of the stopped cars and headed toward
me. A flagman waved furiously and started to get off the
road. I flashed my lights and honked as I edged within an
arm's length of the stopped cars. The lead cars in the
snake broke ranks to my left. I took the dog leg at forty
and accelerated again as I found a groove up the shoulder
beside the opposing traffic. I knew somebody had radioed
the cops by now, but my turn was just beyond the end of
the construction and I thought I'd be okay if I could make
it. I passed the end of the southbound traffic and had
started to swing onto the roadbed when a great yellow
shape emerged through the dustcloud in front of me. As I
hit my brakes, the back of the Wrangler jumped the tracks
and started to swing out to my right. I tried to steer out of
it, but there was too much loose gravel and rock beneath
the tires. I braced myself through the skid as the Jeep spun

around. Over my shoulder, I looked at the big yellow
thing that had been in front of me. It was a front-end
loader, Godzilla-sized, the type they use to move mountains. I regained control of the Jeep a car length away
from the business end of it. A gaggle of construction
workers were watching it, and me; and I realized that
I had not happened on the great machine in the midst of a
routine turn, but that it was maneuvering to try to stop
me. The big scoop went up. A puff of diesel smoke
cleared the stacks and the loader started toward me. A
dozer was chugging up the road to join the party. I gunned
the Wrangler under the loader's scoop just as the driver
started to swing it down on me. The dozer reacted with a
pivot turn, but he wasn't big enough to block me and I
swerved around him. I was in the clear and flying on an
adrenaline high.

It was a long three quarters of a mile from the construction site to the Snowmass road, but I made it without
seeing cop lights ahead of me or behind. I took the turn at
fifty with minimal loss of traction; then floored the accel-
erator and held it there until I couldn't see the main
highway in my rearview mirror.

I figured the escapade at the construction site had brought
me anywhere from five to twenty-five minutes closer to
catching Maitland, depending on how long it had taken
him to get through. It wasn't enough, but I thought that if I
picked up another five or so in the rough terrain past the
monastery, there was a chance I could get to him before
things went irreversibly sour.

As the road began its ascent, I noticed bare-branched
aspens that had been as bushy and yellow as Big Bird two
days before. To the south, the jagged ridge of mountains
that rims the valley stood stark white and defiant across the
Kodacolor sky. I pressed the Jeep along the deteriorating
road and into the foothills as fast as I could, hoping that

with every switchback I was cutting deeper into Maitland's
lead.

Despite better light and a more able vehicle, the road to
Castillo Colorado seemed steeper, rougher, and much longer
than I remembered. When I got to Barron's grove of No
Trespassing signs, I was suddenly overcome by a strange
feeling. I stopped the Jeep, and looked around me. I saw
nothing unexpected, and heard nothing more than engine
noise and aspen leaves quaking in a breeze. I shook off the
feeling and drove on.

The Cyclone fence and gate gleamed incongruously in
the woods ahead of me. Beyond the barrier structure, the
trees thinned and the road climbed a low red ridge dotted
with sagebrush and disappeared over the top. I stopped
short and started honking. There was no sign of life in the
service building that had produced Festus and his associate
on Sunday night. I pulled the Glock from under my shirt
and put it on the seat beside me. I could see now that the
fence ran about a hundred feet into the woods on both
sides of the gate. There was no sign that anyone had tried
to break through. I tried to imagine Maitland drowning his
sorrow at that very moment in some roadside coffee shop.
But if he had gotten this far and abandoned his rescue
plan, I would have met him leaving the valley on my way
in.

I pulled up to the gate. Rockpiles blocked the swath of
land that had been cleared for the fence. There was no way
Ben could have driven around them. I made a hard U-turn
and started back down the road. At the sign grove, I made
another U-turn and headed down the east fork, which was
nearly obscured by tall grasses. The Wrangler rolled like a
storm-tossed dinghy over rocks and washouts. Half a mile
in, the ruts began to climb and turn west, toward Barron's
ranch. At a dip, where water from a spring had collected
in the right track and partially frozen, the ice crust was

shattered and nearby rocks showed signs of being freshly splashed.

I'd punched my speed up a notch and was plotting ways to handle Ben when I saw his car. It was halfway down a steep slope to my right, pinned at an ugly angle against a lodgepole pine. He'd lost control trying to drive around the stump end of a huge tree someone had felled to block the road. From the scarring on the hillside, it appeared that the Aries had slid the first twenty yards, and had just started to roll over when the lodgepole caught it at the back door. The impact had shattered all the glass in the car; the driver door was wide open, pointing nearly straight up. I could see that no one was inside.

I backed up two hundred feet and sighted a line across the bowl of land that had caught Ben's car. It would be steep going down and steeper going up, but I had no intention of going fast enough to set myself up for anything worse than an easy roll. I cinched up the shoulder belt and eased the Jeep over the lip of the bowl. Almost at once, it started sledding on the bed of dry needles under the wheels. I felt the rear end starting to come around. I had no choice, I accelerated out of the skid and went shooting toward the floor of the bowl, bouncing like a bean in a maraca.

From fifty feet below the far lip, I could see nothing but blue sky and treetops through the windshield. I shifted into low low and kept it perfectly straight. I felt the front wheels meet the lip of grass and exposed rock; I petitioned the responsible department for enough power to make it over. Treetops yielded further to blue sky. The whole weight of my body had shifted from seat to backrest. Suddenly, the Jeep's nose dove. The forest floor reappeared in front of me as the back wheels ripped notches in the lip. I was on level ground again and breathing heavily.

It wasn't far from the bowl to the place where the forest gave way to open land. I drove from the edge of the gaunt landscape to the top of a rise. From my vantage point, perhaps a quarter of a mile northwest and slightly down-hill, was *Castillo Colorado,* a grand Southern plantation house, absurdly out of place in the middle of the vast, rocky wilderness that stretched before me. The great, white-columned structure, surrounded by a manicured lawn, sat at the edge of a deep gorge that, like a gaping wound, divided the arid terrain from north to south. Just north of the house, in an area that had been specially graded to protect it from the prevailing winds, were two small heli-copters, Bell 47's, the kind with a bubble on the front end. The rotor on the one closer to the house was turning. Men running from the house were hurriedly loading both of them with small packages.

I drove off the knolltop, cross-country, toward Barron's mansion. The urgency of the men loading the choppers worried me. When I was within five hundred feet, I shoved the Glock under my belt and left the Jeep in an arroyo, out of sight. As I was climbing out of the arroyo, one of the helicopters rose suddenly above the mansion's roofline, then flew almost directly over my head, raising a swirl of dust around me. Using a stable and other clustered out-buildings for cover, I worked my way, running, to an ornate gazebo at the edge of the sweeping lawn. From there, it was a hundred-foot straight shot to the front door. It took me a few seconds to catch my breath. I had seen no one since I lost sight of the loading operation when I left the knoll. In a crouch, I worked my way as far around the base of the gazebo as I could without being seen. It was time to make contact. I gulped the thin mountain air and sprinted across the lawn to the house.

With my back pressed to the wall beside the eight-foot, carved double doors, I gave a knock with the barrel of my pistol. A brisk wind swirled under the portico. I wondered if Barron had a chorus of blacks sing to him from the stable on summer evenings. No one answered the door. I walked along the porch and peered, cautiously at first, into one of the tall, shutter-trimmed windows. I saw a formal fireplace, portraits, and several overstuffed chairs. Everything was in readiness for Rhett and Scarlett, but they weren't there and neither was anyone else. I decided to let myself in. As my hand touched the doorknob, I thought I heard the other helicopter fire up. I wasn't sure. The wind had started whistling through the balusters below the porch railing. I played it by the book going in: arms extended, both hands on the weapon, sweep the area repeatedly, back and front, but the entry hall was as empty as it was pretentious. A grand, curving staircase swept into the chamber and fanned out onto a blue-white marble floor. An ornate grandfather clock ticked solemnly near an eight-foot portrait that looked like the work of John Singer Sargent. The painting reminded me of the Mission Club where the Maitland adventure had started. Suddenly, I felt the air pressure change and heard someone in the back of the house. I ducked into the sitting room I'd seen from the porch and nearly tripped over the corpse of Bobby Barron. I gasped reflexively as I stepped away from his body. My eyes swept the room as I closed the tall, paneled door gently behind me.

Barron was sprawled on the floor, arms thrust into the space beyond his head, knees flexed as if he'd been running. The white leather of his fanciful cowboy costume was drenched with blood from three gaping entry wounds at midchest. The face known to millions of people was frozen, gape-jawed, in a twisted expression of horror and disbelief. One dead eye stared, unseeing, into space. A wreath of dusty footprints, some bearing blood, encircled him on the polished oak floor. Mr. Enchantment's entourage had taken a last look at the mass of useless flesh that had been their meal ticket, and abandoned him.

I took the Glock off safety and listened hard at the door for the sound of approaching footsteps. A cat mewed behind me. I swung toward the sound with my pistol. A small, black and white feline strolled into a sunny spot in the middle of the room and paused to lick the blood from its mouth. On the floor beyond it, in the shadows behind a pair of Louis XV chairs, I saw a forearm and an upturned hand. It was all I could see from where I stood, but it was enough. I recognized the tan safari jacket.

As I stepped closer, a hot, dry thing the size of a fist swelled in my throat. I closed my eyes for a second; then looked into the space behind the chairs. Ben Maitland lay in a dead heap at my feet. There was a four-inch hole in his upturned face where the left side of his forehead had been. He'd collapsed like a marionette without strings. His extended arms formed a gesture of supplication. His legs were tangled oddly beneath his body. The weight of it brought me to my knees. I felt my face flush. There was a single-entry wound in the mastoid region behind the right ear. The forty-five was on the floor nearby. I cursed and turned away from him. It was an unthinkable waste.

I willed myself under control and crossed the empty hall into an extravagant living room with a grand piano and a dance floor at one end. There would be no parties at *Castillo Colorado* for a while. The room was empty. I decided to go upstairs. I wanted to get a look at the remaining chopper and check the bedrooms for Melanie and little Ben. Barron's people wouldn't waste precious passenger space on the surviving Maitlands. They'd kill them or leave them behind. I wondered if they were dead already, or halfway to Utah on a bus.

A fifteen-foot, arch-topped window in the stairwell framed a view of the vast, craggy wilderness to the west. I could see white water rapids in the bottom of the gorge, a nine-hundred-foot drop from the putting green behind Barron's house. A long hallway bisected the second floor. I took the north wing. Two bedrooms, west and east, both empty . . . A john, empty . . . Some decorator had made his life's fortune on this job. I stood in the doorway of a small office and listened. Once again, there was activity on the floor below. I could hear the helicopter. Last bedroom, east side, empty. I went in. From the window, I could see the copter. The rotor was spinning at idle speed. Everything but the pilot's seat was jammed with packages. There were two men near it having an argument. One of them was the guy who'd backed Snyder in the restaurant. Three other men were taking it in. One of them was the gatekeeper. As I turned away from the window, an image of Maitland with his head blown apart flashed into my mind; then one of Barron. I thought of Doe. Her story was still unfolding. The door across the hall was closed. I knocked and stepped away from it.

"It hasn't been five minutes yet," the voice snapped, middle-aged male, Hispanic. "Don't be so goddamned impatient." I wasn't sure how I wanted to play it. He made up my mind. "Come in here, will you? You can help with these bags." I put the gun behind me and pulled my face into a grin as I turned the knob and let the door swing open. It was Montoya, the guy with the flamenco dancer's body, Barron's co-star in the film. He was standing on the far side of an old canopy bed; a canvas suitcase lay open in front of him. There were two others that matched it on the floor near a highboy dresser. I could see that Barron's friend had been grieving. His mascara had run.

"I'm looking for Melanie Maitland and her son," I said. A look of panic spread across Montoya's face. I took short steps toward him, keeping the pistol out of view and the smile glowing. He swallowed hard. "Tell me where they are, Montoya." I stopped moving when we were six feet apart. I was losing him. He glanced repeatedly into the suitcase. I could only assume he had a gun in there. I said, "Honk if you love Jesus, Montoya." His face went wild; he screamed at me. . . .

"BASSSTAAARRD . . ." As he lunged for the suit-case, I dropped to my right knee and fired three rounds into his midsection. The impact of the hollow point bullets knocked him into the west wall of the room. He slumped to the floor. I'm not sure he ever saw my gun. His was still in his suitcase when he died.

I ran from Montoya's room to the south wing, where I rapidly flung open a succession of doors and yelled little Ben's name into empty rooms. One of the doors opened onto a narrow servants' staircase that, I assumed, led to the kitchen. It was clear as far as the first landing. I started down. Halfway to the landing, I heard footsteps coming up from below. There were at least two of them, coming to investigate the shots. I took the stairs backward, ready to fire if there was contact. My right foot was on the carpet of the second-floor hallway when I saw the barrel of a shotgun poke into the airspace above the landing. It grew hands and arms; I fired. There was a howl of pain as I ducked out of the way, slamming the hall door behind me. A second later, the shotgun answered with a blast that blew a hole the size of a dinner plate in the door. The front stairs were not an option. I ran into one of the east bedrooms that had access to the second-story porch that ran the length of the house under the portico. There were French doors, locked. I kicked them open, shoved the Glock under my belt, and crossed the porch diagonally to the fluted column at the southeast corner of the portico. Once over the railing, it was easy enough to straddle the column and slide down. I took it in three-foot drops, using my knees for brakes. I was eight feet from the ground when the front door of the house opened. I recognized the brown leather jacket of Snyder's backup guy. He was carrying a snub-nose big enough to be a thirty-eight. We saw each other in the same instant. As he turned to fire at me, I changed handholds and shoved off with my feet in a rappeling motion. He got off a shot as I dropped to the ground. The bullet ripped through a rib of the column where my hand had been a half second earlier, and showered me with splinters. I rolled toward the steps. The raised construction of the porch shielded me from his view. He fired two more shots for suppression. I heard him moving on the boards above me. I rose behind the column nearest the steps and was about to fire at him when I caught sight of movement overhead. There were men on the porch above me, probably the ones I'd fired on in the stairwell. One of them spotted me and started yelling as he ducked out of sight. I had no good options. I charged up the steps, tenderizing the way in front of me with the Glock. The man in the brown jacket dove into the house before I could get off a straight shot at him. I ran along the porch past the room where Maitland and Barron lay dead, and vaulted the railing. The place where the porch joined the primary structure was a blind spot from inside the house. I stayed there to decide my next move. A hundred yards due north was the protective bowl of land they'd excavated to shield their helicopters from the wind. From four feet in the southeast, the berm rose north and west to an elevation higher than the spinning rotor blades of the remaining chopper. The berm obscured most of the flying machine, but I could see the pilot's head inside the bubble. He had the machine revving hard, within an r.p.m. or two of leaving the ground.

A sudden gust brought the sound of agitated voices from beyond the west side of the house. I'd have to give up the search temporarily, but I could still make life difficult for them. I decided to take a chance that they wouldn't fire on me if there was a chance of hitting the helicopter or its pilot. My insurance company would have disapproved, but I was hurting, and angry. I moved away from the house far enough to see that no one was watching for me from any of the north side windows. As the voices drew closer, I could make out words. Looking every second or two over my left shoulder, I began to run toward the copter. The pilot stared dumbly at me. As soon as I spotted the first of them coming around the corner of the big house, I spun and popped him, a shoulder hit judging by the way he went down. I took off again at a good kick, but I'd seen four others, including Festus with a shotgun and the guy in the brown jacket. A short man with white hair acted in charge. They spread out, running. I was less than a hundred feet from the berm. I sprinted for it. The voices behind me screamed at the pilot to take off. He fumbled frantically with the controls. Bullets kissed the ground around me. The bastards were firing at my legs. The chopper rocked uncertainly as the pilot gave it more fuel. A wind surge whipped across my path and carried off the dust cloud that had billowed below the swirling rotor. As I dove headfirst over the protective berm, the rough ground tore into my hands and forearms like a rasp. I rolled and prepared to fire on them as they appeared. Through swirling sand, I watched the copter rise thunderously above the berm, only to be jarred from its intended vector by the wind. It rocked backward as if reeling from a punch, then rolled hard to its left. The spinning blades of the main rotor caught Festus at the neck as he charged up the berm. Like something from a nightmare, his headless body stood poised to fire the shotgun; then collapsed. The helicopter, lifted by the gusting wind and its own power, shot upward; then, with a strange, sputtering roar, flipped end to end and crashed a hundred feet from where it had taken off.

Anguished cries and curses rose with smoke and flames above the helipad. Neither the remaining three men nor the burning wreckage was visible from where I lay. The crash diverted them, but they'd be coming for me. My death would be a way of showing they could do something right. I got about halfway up; then took off at a stooped run across the floor of the helipad toward the north end. It's hard to run like that and keep an eye on things at the same time, but I got pretty good at it in Vietnam. Scrambling up the rocky side of the embankment, I paused briefly and got my first look at the black and twisted remains of the burning chopper that lay upside down on Bobby's lawn, its rotor blades bent and broken like the ribs of a slapstick umbrella. The guy with the white hair was pacing nearby, hands pressed in desperation against the side of his head. The one in the brown jacket was picking up Festus's shotgun and urging the other man to come along. The third man had been wearing a red shirt. I couldn't see him. It was ten steep feet to the top of the bank from where I was. I knew I couldn't make it without their spotting me. But at that range, the brown jacket didn't have a prayer of hitting me from where he was. I found a hard spot in the crumbling granite with my right foot and pushed off. I heard yelling almost at once. I pulled and pushed myself up the unstable slope like an orangutan. If he ran like hell, the brown jacket might get off one good shot at me before I dropped down the far side. I had my left knee on the very top when I looked back and saw him halfway across the helipad, aiming the scattergun. I threw all my weight to the left and pivoted on one knee, rolling over backward. The shot grazed my right forearm above the wrist. The wound picked up gravel as I tumbled down the back of the embankment. My life did not flash before my eyes, but my forearm was sore as a son of a bitch.

I ran south, circling the berm to the west. A thirty-foot strip of rocky ground studded with yucca separated it from the gorge. Soon, I caught sight of the brown jacket behind me, charging at a dead run from the north. Within seconds, he'd be shooting. Ahead of me, the road was closed. A million tons of unstable earth, weighted by melting snow or summer thunderstorms, had simply collapsed, nearly undercutting the berm. I had three choices: make it easy for the brown jacket by trying to scramble up the berm, sprout wings, or climb down to the bottom of the slide and cross over.

I shoved the Glock under my belt and started down the near-vertical mass of jutting rocks and ledges. The wind was no help. Rushing unobstructed for thirty miles or more, it slammed into me and the craggy precipice, screwing up my equilibrium and blowing stinging sand into my face and eyes. When I felt a gust coming on at a tricky spot, I had no choice but to close my eyes and wait it out.

It was at just such a moment that I got shot. I was working my way down a cleft between two boulders, pressing my hands and feet against their opposing surfaces to support my weight. From two feet at the top, the gap widened to a little over four at the bottom. Overall, the drop was about ten feet. After that, it was a six foot free-fall to an ugly-looking rockpile down below. I'd done the first few feet when the wind came up in earnest. The gap concentrated and reflected it. It buffeted me from all sides. Hundreds of feet below, sixty-foot trees swayed like cattails. I was sorry I looked; and doubly sorry when a swirling wisp of sand and dust rose into my face and blinded me. I had no hand available to clear my eyes. I was wedged there, blinking like a fool, when I heard the shotgun. The pellets missed high and to my left. Rock fragments rained down on me. I strained to see through stinging eyes and dropped down a few more feet until the eyes closed up on me. It wasn't enough. I caught the fringe of the next pattern in the side of my neck and left shoulder. My left hand jumped reflexively from the wall. I started to go down. The buckshot burned in my flesh. I made the hand go back. Tears flushed the grit from my eyes. I stopped dropping, and looked up. The guy in the brown jacket was clambering down from the jagged edge of an anvil-shaped formation above me. Blood ran down my left shoulder and forearm. I was two feet from the bottom of the hole, eight from the rockpile. The muscles in my legs and back threatened mutiny. The brown jacket hit the ground and turned toward me. We were, perhaps, fifty feet apart. He could see my predicament; he could see my blood. The wind had cut back to a stiff breeze. He disappeared behind the upper reaches of the boulder to my right. He'd shoot straight down for the kill. I had almost no chance from that angle. I let go. My heels hit the ground first; then my knees. I struggled to my feet. Lurching forward, I stumbled along a ten-inch ledge down the side of the gorge. It was too steep; I'd had to hold myself too long in the cleft. My leg muscles turned suddenly to linguini as gravity propelled me toward a washout in the ledge. I threw my weight to the right, and with both hands, grabbed onto a man-sized rock embedded in the earthen wall beside me. My legs went out from under me and my butt skidded to a stop six feet short of a free fall to the obituary page. I yanked the Glock from my belt and looked behind me. He was on top of the boulder as I'd imagined. The shotgun had just left his hands and was sailing into open air above the trees. No ammo. I fired at him and missed. He got off a shot at me with his thirty-eight as he scrambled from the brow of the rock. We were making noise at each other. I looked over the edge. Below me, a series of stone slabs protruded like narrow shelves from the gorge wall. It looked climbable. Below the slabs, a ledge resembling a goat path ran north a hundred feet or so to a pile of larger rocks that I could use to continue my descent. I tested the muscles in my legs. Under the blood, my shoulder throbbed; it was getting stiff. I looked over the edge again. Beyond the goat path, it was virtually a straight drop to the canyon floor, seven or eight hundred feet. I could only imagine the roar of the creek as it cascaded over boulders between the trees. All I could hear was the wind.

I slid on my butt to the first of the rock slab shelves. The second was just over a leg length below it. The next

was trickier. I would have to lower myself from the edge
of number two; then, with arms fully extended, let go and
drop a couple of feet to number three. There was enough
of it protruding to catch my size thirteens, and that was it.
I brushed the loose earth and gravel from the edge of
number two where I thought I'd want handholds, and
swung my legs over the edge. My adrenaline kicked in. I
looked up; no sign yet of the brown jacket. If he was
coming. My gut told me he was. I tried not to look down,
all the way down. I sucked in some air, planted my hands
at the appropriate locations, and swung down. Below my
dangling feet, a bird burst noisily from the canyon wall. I
held on. It swooped down and away from the precipice. It
disappeared in space, too small for me to see. I made my
spine and legs perfectly straight, flattened myself against
the wall, and let go. The instant my toes made contact
with the ledge, I sprung forward into the shallow cave
where the bird had been. My heart was playing the attack
theme from *Jaws*.

My cliff dwelling was three feet deep, four feet high,
and about twelve long. View, privacy, likely to be drafty
in the winter. I pressed hard against the back wall. My
breathing returned to normal.

The bleeding had stopped for the most part. There were
no fewer than half a dozen pellets under my skin, and a
half dozen other places where it was shredded. I emptied
some gravel from my shoes and retied them. I looked out
into the canyon. The slope of the opposing wall was more
gentle. It was filled with trees. A soaring hawk passed
through the airspace in front of me. The emptiness welled
again in my heart. Ben's body lay within a few hundred
yards, but I was separated from the place where I had
known him by half a continent. I closed my eyes and
thought of him, and Sonja, of Melanie and little Ben. If
there was any sense or purpose in their pain, it was beyond
me. I looked south. Beyond the canyon, wild and open

country spread endlessly under a radiant sky. I wished my friend well, a good journey to whatever's next, and happiness there.

After nearly fifteen minutes, a dozen pea-sized stones fell at once upon the sunny strip of stone beyond my feet. I pressed both hands firmly against the ceiling of my little refuge and waited. As I had done, he dropped to the ledge and dove for the shadows. But I was there. The look of surprise stayed on his face as my right foot caught him in the chest and sent him flying back into the sunshine. He cried out as he fell. For four seconds. The sound stopped abruptly. On foot, the same distance took me an hour.

I was exhausted when I finally reached the bottom. I was also bloody, battered, sore, stiff, and, generally speaking, wiped out. But unlike the guy in the brown jacket, I was alive. I found a pool by the creek and washed the crust of blood and dirt from my shoulder with cold, clear water. I washed my face and my feet, too, and shook the stones from my running shoes and socks. It helped.

I found a footpath that meandered through the pines along the east side of the creek and started walking toward the mouth of the gorge. After half an hour on foot, I could see the roofline of Barron's house high above me. My eyes followed the first part of my route down. Directly below the series of ledges, not a hundred feet from me, was a flat-topped rock shaped like the stern of an old sailing ship. Tiny rills of a dark liquid had traced a cobweb pattern in a two-foot section of the rock's surface below the top. I didn't have to speculate, as would hikers in the future, about the nature of those peculiar stains, nor about what I'd find if I climbed up there to investigate. As I turned to start down the path again, a crow landed on the flat, upper surface of the rock, setting off a great outburst among what sounded like a large group already gathered. A half dozen of them rose into the air, cawing and flapping in protest. Their demonstration was as brief, however, as it was vehement. I guess they realized that nobody would leave the party hungry.

The valley floor widened as it dropped. Golden cottonwoods appeared among the aspen and pine. There were beaver ponds eventually, and willows. I caught whiffs of the rich, peaty smell I associate with hardwood forests in the East. Then, above the rush of wind through the trees and the roar of cascading water, I heard a radio. Soon, I spotted a picnic table. And another one. And an outhouse. I saw a pale green Forest Service pickup as I rounded a bend in the loop road. And three civil servants closing up the campground for winter.

The top man told me his name was Leroy Clemmons. I showed him my license and told him enough of what had happened that he dropped his keys twice trying to get the truck started.

·· Chapter Seventeen ··

The telephone belonged to a red-headed widow who lived alone on a ranch six dirt-road miles from a tiny settlement called Redstone. After we were properly introduced, the widow directed me to a straight-back chair at her kitchen table and brought me a telephone, which she said I could use as soon as I had given her permission to tend my shoulder. While I reported the morning's carnage to an incredulous sheriff's dispatcher, she cut away my shirt and worked me over with peroxide and gauze bandages.

Before I finished my conversation with the Sheriff's Department, a senior deputy and a ranking member of the major crimes team had joined the dispatcher on the line. I said I'd meet them at Barron's place and walk them through my part of what had happened.

When I was ready to go, the widow presented me with a red, hooded sweatshirt she'd mail-ordered for her husband a few weeks before he died. It fit me perfectly. She wouldn't take money for it, but I left some in her bathroom with a note of thanks. If ranching had been good to her, it didn't show.

The gate on the road into *Castillo Colorado* was wide open and swinging free. There was no indication that it had been forced. It seemed like a good bet that the guy with the white hair had taken off as soon as his colleague started down the gorge wall after me.

The sky was gray now; the wind colder. Barron's house looked like the setting for a Hitchcock movie when it came into view as we topped the crest of the first hill beyond the gate. I thought of Maitland and the others, six in all. Two of them, mine. A thin band of golden sunlight gleamed at the horizon. Fat raindrops splattered the windshield of Leroy's truck. There was no sign of the cops. When we got to the house, I told Leroy to put his hands in his pockets and leave them there until he was outside again. I went in first and closed the door to the room that held the bodies of Ben Maitland and Bobby Barron. I told Leroy that room was off limits, but said it was okay for him to look around the rest of the house for a couple of minutes while I called Doe.

She cried when I told her about Ben Maitland, not because of her feelings about him, but because of mine. I tried to comfort her. I told her I felt lousy, but that it would be okay. The shock of his death would pass. The sadness and sense of loss would be harder to shake. I'd been through it before, both parents, a brother, and too many friends in Vietnam. It's not something I want to get good at.

I told Doe it appeared that Ben had murdered Barron in a confrontation and then turned the gun on himself. I told her about the fallen helicopter and its suspect cargo. It was enough to get her started. She could tell the world. I said the cops would probably hang on to me for a couple of hours, and then I'd be coming home, by way of the emergency room.

I found Leroy in the kitchen, trying to open the refrigerator door with his foot. He got red-faced and said he was hungry. I found him a cold Beck's and a package of Swiss cheese. We went outside.

Huge snowflakes mingled with a light rain. I pulled the red hood over my head. Barron's lawn began to turn white as grass blades skewered the big flakes and held them aboveground. Leroy washed down a mouthful of cheese with his beer and said he thought he ought to go rescue the two men on his crew from the rain. We shook hands. I watched him drive off. He was lucky. Death hung over that place as certainly as the damp air. The wind had stopped. The snow fell straight down, heavily enough that I could no longer make out terrain features in the gorge. Barron's house, a dark-windowed hulk, collected its share of the white. I felt cold. The world was dead silent. I wandered into the cluster of outbuildings, and then I heard the little boy cry.

The sound came from a tack room at one end of the stable. It was padlocked. I found a spade in one of the empty stalls and knocked the hasp from the door. Melanie and little Ben were sitting on the dirt floor in opposite corners of the small, dark space. She cringed as I swung the door open, started to say something when she recognized me, then looked away. I walked past a neat row of saddles to the corner where little Ben was. He stared at me with red eyes through a tangle of bridles. The musty air between us smelled of raw earth and old leather. I extended my hand to him. He looked at it and pulled deeper into the shadows.

I said, "Ben, it's going to be okay now. The bad men are all gone. You can come out. It's snowing." I stood and went to the door. I thought he might be willing to leave the corner if I gave him some space. "Are you all right Melanie?" I said. "Are you hurt?" Her jeans and baggy, plum-colored sweater were smudged with dirt from the tack room. She pulled her knees up under her chin and stared at her feet. She shook her head. I wasn't sure how much she knew, although it seemed likely that they'd locked her up following the deaths of Barron and her father. Through the snow, I saw the headlights and flashers of three police cars approaching the house. "The police are here, Melanie. I called them. They'll want to ask you some questions. Is there anything you'd like me to say for you?" She started to sob. Her shoulders shook. She wrapped her arms tightly around her knees and began rocking for comfort. I approached her. When I put my hand on her shoulder, she recoiled so violently that her head slammed against the wall behind her.

"Get AWAY from me!" she screamed. "GET AWAY FROM ME!" I drew back. Her eyes bulged; her body was trembling. Little Ben was still huddled in his corner.

"Let's go into the house," I said. "It's warm and you guys could probably use something to eat." I took a couple of steps back and showed her what I hoped was a persuasive smile.

"Have you got a cigarette?" she said. Her voice was so low I had to ask her to repeat the question. "HAVE YOU GOT A CIGARETTE?" she shouted.

"Sorry. I don't."

"Then get out of here. The kid stays with me. He's my son and don't you ever forget it."

Ben and Melanie needed someone with talent and training that I don't have. The officer in charge of the investigation agreed to send for a psychiatrist and said he would assign someone to stay with the young Maitlands until the doctor arrived.

I reviewed the facts three times with a crusty sheriff's investigator named Engel. I gave him references on the Santa Clara, Palo Alto, and San Francisco police departments. He was appropriately disapproving of my methods and tactics, but underneath the dour facade beat the happy

heart of a career civil servant whose job I was making a lot
easier. His men had no more luck with Melanie and little
Ben than I had. When the sky began to clear a little after
three, they called in a Flight for Life helicopter, which
arrived twenty minutes later bearing a psychiatrist. The
FBI and the DEA showed up at about the same time the
helicopter left with the two Maitlands, whom the shrink
was dispatching to Aspen Valley Hospital for observation.

About the time Engel released me from the fancy living
room where he and his federal colleagues had been questioning me, men from the coroner's office were removing
two heavy body bags from the sitting room across the hall.
I looked away and followed a coffee smell to the kitchen.
Engel had said that as long as I didn't interfere with the
investigation, I was free to wander around until he gave
me the all-clear to leave.

In the kitchen, I stood watch with a DEA guy while a
fifteen-cup Mr. Coffee brewed up a fresh batch, compliments of the late Mr. Enchantment. While the carafe
filled, I learned that what Barron's men had loaded onto
the two choppers had barely dented the horde of drugs at
Castillo Colorado. The feds were elated, not so much by
the sheer size of the discovery as by the extensive records,
including a cabinet full of floppy disks, that had been left
behind. They'd also found a large basement chamber full
of floor-to-ceiling racks jammed with pornographic films
and videocassettes. Adjoining it was a well-equipped ship-
ping room with a heavy inventory of plain, brown wrap-
pers. Upstairs, in what appeared to be Barron's office, was
a large safe, which would be drilled as soon as the safe
guy, who'd just arrived, got upstairs with his equipment.
As we talked, I got the feeling that the assorted cops
combing the place were having as much fun as kids on a
field trip to Santa's workshop.

All we could find for our coffee were black pedestal
mugs monogrammed ''B.B.'' Under the circumstances, I

would have preferred leaky Styrofoam. The DEA's man had no such problem. I sensed that at least one of the mugs would make its way to his house as a souvenir.

I went outside. The air seemed full of life after the cold rain. Mist clouds hung like whipped cream over the gorge. I could see my breath. Without thinking where I was going, I walked across a large flagstone patio and through a rose garden that bordered the putting green. I wondered what would happen to all of it. Was Barron even the legal owner? Or did the place belong to someone's retarded niece in Jersey City, or an anonymous safe deposit box in Luxembourg? Would the state convert *Castillo Colorado* to a retreat for victims of sexual abuse? Would a carload of heartbroken grandmothers burn it down?

As I rounded the end of the house, I confronted the charred skeleton of the fallen chopper. They were taking pictures of it. What remained of the pilot was still inside. An open body bag was waiting on the ground nearby. I got close enough to hear one of the coroner's men say that it looked to him as if the pilot had been shot in the left eye. With a bullet intended for me.

I walked to the front of the house and up the front steps. There were no less than a dozen cars parked on the drive. I could hear another helicopter coming in. My shoulder was starting to ache. I wanted to leave. There was still the drive back to town and a visit to the emergency room.

The front hall was empty. I heard laughter. I followed the sound upstairs to the room that had been Barron's office. There were at least twenty of them gathered around a big screen TV. On the screen, Barron and a little Mexican boy, about eight, were cavorting naked on a canopy bed. It looked like the one upstairs in the room where I'd shot the flamenco dancer. As the cavorting became foreplay, the room fell silent. There were curses of disgust as the little boy set his mouth to Barron's erection. He seemed to know exactly what to do. The camera zoomed in to the boy's lips. Several people left the room. I found Engel and spoke to him. He looked embarrassed.

"It's from the safe," he said as if apologizing. His eyes went back to the screen.

I said, "I want to leave. I need to get the shot dug out of my shoulder. You know where to reach me."

The camera zoomed back as the little boy withdrew his lips from Barron and looked up expectantly for approval. "The damn safe is full of this shit," Engel said. "Every cassette's got a name on it. This one said 'Manuel.' There was a date last July under the name."

"Can I go?" The camera stayed on the boy. I could hear Barron and the flamenco laughing.

"I guess I can't think of a good reason to say no. You don't leave town without my say-so. Got that?"

"Sure."

"We probably ought to give you a damn medal, but don't hold your breath. I'll say one thing, I always hated that bastard's singing."

Outside, long shadows striped the lawn. Though it was chilly, warmth radiated from the ground had melted most of the snow. I headed southwest toward the arroyo where I'd left the Jeep. When I was halfway to the gazebo, the sound of indignant bird squawking made me turn around. A pair of peacocks were caught in a circle of pop-up sprinkler heads that had just come to life in the front lawn. Ahead of me, a tall black woman in a dark-blue designer business suit was steaming my way from the direction of a helicopter that had landed in the prairie grass beyond the stable. When the distance between us was down to about three paces, she extended her hand and spoke.

"Hi, I'm Camilla Monroe from the *National Globe*. Is my photographer here yet?" She shook hands like a longshoreman. "Thanks so much for coming out to meet me."

"Sorry to disappoint you. . . ."

"That's okay, I have a camera in my bag here. I just

want to get a shot of the body before they take it away. Is
it there in the house?'' She was breathless.

''It's gone.''

''Shit. Where'd they take it?''

''The *Enquirer*'s got it.''

''Huh?''

''I understand they're going to do a nude layout in their
next issue.''

She gave me a hard squint and said, ''Go to hell.'' I
didn't blame her.

I drove the Jeep overland to Barron's driveway. Two
sheriff's cars blocked the road inside the gate. Beyond
them, a dozen or more civilian cars and TV news wagons
were waiting to get in. The deputies radioed the house and
got an okay from Engel to let me through. As the junior
deputy on the scene prepared to back one of the patrol cars
out of the way, the reporters and photographers beyond the
gate formed a gauntlet ahead of me. I drove into the glare
of the camera lights without slowing or even looking at the
people behind the barrage of questions. I was a couple of
miles down the road before it even occurred to me that one
of them might have been Doe.

The heater was out in the Jeep. I was cold and yawny
when I pulled into the parking lot of Aspen Valley Hospital. It was nearly dark. The hospital is a contemporary,
one-story brick structure on a rise of land just south of
downtown. I was glad to see that the emergency-room
waiting area was empty. Once the receiving nurse had
satisfied herself that my insurance was paid up and had
warned me that she was obligated to notify the police of all
gunshot wounds, I received excellent and relatively painless attention from a young Korean doctor, assisted by a
pair of nurses. In exchange for a few crumbs about the
day's doings at *Castillo Colorado,* they told me everything
they knew about Melanie and little Ben.

After Melanie attacked a nurse who was trying to draw

some of her blood, Dr. Goldschmidt, the psychiatrist, had put her on a regimen of Thorazine, seventy-five milligrams every six hours. En route to Aspen, they said, she had tried to jump out of the helicopter. The initial bloodwork and examination had not turned up anything wrong with Melanie physically other than symptoms of chronically inadequate hygiene and nutrition.

Like his mother, little Ben was in a private room and was sleeping with the help of a mild sedative. The internist who examined him felt that he was in good shape physically. Dr. Goldschmidt had noted symptoms of depression. Sonja Ridgely was identified as the "responsible party" for both patients.

Hearing Sonja's name stirred rumblings of guilt in me. I hadn't given her a thought, not directly. My mind had been preoccupied with the immediate. I should have been the one to break the news, but it was too late for that and I was in no shape to function as a supportive friend. I needed a half dozen myself.

The doctor retrieved two pellets from my neck and seven more from my shoulder. When he confirmed with X rays that there weren't any more, he put the nine in a specimen jar and gave it to me for a souvenir, along with my walking papers.

Freddie's house was dark. I wasn't surprised, but I allowed myself a moment of disappointment. Doe's note said she'd hired a local photographer, and the two of them were about to leave for Barron's ranch. She'd phoned the story to *Excelsior* using the information I'd given her and the background she already knew. She thanked me for enabling her to break the news and again expressed her sympathy about Maitland.

It was a nice enough note. I'm not sure why it made me feel worse. Probably because it was a note and not her, and because it could be hours before I'd see her. Duty calls. I could have phoned Maggie to commiserate.

I thought about showering, fresh clothes, and going downtown to drink myself senseless with the beautiful people. But no. When I am too long with the beautiful people, I get angry, and I was angry and sad and frustrated enough already.

We hadn't gotten around to stocking Freddie's bar with our personal favorites, so it was well drinks or a trip to the pop shop. That was an easy decision. I floated three ice cubes in Dewar's and fed the CD a copy of *Die Walküre*. I went upstairs. Ben had left the door to his bedroom open. As I closed it, an icicle slid down my throat, melted, and refroze in my stomach. I turned on lights in all the other rooms. Doe would not come home to a darkened house. The tub in our bathroom was big enough for a *ménage à trois*. I started it filling and went down to restart the Wagner at higher volume and top off my drink.

Thanks to a big amp and a pair of immense ADS speakers, I got the whole place shaking. I added a splash to my glass and brought along the bottle in the interest of efficiency. Our first night on the premises, I had noticed a box of Cuban cigars in Freddie's freezer. I thought the matter through during a swallow of Scotch and decided to indulge myself. It's not every day you lose a good friend.

I brought one of the cigars to room temperature in the microwave, cut the tip, and lit up. Whatever physical harm I was doing to myself was well worth it. At the foot of the stairs, the door to Freddie's office caught my eye. Engel had scolded me for carrying a concealed weapon. I assured him that I had made little or no effort to conceal the Glock, except to spare innocent Aspenites unnecessary alarm. As a matter of course, he had taken the gun to hold as evidence. It was standard procedure. If my story held up, the D.A. would return the pistol to Freddie in a month or so. I went into the office and opened the door to the little room where my host kept his arsenal. I didn't think I'd need or want a gun following the collapse of the House of Barron; I'd even told Engel so. Now I wondered. They couldn't put Humpty-Dumpty back together again, but men were dead because of me. A very rich operation lay in ruins. I'd told Doe we wouldn't be targets for revenge. Now I wasn't so sure. There was only one gun with adequate knock-down power for which I could find ammunition: a double-action Smith and Wesson Model Twenty-Five revolver. It looked like a collector's piece, with gold engraving in the shiny-blue gunmetal and a six-and-a-half-inch barrel that made it a bit hefty for law enforcement. Its diet was forty-five caliber long Colt ammunition of which I found a nearly full box. Freddie had even bought it a fancy, studded gunbelt and quick-draw holster, though no Old West gunslinger ever laid his hand on such a gun. I dropped six shells into the cylinder and headed upstairs.

Hot water was lapping at the overflow port in the huge, red tub. I switched on the Jacuzzi, stripped, and settled into the swirling water, cigar and Scotch in hand. The little joy jets worked their magic on my weary flesh. The warm water seemed to draw a pleasant buzz from the Scotch. I'd had much less than it usually takes, but then I hadn't eaten all day. If the place had had room service, I'd have ordered a four-pound lobster. But, alas, there was no room service, nor any companion with whom to celebrate Ben's memory. There was only Wagner, who was also dead. So with another splash for company, I settled back and blew smoke rings into the steam.

·· Chapter Eighteen ··

G—

Sorry I got back so late last night. (Do you remember?) The paper here said I could use their Fax machine to transmit pictures to Excelsior, but by the time we finally got a line open, the machine wouldn't work! Then I waited for an hour while they tried to fix it, but still no luck. I'm off to try again now. (Rented a car yesterday at the airport.)

Bad news: Julio, my boss, wants me back there tomorrow. I told him that one of Barron's victims in Mexico City had committed suicide. (I hope Maria and Juanita will talk now.) Julio wants me to do the story and supervise all the coverage in M.C.

Also, I thought you'd be glad to know that the FBI has picked up your friend Jim Snyder. He must have been on the helicopter you saw leaving the ranch when you first got there. Barron's pilot flew him to Las Vegas on The Rising Star, *and the FBI arrested him a few hours later. After I send the pictures, there are a few things to follow up from yesterday; it shouldn't take long. (I hope.) I'll call you later.*

Kisses,

Doe

P.S. Shall we try the hot tub tonight??

I felt like shit. My sinuses were plugged. A molten spike sizzled in the top of my head. Someone had started a compost heap in my mouth.

I was offended by the busy competence of the note Doe had turned out on Freddie's word processor and left for me on the kitchen counter under a bottle of aspirin. But I used the aspirin, four of them with a quart of orange juice as a chaser. Then I plugged in the coffee maker and watched it do nothing for ten minutes, while the seven dwarfs turned big ones into little ones inside my skull, and while I wondered if it was due to cruelty or bad timing that God had chosen this particular morning to dramatize the evil of drink. It seemed fitting that I ponder the question over a stiff belt at Freddie's bar, and I was actually headed that way when I realized that I had omitted an important ingredient from my coffee recipe: water.

By my third mug, the aspirin had kicked in and things began to improve. I tied my bathrobe and ventured out on the side deck to set up the hot tub. My eyes seemed to shrivel in their sockets from the glare. The tub lid was fiberglass trimmed with redwood, hinged in the middle. I raised one side and took great care to lower it without making a noise. There was a hose nearby. I turned it on, and as the tub began to fill, I set the thermostat on the side of the unit to a hundred and four.

I was plodding upstairs to take a long shower when the telephone rang. I could not decide immediately whether to go down or up to answer it. At the beginning of the third ring, I decided that up was the more constructive choice and made myself press onward at a jog. Almost immediately, however, a bowling ball broke loose inside my forehead and began to carom between opposing sides of my skull. I slowed down. It was either that or suffer additional severe brain damage.

The telephone was on the floor by my side of the bed. I picked up the handset as I sat and carefully rolled to a reclining position as I brought it up to my ear.

"Hello."

"Hello. This is Sonja Ridgely. I'm trying to reach Gardner Wells. Is he there?"

"What's left of him, yes. Hello Sonja, I'm afraid I overtrained last night."

"I'm so glad I found you. . . ."

"I should have called you yesterday, but by the time I got back to civilization, you already knew and I don't think I would have been worth much as moral support. . . ."

"There's no need to explain. I've spoken with the police. You're lucky to be alive. I'm very thankful for that."

"How are you doing?"

"I would never have expected to feel his loss so deeply, after . . . everything. Friends and enemies, we meant a lot to each other. I was a jellyfish last night. Jack was great about it. Dammit, Gardner, Ben and I started down the Yellow Brick Road together. First love, first marriage, Melanie, the business . . . all those years."

"He would never have left you if he'd been in control. In all the years since you and he split up, I don't think there was a time I saw him when the regret wasn't there." I heard her light a cigarette.

"We'll all be so much wiser next time around, won't we? No mistakes."

"Happy endings for everybody."

"I need to ask a favor, Gardner."

"Anything."

"I want you to bring Melanie and Benjamin home. I've spoken to the doctors there. I can't say that the psychiatrist who admitted Melanie was enthusiastic about letting her go, but I'm going to make arrangements so that we can take her directly from the airport to a psychiatric hospital out here. He seems very concerned, but if it's going to be a long course of treatment . . . Dr. Goldschmidt says they'll keep her in the Aspen hospital tonight. With the medication he's given her, he says she'll be docile. . . ." Sonja broke down. I let her cry it out. "Can you help me, Gardner?" she sobbed. "I don't trust myself anymore."

"You're doing fine, Sonja."

"Do you think that deviate touched my grandson?"

"Melanie says not."

"What does that mean coming from her? In some ways, I'd feel better if she said he had. Virtually everything she's said to us for years has been a lie."

"Have the doctors here talked to Ben about it?"

"They say there are no acute symptoms, mental or physical. Apparently he didn't witness any of the violence. I'm thankful for that. Dr. Goldschmidt thinks Ben would benefit from seeing someone for a time, whatever happened.

"It's natural enough that you'd want to know about Barron. Ben did, too, but give it time. I take it the doctor thinks he's okay, at least on the surface."

"That's the impression I got. You know psychiatrists."

"Most of what that kid's got going for him, he owes to you. You might do well to remember that while you're having all these self-doubts. You've been the major source of love, strength, and stability in his short life."

"Thanks."

"Will they release him to me today? I'm sure he's ready to get out of the hospital."

"I think that's an excellent idea. I'm sure I can arrange it."

"You'd like me to bring them home tomorrow?"

"Will that be convenient?"

"Very. Assuming the cops here don't arrest me for anything."

"You don't think they will, do you?"

"Probably not. It's a clean case, my part of it anyway. All the evidence is intact. Not much for the cops to do really except fight over who gets the credit."

"I made plane reservations. Ten-o-five tomorrow morning. United. You change in Denver."

"Thanks."

"Thank you."

"Did you talk to Melanie?"

"I think so. They handed her the phone. She didn't say anything. I told her I love her. It was different with Benjamin."

"I'm sure it was."

"He's a wonderful boy."

"You may have a different opinion when he's seventeen."

"That seems so far away."

"What about Ben? I assume you're not involved in those arrangements."

"I've talked with his lawyer. You know, Ben hated funerals. The body will be cremated there and the ashes flown here for burial. His family will probably have a memorial service. I may call his sister later. I'm not sure."

"Be kind to yourself, lady. You've got a little boy to raise."

"When you get back, I want to have dinner. Just the two of us. There's a little Italian place near Stanford with huge booths and a great wine list. They expect you to spend the evening. We'll have our own private memorial service for Ben. Jack will understand."

"I'll look forward to it."

"Other than the hangover, you're okay?"

"I'm getting there. It's nice to hear a friendly voice."

"Have you talked to Maggie?"

"No."

"Call her, Gardner. I'm sure she has no idea how to reach you. Your name was in the paper. She must be worried."

"Thanks for the suggestion. You can tell the hospital I'll be there in forty minutes."

"Okay, but don't just dismiss what I said about Maggie."

"I'm here with someone else, a Mexican reporter. She's been researching a series on Barron. We started helping each other, and it got personal. At least I think that's what happened. She's going home tomorrow. I'll call Maggie from Half Moon Bay."

"I'll be at the gate when your plane lands. Would you like me to bring her along?"

I wanted to say yes, but it came out, "No."

My stomach rumbled warily as I stepped over the Dewar's bottle into the tub. Despite the hose filling the hot tub down below, the water erupted forcefully from the showerhead and held a steady pressure that seemed more than sufficient to revive my flagging life systems. For fifteen minutes, I turned like a roast under the needle streams of hot water. It seemed to be working; I wouldn't know for sure until I got dressed and started trying to function like a real person. After I shaved and drank a quart of cold tap water, I put on my last clean shirt, a blue-on-white tattersall plaid; a pair of Levis; a navy-blue wool sweater I borrowed from one of Freddie's closets; and my Topsiders, sans socks.

I decided I felt up to making a phone call and dialed the number I had for Chaco Aguirre's priest friend in Mexico City. The connection wasn't great, nor was my Spanish at its sharpest, but I was able to get across the message that I thought it was time for Chaco to come out of hiding and peddle his wares. I left my home number and the office number in L.A. of Missy McLeod, a very successful packager and promoter of deals in the world of show biz. Missy was having an affair with my former business partner when he went to prison. They were a perfect match: ruthless, avaricious, and without scruples to interfere with their deal-making. Nonetheless, I thought that whatever Missy took him for, Chaco would net a hell of a lot more money with her fronting for him than he would on his own or with anyone else I could think of brokering the deal.

It was another pretty day, a bit overcast and chillier than the day before, but nothing for the chamber of commerce to be ashamed of. As I lowered myself into the driver's seat of the Jeep, I realized that I had started looking forward to going home. The clump of aspen at the end of Freddie's drive was nearly bare. Downtown, the air was redolent of charbroiled burgers. I was seized suddenly by a ravenous hunger. A couple of days without food will do that to a person.

Despite the hunger, I decided to wait. If Ben hadn't eaten, we could do it together. The receptionist in the hospital's small lobby gave me room numbers. Melanie and her son were in separate wings. I went to her room first. My knock was unanswered. I pushed the door open and went in. The television was on, a soap opera. The pretty man was threatening to tell everyone how the pretty woman got her big promotion. Melanie, curled up in her bed, paid no attention. Outside her picture window, a dozen chickadees frolicked in an old blue spruce. The unblinking eyes in Melanie's pale face seemed locked on the commode chair beside her. I wasn't sure she knew I'd entered the room. I said hello and went to sit in the high-backed chair between her bed and the window. She lay motionless. I could see a triangle of bare back between the worn edges of her hospital gown.

I said, "I won't pretend to know how much all of this has hurt you, Melanie. I just want to say that your father loved you. He knew he was responsible for a lot of your pain, and I think if things hadn't gotten out of control, if you'd been willing to give him a chance, he could have proved his love to you. He knew he made mistakes in his life, choices that hurt you and your mother in ways he never intended.

"Your mother has asked me to take you and little Ben back to San Francisco tomorrow morning. The doctor says he's doing just fine, so your mom and I think it would be a good idea to get him out of here. He'll spend tonight with me, and the two of us will come for you in the morning. I hope you think that's a good idea." I had no idea whether she understood anything I said. She just lay there. I might have been talking to a doorstop. I rose from the chair and went to stand where she could see me. "Is there anything you'd like to say, Melanie? Any questions? Anything I can do for you? Anything you need?"

There was no response. The young woman curled up fetally on the hospital bed could have been Melanie's ghost. I wondered if it had occurred to her that the life she had made playing the promiscuous delinquent to defy her old man was pointless now. Hating Ben Maitland was no longer a viable career. Maybe she was lucky, although it was hard to look at her and believe that. I said good-bye.

From the number of empty rooms I passed on my way to the pediatric section, it appeared that Pitkin County was suffering from an epidemic of good health. The head nurse in little Ben's area seemed glad to have something to do. She had me sign half a dozen forms as "the representative of the responsible party," then put in a call to Dr. Goldschmidt's pager.

"He wants to talk to you about Benji," she said. "He's

such a cute child. What a shame he had to go through something like this." The name tag on her uniform said "Doris Sanders." She was five-six, about fifty, with graying brown hair pulled into a large bun behind her head. A pair of half–eye glasses hung from her neck on a chain of fake pearls. She double-checked the station's direct-dial number, fed it to the pager, and hung up. I decided I'd poke my head into Ben's room and say hello while we were waiting for Goldschmidt, but Doris called me back. "I'm sorry," she said, mustering the authority of her uniform. "The doctor feels he should speak with you first."

"Before I say hello?" She leaned toward me over the tall counter. The facial expression said she was about to take me into her confidence.

"I think the doctor's concerned that someone might say something to Benji that could upset him, after what he's . . . been through. I'm sure the doctor just wants to warn you, that's all. It's unusual for us to have a psychiatric patient here. Of course, now with the mother, we have two. She's in quite a bad way I understand. . . ." I got the feeling that Doris was aching to shed her professional airs and engage me in a down-and-dirty discussion of the Barron scandal. Fortunately, Goldschmidt was quick to answer his page. After he'd spoken with her briefly, she handed me the phone. It sounded like he was calling from a restaurant. I said hello.

"Don Goldschmidt, Mr. Wells. You'll be taking young Ben with you today?"

"That's the plan. His grandmother and I felt he'd be happier away from the hospital with someone he knows."

"How well do you know the boy, Mr. Wells?"

"Hardly at all, but then, better than anyone else here. His grandfather, Ben Maitland, and I were friends. I'm an investigator. When Melanie took Ben from his grandmother's house, where he'd been living, Ben, Sr., asked me to find both of them. We followed them here from Mexico City.''

''You've lost a friend, then. I'm sorry. It's a terrible business. Of course, my immediate responsibility is to the boy and his mother. I told Mrs. Ridgely, and I feel I should tell you, that it's very hard to know what's going on with Melanie right now. Clearly, she's been devastated. She can't function normally. She won't communicate. You may be aware that she tried to jump out of the helicopter when we brought her in yesterday. Later, she threw a nurse to the floor and tried to strangle her. We've been working with the medication, checking levels, and so on. I think we've found the right dosage, but you can't be sure immediately. Her history of drug abuse makes it trickier. My opinion is that it's a mistake to try to take Melanie to San Francisco tomorrow.''

''How did Sonja respond to that? Mrs. Ridgely.''

''She has great faith in you. She wants to go ahead with it tomorrow. In situations like this, especially when there's been a death, many people feel a great need to do everything they can as quickly as they can. . . .''

''Even when it's ill-advised.''

''Yes.''

''What are the risks to Melanie in my taking her, as opposed to waiting?''

''That's where I lost Mrs. Ridgely. I can't give you a definite answer. 'If we do this, X will happen. If we don't do that, Y will result.' Do you see? The problem is, we have no idea what's going on in Melanie's head. Her mother told me some of the personal history. This was a very complex and troubled young woman before yesterday. Now, who knows what she's thinking? We know she's potentially violent, suicidal. You see, I have no reason to think that the gears aren't turning in there. In fact, there's every reason to think they are. She just doesn't want to let any of us in on what she's thinking. That's where the danger is. We have no idea what she saw at Barron's ranch, or how she interpreted it.''

"I'll have her at the hospital in San Francisco in time for lunch tomorrow. I'll play it completely neutral, no questions, no judgments. Between me and the Thorazine, no sharp edges, I promise.''

"Absolutely no alcohol. She'll have medication before she's discharged. I'll dispense two more doses. That will cover her for twelve hours. Avoid touching her. A lot of what's going on with Melanie is probably sexual. We found evidence of self-mutilation—lacerations of the labia and vagina; some fairly recent; some probably going back several years, where there's mature scar tissue now.''

"How can you be sure it's self-inflicted?''

"We can't be sure. The fact that it appears to be a chronic problem points us that way, also her history: violence; promiscuity; hatred of the father, probably tied in with strong sexual attraction; the parents' divorce, for which she may have felt she was to blame. The composite isn't all that unusual I'm sorry to say. The extreme behavior is. Melanie has no coping ability, no way to process all her feelings in a healthy way. I don't like to see someone as young as she is so thoroughly trashed out. Forgive the language. Most people headed for the place she is at twenty don't get there until much later in life, maybe ten or twenty years later. You can be sure that all the pain she's caused other people is nothing compared with her own suffering.''

"I appreciate the candor. Does she have a chance?''

"I wouldn't write off anyone that young where there's no permanent, physical damage. She may never be what you and I think of as a happy person, but she could develop coping skills where now she has none. If she makes some friends, it could be okay for her, maybe not great, but worth living. I told her mother I'd get her the

names of some good people out there. We can do a lot
with medication. You may see a change fairly quickly, on
the surface at least.''

"What about Ben, any special instructions?''

"Not really. I'm also going to give Mrs. Ridgely the
names of some people who specialize in kids. Of course,
you probably know, he's in much better shape than his
mother. Her rejection of him was probably a good thing,
crazy as that sounds. I seriously doubt that he'd be func-
tioning as successfully if she'd been dragging him through
the mud with her this past year. The three–four year is
very critical, very sensitive.

"As to care, I'd echo what you said about Melanie: No
sharp edges. Keep it light. Don't bring up what has happened; let the therapist do that, but let him talk about it as
much as he needs to. Be supportive. Don't judge him. . . .''
The more he talked, the more I wanted to ask him, but he
had a lunch to get back to and I had a kid waiting for me
in a lonely hospital room.

Ben's room was identical to Melanie's except that the
white walls had been painted with bright-colored birds,
balloons, and a huge rainbow. Ben was staring out the
window, already in his street clothes, a yellow cotton shirt
and blue jeans. His few belongings had been wadded into
a brown plastic trashcan liner, which sat on the foot of the
bed. He did not turn around when we came in.

"Hey, Ben," I said, "ready to bust out of here?'' The
sound of my voice startled him. He turned toward us with
a jerky motion, and spoke.

"There was a man taking my picture through the window. He told me his name is Ben, too. He asked me if I
knew which room my mom is in, but I don't.'' Without a
word, Doris picked up the telephone on Ben's nightstand
and dialed an extension.

"What did he look like, Ben?'' she asked. "That man
shouldn't have been bothering you like that.''

"He wasn't bothering me. I liked him."

"What did he look like?"

Ben glanced out the window and said, "He's fat. See?" Doris told whoever answered the call to hold on. She went to the window. I followed her. By putting our heads close to the glass and looking along the wall of the building, it was possible to make out the starboard side of someone who might have been mistaken for Michelin's tire man. Over fluctuating fat rolls, he wore a too-tight gray sweater that had retreated several inches from his belt line. What appeared to be a camera bag hung from his shoulder. He was waddling away from us in no particular hurry. Doris went back to the telephone and reported him to hospital security. I indicated to her that we'd be leaving. She nodded. I picked up Ben's bag and we started to go. At the door, he pulled on my sleeve. "Hey, I forgot," he said excitedly, "they told me I get to keep my pitcher and stuff. The toothpaste is really gross, but I want the pitcher and that dish. You want my toothpaste?"

"Sure," I said. "Gross toothpaste is my favorite." In addition to the pitcher and crescent washbowl, a miniature box of Kleenex, gross toothpaste, a thermometer cover, a plastic cup, one plastic glove, and a Styrofoam cup got packed into Ben's trashbag suitcase.

On our way to the lobby, I wondered what, if anything, to say to Ben about his mother. Most kids, under the circumstances, would welcome assurance that mom was okay and that the two of them would soon be together. But this was not a mom in the June Cleaver tradition. It seemed like a good bet that Ben would feel more threatened by the prospect of seeing Melanie than not seeing her. I kept my mouth shut.

As we stepped from the curb into the parking lot, I reached down and took Ben's hand. The sight of it did not prepare me for how tiny it felt in mine, and how vulnerable. Suddenly, the responsibility of caring for him seemed quite large and growing larger with each step we took away from the hospital. He lit up like Christmas morning when he saw the Jeep.

I helped him with his seatbelt and asked him what he'd like for lunch. He said, "Not ice cream. They kept bringing it to me in the hospital. I told them that's not good for you." We decided on pizza.

A pair of giggly secretaries who climbed out of a blue RX–7 half a dozen spaces away from us recommended Gepetto's, a place downtown with "great gourmet pizza and a hundred kinds of beer." By the time we walked in, the lunch crowd had thinned. We grabbed a big booth up front where Ben could keep an eye on the street action and I could watch the buxom bartender practicing her dart game. I had a feeling I'd been there before.

I figured our waitress for a leftover 'Nam era snow bunny. Class of Reds and Acid. Came out for spring break and never went back. To make it through a dozen-item list of pizza toppings, she had to check her crib sheet twice. Ben ordered pepperoni and artichoke hearts. No doubt, this was Sonja Ridgely's grandson. I stumped the bar by asking for an Eau Claire, a lyric beer from the Wisconsin town of the same name, and settled happily for an Anchor Steam. We sipped as we waited for our pizza, me on my beer and Ben on a raspberry seltzer. After a couple of minutes, I noticed that Ben was staring quizzically at me. Before I could ask why, he said, "What's your name?"

"Gardner Wells. I'm sorry, Ben. I thought you knew."

"I forgot."

"I was a friend of your grandfather's, remember?"

"Uh huh."

"Tomorrow, you and I and your mother are going to fly to San Francisco. Your grandma will be at the airport to meet us. You'll go home with her. They told you that at the hospital, didn't they?"

"They said you were coming to take me home."

"After we eat lunch, we're going to do a little grocery shopping. Do you remember my friend, Doe?"

"Yes." He was twisting his plastic soda straw into a pretzel shape.

"Well, you and I are going to make dinner for the three of us. We'll be spending the night in the same house where you slept night before last."

"My mom woke me up and we sneaked out of the house when everybody was asleep. It was scary."

"Then you walked a long way and called somebody from a pay telephone, right?"

"Yeah. My mom said it was a trick on Granddaddy. My granddaddy's dead now; so's Bobby."

"I'm sure that makes you sad."

He nodded. "They're in heaven. Are they going to hurt that fat man?"

"The one who took your picture? No, I don't think so. If he can prove he was only trying to do his job, they'll probably just scold him and say, 'No doughnuts for a week!' "

Ben laughed. "Can I taste this?" he said. It was an envelope of artificial sweetener.

"Just a little, okay? It's meant for coffee or tea."

"I know." He tore off a corner, poured a little on his hand, and licked it up. "I'm hungry."

"Me, too. Maybe we should have gone to McDonald's."

"Can I pour this in here, Mr. Gardner?"

"Sure. Just call me Gardner; it's my first name." He poured the rest of the sweetener into his glass of ice water and stirred it with a knife. "Will my mom still be crazy when she comes out of the hospital?"

I looked, but there was no one to punt to, nor any good reason I could think of to challenge the characterization of Melanie's mental condition. I said, "The hospital is keeping your mother safe and comfortable. Her problems are not a kind that can be fixed quickly. She'll go to another hospital when we get to San Francisco tomorrow. They're going to try very hard to help her, to make her well. Sometimes it takes a long while. Your grandma will take good care of you.''

"I know. She loves me, and I love her.''

For twelve bucks, the large pizza looked kind of medium-sized, but it was good. I complimented Ben on his choice of toppings. The artichoke hearts were a winner.

It was after two when we felt sunshine again. The haze had burned off and the temperature had climbed into the seventies. A stroll seemed in order. I let Ben call the turns. He pointed us toward the mall. Even on this off-season, weekday afternoon, the sun lovers and people watchers were out in force. In Wagner Park, we found a play structure built of six-inch timbers that had a rope bridge, a tire swing, balance beams, a slide, a sandbox, and other goodies sufficient to occupy the interest of a four-year-old for nearly an hour. All that was required of me during that time was an occasional helping hand or word of appreciation. As Ben created a fantasy world and joyously entered it, playing every part himself from Peter Pan to The Masters of the Universe, I marveled at how he appeared to have bounced back emotionally from what for most adults would have been a devastating series of direct hits. I had no idea whether to credit him, or being four, or some of each; or whether to doubt my ability to interpret what I was seeing.

When Peter Pan had gunned down the last laser-eyed invader from outer space, he climbed onto my back for a piggyback victory march along the Cooper Avenue Mall. Despite his feelings about slack nutrition at the hospital, I prevailed upon him to have a cone of bubble-gum ice cream. Then he prevailed upon me to let him check out the goodies in a very upscale toy store, and in doing so, I

learned one of the benefits of parenthood: You get to have
toys again. All you have to do is pretend they're for your
kids. We bought an all-terrain vehicle with doughnut tires
and wireless remote control. I think I was more anxious to
get it back to the house and try it out than he was.

By four, the town's bars were coming to life and the
scent of woodsmoke pervaded the air. We got the Jeep and
drove over to the supermarket. On the way in, I noticed
vending machine copies of the *Rocky Mountain News* and
U.S.A. Today with Bobby Barron's picture on page one
under lurid headlines. Fortunately, Ben was more interested in the coin-op lion ride. We bought all the makings
for a steak dinner and an extra set of batteries for the
ATV. Near the bottom of the hill, I stopped briefly at a
little grog shop and bought some wine.

I had hoped Doe would be at the house, but the place
was as empty as I had left it. While I started a pot of
coffee and put the food away, Ben got the job of unpack-
ing our new toy in the living room. I realized I had mixed
feelings about seeing Doe. Along with the sex, steak,
wine, and childcare, our evening's agenda included saying
good-bye. As I poured coffee into a mug that said, "Creative Financing," I asked myself whether I should have
kept things with Doe strictly professional. The answer was
a definite yes and no.

A faint afterglow in the western sky was the only source
of light in the living room when my mug of coffee and I
went in there looking for Ben. I'd puttered longer in the
kitchen than I anticipated and was feeling sheepish about
leaving him alone for so long. There was no answer when
I called his name, no sign of him among the gray shapes
and shadows. The toy box sat unopened on the coffee
table where I had left it. I started across the room toward
the light switch by the front door, but stopped short when I
thought I heard something. I stood still and listened and
heard it again. I spoke his name, and in the same moment

saw his shape in the darkness. He was curled up like a ball on the floor beside one of the big wingback chairs, clutching the tattered, cotton security blanket he told me one of the hospital nurses wanted to throw out. I put my mug on the mantel and approached him slowly. He looked tiny as a cat. I lowered myself and sat cross-legged beside him. After I'd rubbed his back for a minute, he climbed into my lap and said in a very small voice, "I want my granddaddy." Then he started crying again and buried his face in the place between my chest and arm. While he cried, I held him, and watched the twilight fade slowly from the sky.

·· Chapter Nineteen ··

I was slicing tomatoes and little Ben was washing lettuce when Doe came in, a little after seven. She reported that the local paper had granted her desk and telephone privileges, but most of the day, she'd been out racing across the landscape with her hired photographer. At *Castillo Colorado,* they took enough shots to fill an entire issue of *Architectural Digest.* They'd been to Glenwood Springs twice chasing the top FBI guy on the case; and, cumulatively, had spent in excess of ninety minutes waiting in line at the road construction on Route 82. She said I owed her a large favor for keeping my whereabouts a secret from her colleagues. I said I'd filled and preheated the hot tub and didn't know what else she could possibly ask. She assured me she'd think of something.

There was an awkwardness between us when she first came in. Little Ben's presence necessitated adjustments in the way we were with each other. There hadn't been time in our budding-ending romance to create tactics for dealing with a kid, and I couldn't very well send him to his room. Our imminent parting and unshared experiences of the past thirty-six hours just hung over us, conversations we couldn't have.

But as we talked and laughed, it got better. The good feelings took over again. We warmed to each other. Doe and Ben built a salad while I boiled fresh fettuccine and Charmglowed steaks. By the time we sat down to eat, Doe and I were trading yarns about our growing-up years and enjoying it just as much as our audience. By bedtime, my repertoire of G-rated stories was depleted and Doe had segued into Aztec legend. At first, Ben seemed more fascinated than ever, but soon the eyelids got heavy and Doe polished him off.

With our charge bedded down for the night, we headed toward the living room, congratulating ourselves on our knack with kids. East-facing sections of the broad, hardwood floors were bathed in moonlight, but otherwise it was dark. Doe started to turn on lights. I said that if she'd give me just a couple of minutes we could bask in the glow of a crackling fire. She poured us each a splash of Remy Martin while I made like a boy scout, skillfully crumpling up pages from a four-month-old copy of *The Wall Street Journal*. Building fires in a place as dry as Colorado is very gratifying to the male ego. The logs of split piñon were already popping when I sat down beside Doe on the big sofa. She handed me a snifter.

"To your friend, Ben," she said. We touched glasses and drank. The firelight danced across the soft, ripe features of her face. Her hair gleamed. The nipples of her breasts asserted themselves behind the raspberry-colored knit fabric of her turtleneck. The sheer hose covering one exposed knee glinted with light from the hearth.

"He approved of you," I said. "So do I."

"Has it been hard for you today?"

"Not in the way you're thinking. I said good-bye to Ben yesterday. I guess I've seen enough death that I've made some sort of peace with it. I don't like it, but there it is. Ben and I weren't actively involved in each other's lives, but we had a kinship. I'm going to miss that."

"Is little Ben going to be okay with his grandmother?"

"Yes. Sonja is pretty stable these days. She's done a lot of growing up in the last few years. I guess it's never too late."

"You mean there's hope for you?"

"I wouldn't go that far. . . . Your editor's pleased?"

"Well, he's not exactly the effusive type, but, yes, in his own way, I think he is. He said, 'We broke the story to the world. We've got the franchise.' From Julio, that's high praise, and gratitude."

"I hope they give you a hero's welcome."

"Thanks."

"Does he really talk like that, 'We've got the franchise'?" I took a course in small talk at community college.

She laughed, "Oh, definitely. He watches all the American TV shows. He probably got that one from 'Dallas.' " She looked down, and back up at me. "Gardner, I have a confession to make. I stayed away a lot longer tonight than I needed to."

"I noticed."

"I'm not very good at making commitments, or saying good-bye."

"Neither am I." One big tear rolled slowly down her left cheek. I took her hand. "It snuck up on us, didn't it?" She nodded. "To you," I said, and finished my drink.

"To the hot tub," she said, and drank the rest of hers.

We went upstairs to shed our clothes and get robes. On the way, we checked Ben. He was sleeping with his butt in the air; his thumb in his mouth; and the security blanket clutched to his little chest; but he was sleeping.

I had already changed and was enjoying the view from our bedroom when Doe emerged from the bathroom in her robe and slippers. All the Roaring Fork Valley was brilliantly illuminated in moonlight. The Fourteens towered majestically like white-capped waves. We had a kiss, and I gave myself a little lecture about patience.

From the front door of Freddie's house, you walk east along the wraparound deck, and then north to the hot tub, which is tucked against the hillside toward the back of the house. Very private.

Steam rose from the tub as I uncovered it, and more when I switched on the jets. There were switches in the control panel for underwater and deck lights, but both options seemed contrary to the kind of party we had in mind. I poured each of us a fresh splash of cognac and put them in appropriate locations. The magic moment had arrived.

"You first," I said.

"No, you!" she laughed.

"Count of three? Okay! One . . . Two . . . THREE!" The robes fell to the redwood and we marched forward, Doe much more quickly than I'd have liked. I tried to watch her in slow motion, making freeze frames in my head of each moonlit orb of her anatomy, but it was too damn cold. She practically jumped in, squealing like a kid.

The water temperature was ideal. I handed her her glass and she snuggled next to me on the subsurface ledge. It took us a moment to adjust ourselves so that only minimal areas of skin were exposed to the cold air. Above us, beyond a bower of rustling aspen leaves, a fat harvest moon crowned the clear night sky.

"It's perfect," she said, and kissed my shoulder.

"And to think I charged everything on my American Express."

"I may change my mind about going back, and never leave this tub."

I put my arm around her shoulders; she hitched a leg over my thigh. We sat like that for several minutes; just sipping, soaking in the ambience, and chatting about nothing in particular. It seemed very casual, but that was a lie. There was a palpable sexual tension between us. Resisting it was somehow part of the fun. When we'd both had enough of self-restraint, I put my arms under her and swung her to a sidesaddle position on my lap. She pressed close to me and tickled my lips with her tongue. In that instant, our horniness reached critical mass. We kissed, and by the mere touch of our lips, lost control. Any notions about an orderly escalation of romance were happily abandoned, and we surrendered to our simple, glorious lust for each other.

With our lips locked, she found my hand and put it to her breast. She cooed when I rolled her tumid nipple between my fingers, then pulled back and got astride my legs, squeezing my thighs hungrily between hers. While I supported her buttocks with my hands, I arched forward and entered her. She sighed extravagantly and shuddered as I gathered her closer. I felt her legs lock over my ass. Then, half-floating, half-supported by my body, she stretched out before me in the rushing water. Her ripe, moonlit body, radiating pleasure, called up every impossible sexual fantasy I'd had as a kid. For a long moment, we were still, moved only by the swirling water, joined and savoring our union. Then she took my hands and pulled herself up until she had her arms around me and could kiss me. As our tongues found each other, I withdrew all but the very tip of my erection and with that, probed her playfully.

"Don't stop," she commanded. "You're killing me."

But a few seconds later I did. Doe was facing the wrong way to see them standing there in the moonlight. She squeezed me tighter and made little whimper noises to protest when I stopped moving. I wanted to deny them, to will them out of my sight, but they were there, and real enough. Melanie had Freddie's forty-five in her right hand, the one I'd borrowed. She held little Ben's hand in her left. "It's Melanie," I whispered to Doe. "Stay as low in the water as you can." I heard her say, "Oh, Jesus Christ," as she slipped away from me. I caught her right hand and held it as she turned to face them. She gave my hand a strong squeeze and threw me an apprehensive smile. Only our heads were above water.

They were standing on the middle of the deck about fifteen feet from us. Melanie's short, uncombed hair appeared white in the moonlight. She had on what looked like jeans and a short, dark jacket. Her hospital gown was loosely tucked in at her waist. Little Ben was barefoot, still in his pj's. He looked scared.

"How can I help you, Melanie?" I said. "What do you need?"

"Get out of there," she said, gesturing with the pistol.

"How about turning off the jets?" I said. "There's a switch in the control panel, right over there, top one." She moved with a strange, loping gait, and turned off the jets. It was suddenly still and very quiet. "Thanks. It was hard to hear you." She raised the gun and pointed it at me.

"Get out."

"It's cold out there. Would you hand me my robe?"

"Get out of there. NOW!" I stepped out of the hot tub steaming like a plow horse on a cold day.

"My robe?" She nodded. I picked it off the deck and put it on. "How did you get away from the hospital? They'll be looking for you."

"I walked," she said. "They took my temperature at nine and I just walked out, where they take the trash. It was easy. . . ." I halved the distance between us, to eight feet. "Tell her to get out," Melanie ordered. She took a step back and made a wobbly gesture with the big pistol. As I was about to speak, Melanie's face twisted in anger. "GET OUT OF THERE!" she screamed. Doe emerged trembling from the water. Her eyes implored me to act, but Melanie was too well-focused, a yard too far away. I couldn't risk it. "I didn't take the pills the last two times," Melanie bragged, "which is funny because I used to eat that junk like M&M's. . . ." I smiled at little Ben. He started to speak. Melanie shook him. "Don't say a word," she warned, and turned to me. "He's not your problem." Ben started to cry. Melanie went on, speaking faster. "When you were in my room today? Working your mouth? I wasn't zoned out like you thought . . . HEY!" She swung suddenly and fired. Doe went down. I lunged at Melanie, who was stunned by the weapon's sharp kick. She jumped back and waved the gun barrel in my face. "DON'T MOVE!" she screamed.

"No, Gardner! Don't," Doe sobbed behind me. Her voice brought me back. I turned toward her. The last echoes of the gun's report reverberated in the darkness. Doe's face was full of tears. She'd dropped to one knee and was leaning hard to her left, supporting herself with her left arm. Blood streamed down her right hip where the bullet had grazed her. "I only wanted my robe. . . ." she sobbed. I squatted beside her and covered her with the robe. She couldn't stop crying. I put my arm around her.

"I was planning to do you both in bed," Melanie said, "but this is cute. I like this. In the moonlight." She smiled approvingly and took three steps forward. "Now say what you mean." I pulled Doe a little closer.

"What?" I said.

"You know, say you're sorry."

"What am I sorry for, Melanie?"

"Do you think I'm stupid? For killing Bobby, of course."

"I didn't know what you meant. . . ."

"I had a chance for a new life. Bobby cared about me."

"I know. . . ."

"He didn't want to fuck. . . . Look at the moon on that water. It's like the ocean. Look at it." We did. For an instant, I glimpsed the terror in Doe's eyes. "What was wrong with my being happy?" Melanie asked.

"Nothing. You deserve to be happy."

"Then why couldn't you stand it?" She raised the tip of the gun barrel just enough that I was staring directly into it.

"I don't know what you mean."

"Nobody ever loved me."

"That's not true. . . ."

"Stop talking to me." She took a step back and gestured with the gun. "Stand up." Doe began quivering as I helped her to her feet. I held her hard against me. Melanie kept talking. "Ramon didn't believe I'd do him, either. I'm not bragging. He made that man get killed. He would have wrecked Bobby with that film. . . . I'm not wrong. I knew about you when you came in the hospital. I heard you in his voice."

"What did you hear?"

"QUIT LYING, DADDY!"

"Melanie, I'm not your father."

"LIAR!" she screamed.

I could see the disbelief in her eyes, but there was something more. The blood drained from my face when I realized what it was. I said, "You killed your father, didn't you, Melanie?" Doe shuddered as I spoke the words.

"You know I did," Melanie said bitterly. "That's when he got in you. Now, we're all poisoned. . . ." I would not have guessed that anything could have made me feel worse about Ben Maitland's death, but this did. "God, why is it so noisy?" she moaned. "Please stop talking to me." She looked around as if addressing others only she could see, then focused sharply on us. "Say you're sorry," she ordered. "I don't want to kill my baby. . . ." She spoke before we could. "I've got to. . . ." She couldn't hold herself back much longer. The twelve feet between us looked like forever. At that range, any hit by a forty-five would stagger me; the next would finish me off. "Just say you're sorry," she begged, "please."

"I'm sorry, Melanie," I said. My own voice sounded odd to me. My throat felt small. She extended her arm and aimed the gun at me. My mind locked up. The hammer came back as she squeezed the trigger. "Bobby Barron should never have been killed," I said. I stumbled over the words. My legs began to shake. "Your friendship with him was something very special. . . ." She let go of Ben. It was happening too quickly. "Bobby brought so much joy to so many people. . . ." Tears poured from Melanie's eyes. "It was tragic that his life had to end." Ben stared at his mother with huge, terrified eyes. "I'm sure he loved you," I said. Her gun hand began to tremble.

"He wanted to get rid of me," she said in a tiny voice.

"Don't kill us, Melanie," I said.

"No, Mom," Ben said, "you can't."

"He LAUGHED at me," Melanie cried. Then her eyes went wild and I knew we were out of time.

I yelled, "The gun, Ben!" and leapt. As he grabbed her arm, she fired into the deck. I dove at her sideways. The muzzle flashed in my face as she fired again. The impact of my body knocked her flat. Ben tumbled away from us. She fought wildly under me, all knees and elbows. I was across her, trying to pivot like a wrestler to get control. I felt the gun under my belly. With animal fury, she struggled, groaning and cursing, to pull it free. As I reached between us, she bit my shoulder. If I could not immediately wrest the gun from her, I could try to keep her from firing it through my gut. I grappled for it, but my one hand

was no match for the strength of madness. She began
sobbing as she pulled the gun up along her stomach to her
chest. My hand found hers and I heard myself yell "NO!"
as she raised her head and fired a single round into her
mouth. I felt the life go out of her. I turned away from the
horror that had been Melanie's head and shut my eyes. I
couldn't move. For a moment, the world was still.

The first thing I heard was Ben crying. The first thing I
saw was his eyes.

I will never forget his eyes.

·· Chapter Twenty ··

My own house felt unfamiliar to me, like an estranged friend. Though the evening was mild, I built a small fire in the fireplace. It seemed to help. I was just back from two weeks in Japan, dog tired, and in the midst of repacking my suitcase for an eight o'clock flight the following morning. Jimmy Tanaka had been very nice about my showing up a week later than we'd planned, but he wouldn't budge an hour on the original deadline, which meant that I had to do three weeks' work in two. I had seriously considered telling the unreasonable bastard to kiss off, but at the end of the two weeks when he handed me a check for twenty-seven thousand dollars to cover my fee and expenses, I decided that, for an unreasonable bastard, this was not such a bad guy after all.

After the packing and some minimal house care, I had one objective: sleep. I did not care that it was only a little after eight and that only red-necks, geriatrics, and small children go to bed that early; I was tired. I stretched out in bed and was listening to the little crackles and wheezes from the fire in the next room when the gentle darkness in my bedroom was breached by headlights on a car bouncing down the long lane to my house. The pinging chatter of the little air-cooled engine gave me a clue, but when the convertible swung into its old spot under the big live oak tree near the front door, I knew that my unexpected visitor was Miss Maggie.

I had a pair of Levis and a madras shirt hanging on the silent valet by the door to my bathroom. I pulled them on hurriedly and got to the front door just as she began a second, and more insistent, barrage of knocks. Even in the jaundiced glow of the overhead bug light, she looked great. The clothes were the same: jeans and a workshirt, hanging out at the waist, but the hair looked a little shorter, the lips a little redder. The fragrance was different, too. Jasmine instead of turpentine.

"I shouldn't be hugging you like this, Wells," she said, after she apologized for getting me out of bed.

"Why not?"

"Because I like it too much, and I'm mad at you, besides." We parted. I began buttoning my shirt. "Would you consider it pushy if I turned on some lights?"

"Please." A smile came to my face as I watched her bustle from one switch to the next until she had enough lights burning for a bingo party. I tossed a couple of fresh chunks of wood on the fire. "How about a beer?"

"No thanks, I can't stay. I really just came by to check on you." She blushed. "I didn't mean that the way it sounded." She stood awkwardly in front of the chair where she used to sit, a small upholstered piece by the fireplace. "I meant I came to see if you're okay. I've been calling for days. Finally, I talked to Sonja. She said you'd gone to Tokyo. That was over a week ago."

"I got back today. Why didn't you leave a message?"

"You know I hate those things."

"So does anyone with taste, or concern about the loss of individual dignity in this impersonal age, but 'those things' work. Please sit. Rum and tonic?"

"Okay, but just a short one." She sat in the chair and swung her legs across the arm toward the fireplace, just as she'd started doing the first week after she moved in. I wandered off to my little kitchen to get our drinks. "You know," she called after me, "I just have to say I think you're a sorry shit for not even calling me during all this, just to let me know you're alive. Just because we're not living together anymore, doesn't mean I don't care about you, you know." She got out of the chair and followed me as far as the door to the kitchen. "I'm sorry about Ben, Wells, I really am."

"Thanks."

"Are you doing okay with it?"

"I guess. I thought I'd shaken it off, but he keeps coming back to me. And I keep asking myself 'if' questions. 'If I'd done this, or that, would it have turned out differently?' I was supposed to be running things, after all. Here."

"Thanks." We took our drinks into the living room. I liked the way the house felt with Maggie in it. I lowered myself into the bentwood rocker and stretched my legs across the coffee table. She said, "If it's ever bugging you and you want to talk about it, you know you can call me, anytime. You know I mean that."

"Yes, I do, and it's very damn good to see you."

She raised her glass. "To us," she said, "when it was good, it was very, very good. . . ."

"And when it was bad, it was torrid." We drank. "How's Sonja?"

"I guess she's been better. . . . She and Jack have decided to adopt Benjamin."

"Good."

"Benjamin likes his therapist. He's having a lot of

trouble sleeping, but he's so young. . . . It's got to get better. Sonja really wants to see you, Wells. She said you and she are supposed to have dinner.''

"I'm planning on it.''

"She can't believe Melanie murdered her father. She can't believe she was that . . . what was the word she used . . . 'depraved.' ''

"Can't believe it, or doesn't want to believe it?''

"I'm not sure. You'd know better than I would.''

"Melanie's fingerprints were all over the gun. She told the cops she tried to take it away from Ben when he threatened to shoot himself. They believed her. It was a normal enough thing for a man's daughter to do under the circumstances. But 'normal' applied to Melanie only in contrast to what she was really like. I don't think any of us realized how sick she was.''

"Were you able to follow the story in Tokyo?''

"Only in a limited way. I was pretty busy. Barron was big over there, though. I got the impression there was a lot of coverage.''

"It's been incredible here. Today on the news they announced that some big foundation, the World Children's Federation, or something like that, is going to take over all of Barron's charities, the orphanages and clinics, and so on. Did you hear about that?''

"They were selling kids to anyone with the right connections and deep pockets regardless of intent, right?''

"Something like that. There have actually been public burnings of Barron's records.''

"The kids he raped will be glad to hear that, so will the people hoping to make a killing on Bobby Barron memorabilia in twenty years.''

"Okay, cynic, what do you expect people to do?''

"Nothing. For a few weeks, a lot of folks are going to enjoy feeling superior to Bobby Barron, and then it will all be forgotten.''

"Is that so bad?"

"It's good. It's also good that a major drug and smut depot has been shut down, and that some very dirty people are headed for the slammer, or at least worrying about it. See? I can look on the bright side."

"You make me proud."

"It's your good influence, my dear."

"I'm happy to be of service."

"Then why do you keep looking at your watch?"

"I don't know," she said, a little flustered, "just habit, I guess."

She stayed exactly one hour. It was a good visit, a very good visit, but I was aware that she was keeping the conversation, like the time, within preset limits. When I tried to find out how and what she'd been doing, she was terribly charming, and terribly evasive. I didn't pressure her. I really appreciated her coming, so much so that I found myself wondering if my skepticism about our ability to maintain a simple friendship had been misplaced. When it was time for her to go, she acted like Cinderella at ten seconds to midnight. I figured I'd be lucky to get a handshake, but once again, I misjudged the lady. As we stood under the stars making awkward small talk beside the open door of her beloved convertible, without warning, she laid upon me a seismic kiss with a surprise ending, and then drove off like the proverbial bat.

I hadn't said anything to Maggie about Doe. What, if anything, she'd heard from Sonja, I had no idea. I told myself it didn't matter, but somehow it did, still.

The next morning, as Mexicana 977 climbed out of the haze over San Francisco, I arranged myself comfortably in the big seat and closed my eyes to daydream about the four-day weekend with Doe that lay ahead of me. When the plane landed that afternoon in Puerto Vallarta, Doe would be there to meet me; we'd board a puddle jumper and fly off to make happy memories in a little paradise she knew an hour's flight down the coast, a place not even blessed with a brochure.

We'd had a hard time staying in touch since I put her on the plane in Aspen. I did reach her once when I was in Tokyo. She was beginning her day; I was ending mine. Such things make a difference, but it was good to talk to her. She told me that she'd done a story on Juanita, the little girl who'd blown the whistle on Barron after her friend committed suicide. Several families had been touched by Juanita's bravery and had offered to give her a real home. I felt good about that.

Doe also reported that Chaco Aguirre and Missy McLeod were planning to make beautiful money together. I felt good about that, too. I wouldn't ordinarily promote trafficking in dirty pictures, but these had cost Chaco his brother. It seemed to me that the man deserved anything he could get.

When our weekend was over, Doe would go back to her life, and I'd go back to mine. But while we were together, we'd walk the white sand beaches, collect shells, and spend afternoons baking in the tropical sun. At night, we'd watch the moon set in the Pacific. We'd drink, talk, dance, and make glorious love. It wouldn't last forever, but then nothing does.

RULES OF PREY

John Sandford

THE TERRIFYING NEW THRILLER!

The killer is mad but brilliant. He kills victims for the
sheer contest of it and leaves notes with each body: rules
of murder. Never have a motive. Never kill anyone you
know...

Lucas Davenport is the cop who's out to get him. And
this cop plays by his own set of rules.